NORA QIN

Yes To The Spanish Reboot

Acknowledgments

This book exists because a handful of people believed in it long before it looked like a real thing, and because one person believed in me even on the days I absolutely did not.

To my husband: thank you for loving me through every version of this book, and every version of me while I was writing it. Thank you for the patience, the calm reassurance, the steady belief, and the countless small acts of support that made this possible. For listening to half-formed plot ideas, reassuring me during spirals of self-doubt, and never once asking when I'd "be done already." Thank you for making space for this dream, for holding the fort when writing took over the house, and for reminding me that I could do this. This book may have my name on the cover, but it carries your fingerprints on every page.

To my early readers: thank you for bravely reading drafts that were occasionally chaotic, always earnest, and very much in progress. Your feedback, encouragement, and enthusiasm made the story sharper, stronger, and more itself.

To my friends and family: thank you for your patience, your encouragement, and for believing in me even when you didn't always understand what I was working on.

To the places and experiences that shaped this story, especially the ones that challenged me, thank you for the inspiration, the growth, and the reminder that reinvention is rarely tidy, but always worth it. This book carries pieces of a life lived bravely and imperfectly.

And finally, to you, dear reader: thank you for choosing this book. I hope it makes you laugh, feel seen, and maybe believe, just a little more, that starting over can be both terrifying and beautiful.

CHAPTER 1 – Breaking Up with Predictability

The first time I cried in Barcelona, it was over an omelette.

It wasn't even quiet crying. No, I mean full, glassy-eyed, nose-running, what-is-my-life crying. In public. At a café.

The waiter had just placed a small ceramic plate in front of me, steam rising gently from the thick golden wedge of *tortilla*. It looked harmless. Lovely, even. A glistening, eggy slice with crisped edges and the promise of warm potatoes tucked inside.

I took one bite.

And it just hit me. The jet lag. The loneliness. The fact that I had moved halfway across the world with no job, no backup plan, and zero ability to hold a conversation in Spanish.

The *tortilla* was soft and buttery. It was unfairly good. And suddenly my face was leaking.

The waiter, mid-20s, kind eyes, one earring, froze beside me, holding a glass of orange juice.

"*¿Estás bien? Ok?*" he asked, alarmed.

"I'm so sorry! Yes, I'm ok. Good," I blurted, dabbing at my face with a paper napkin that immediately disintegrated. "It's not the *tortilla*. The *tortilla* is incredible. It's... it's actually perfect."

He looked mildly concerned and offered the juice like it was a peace offering. I took it.

"*Gracias,*" I sniffled as I thanked him.

He nodded slowly and backed away like I was a precarious Jenga tower, one wrong move from total collapse.

As soon as he disappeared into the kitchen, I laughed. One of those short, broken laughs that comes out sideways.

Of course my first emotional breakdown in Barcelona was at a café surrounded by strangers who just wanted their morning coffee and not, say, a front-row seat to a live-action breakup with reality.

This wasn't just about food. This was about everything I had left behind. Everything I was trying to outrun.

And still, I took another bite.

Because honestly? That *tortilla* tasted like the first right decision I'd made in a very long time.

I sat there, fork in one hand, napkin in the other, wondering how a plate of eggs and potatoes could feel like a personal intervention. Maybe it was because, for the first time in months, I wasn't thinking about my failed engagements. I was just... here. Alone in Barcelona, eating something warm and safe while the rest of my life felt like an unsolvable math problem.

And then it hit me, hard enough to nearly choke on a piece of potato.

What if this is the biggest mistake of my life?

It's been a month since I arrived, and I'm still not sure if I made a bold, inspiring life choice or if I'm just spectacularly bad at crisis management.

Sure, things look dreamy on the surface. Winding cobblestone streets. Cafés buzzing with laughter and the smell of fresh bread. Street musicians strumming guitars like the entire city is flirting with me.

And then there's me, a girl from Singapore, standing awkwardly in the middle of it all like a human pop quiz on Spot the Foreigner.

Still, there's a small, stubborn pride in the fact that I even got here. I moved out. I crossed continents. Adulting level: expert.

But underneath the charm and bravado, there's a whisper I can't quite shake. Was this a terrible idea?

Growing up in a traditional Asian household, the life plan was about as flexible as a steel beam. You live with your parents until marriage. You follow the script of good grades, good job, good spouse, good kids. Deviate, and suddenly everyone's acting like you announced you were moving to Mars.

Independence wasn't necessarily celebrated the way it might be in the West; it was actually frowned upon. When I once mentioned wanting my own apartment, my mother winced and said, "Why? That's for people with no families."

So I played along and tried to check the boxes. In the meantime, everyone around me seemed to be checking off milestones like it was some cosmic bingo game. By 25, they were planning weddings, buying condos, posting pictures of their fiancés posing awkwardly in botanical gardens.

And me?
I was there too. Almost.

I got engaged. Twice. Yes, twice. I like to commit to poor decisions thoroughly.

The first time was Remy, stable, kind, and most importantly, the one who passed the all-important "Would Mom Approve?" test with flying colors. Within two years, we were engaged. I had the checklist. The ring. The social approval.

Unfortunately, I also had a gnawing feeling in my gut that said, *this is not it*. A feeling I mostly tried to drown in wedding Pinterest boards.

Turns out, gut feelings are loud for a reason.

One night, while he was in the shower, his phone lit up with a text.
   "I miss you. Can we talk?"

In a way, I almost admired how classic the whole thing was. No cryptic codes, no secret aliases... just a good, old-fashioned I'm-a-cheater text message.

When he came out of the bathroom, towel slung around his waist, I confronted him. My voice was barely above a whisper, but the words felt like they weighed a thousand pounds.

At first, he denied it. Of course, he did. Then, as I stood there, my stomach in knots, he crumbled like an overbaked soufflé.

"It was a mistake. It didn't mean anything."

But it did. It meant everything.

Calling off the engagement shattered me, but it also cracked something open: the realization that a perfect-looking life could still be completely wrong.

I swore I'd never make that mistake again.

And yet, two years later, there I was, engaged again.
Henry was the "safe" one. We'd been friends long before we became something more, so I told myself it was different. He knew my history, promised never to hurt me, and I believed him.

I ignored the tiny voice in my head that asked if I was in love with him or just the idea of stability. I wanted so badly for it to work, to prove to myself that I was capable of love and not some cursed tragic figure doomed to a life of being alone.

But love built on fear isn't love at all.

I found out about the other affairs through a mutual friend, Nina. She delivered the news the way you might tell someone their favorite restaurant had closed down: soft, apologetic, bracing for impact.

"Are you sure?" I asked, my voice oddly detached.

"I'm sorry," she said, her face pinched with sympathy. "I thought you should know."

And just like that, history repeated itself.

I wish I could say I handled it gracefully, that I walked away with quiet dignity, a poetic one-liner, and a swish of my coat. But no. I yelled. I cried desperately and begged him to stay with me. In those moments, I was nothing but raw emotion.

But the worst part wasn't even the betrayal itself. It was the fact that it had happened again. And that's when the spiral began.

The self-doubt came in hot, like an uninvited guest who eats all your snacks and then asks why your couch is ugly.

Was I really that clueless? How did I not see the neon warning signs flashing above his head? Was there some cosmic sticky note on my forehead that said, *"Hi, I specialize in choosing men who will emotionally body-slam me"?*

And the worst thought of all, the one that crawled into bed with me at night, was *Maybe I wasn't just unlucky. Maybe I was unlovable.*

I replayed every conversation, every lingering glance, like I was the FBI reviewing footage for a case I was destined to lose. Maybe I laughed too loudly. Maybe I wanted too much. Maybe I was just… too much.

Some mornings I woke up feeling like I'd been run over by a truck made entirely of invisible bruises. Each one whispered the same thing: *You messed up. Again.*

And in Singapore, nothing stays private. At weddings or

family dinners, I could feel the whispers brushing against me like flies. *"Didn't she have a fiancé last year? Or was it the year before?"* Someone would smile and ask, *"So... still single?"* in the same tone you'd use for, *"So... still unemployed?"*

The shame clung like humidity. Everyone else was moving forward, happily checking their adulting bingo cards—marriage, condos, babies. Meanwhile, I was sitting there with two broken engagements and a track record that screamed, "Professional Red Flag Collector."

It wasn't just heartbreak. It was humiliation stitched right into my skin, and it started bleeding into everything else.

Food became optional. Everything tasted like cardboard. I lived on instant noodles, caffeine, and something dangerously close to resentment.

I kept telling everyone I was fine. "Totally fine!" I even added an exclamation point sometimes, which we all know is a dead giveaway that I was absolutely not fine.

And okay, there may have been some drinking. Not the classy kind with clinking glasses and good lighting. No. The kind where you sit on your kitchen floor at 2 a.m. in an old t-shirt, drinking tequila straight from the bottle and crying because you can't find the other sock.

There was also a brief experiment with smoking, which lasted approximately three puffs before I nearly hacked up a lung and gave myself a nosebleed. Super chic.

And then there was the flirting. Mindless, harmless, absolutely ill-advised flirting. Because apparently, attention is my favorite band-aid.

But the thing about spirals is they don't stay contained. They leak. Into work. Into friendships. Into family gatherings.

My sisters exchanged glances they thought I didn't see. My mom's mouth tightened the way it did when she wanted to scold me but didn't want to cause a scene.

And then, one night at dinner, Kyra finally broke the silence.

"How much longer are you going to keep numbing yourself like this?" she asked, her voice sharp enough to cut through the clinking of cutlery.

I froze and looked up. Everyone at the table was watching me.

And in that moment, I wasn't just the girl with two broken engagements. I was the girl whose family had started to wonder if she was breaking too.

The memory snapped shut like a book I didn't want to be reading anymore. When I blinked, I was still in Barcelona, still sitting at a tiny table with tear-streaked cheeks and egg on my fork.

The waiter gave me a tentative thumbs-up from across the café. I raised my juice glass in return, like, *Yep, still alive, still embarrassing myself in public. Carry on.*

If my family thought I was breaking, fine. Maybe I was. But at least here, no one knew me as "the girl with two broken engagements." Here, I was just the weirdo crying over an omelette. Which, frankly, felt like an upgrade.

CHAPTER 2 – No Gloves, No Script, No Clue

"*Señorita*, you cannot ride the luggage carousel."

That was my welcome to Barcelona.

In my defense, I wasn't riding it so much as trying to wrestle my overstuffed suitcase off before it made a second lap around the airport. The bag was winning. A kind man in a wool coat finally took pity on me and yanked it free, nodding politely as if helping confused foreigners was part of his cardio routine.

By the time I made it outside, the air hit me like a slap and a kiss all at once—cold, dry, and completely unrecognizable to someone raised in the steamy arms of Singapore. My skin immediately started drying out like a sad piece of bread left out overnight while my lungs tried to decide whether to throw a party or file a formal complaint.

The smells of roasted coffee, cigarette smoke, and something vaguely sweet, like caramelized sugar lingering in the air hit next. I stood there inhaling deeply while my body screamed, *"WHERE'S THE HUMIDITY?"* and my brain whispered, *"Don't panic. Europeans are allowed to smell nice."*

The taxi ride from the airport was a blur of gorgeous chaos.

I pressed my forehead against the cold window, eyes darting from one crumbling balcony to the next, watching laundry flap dramatically like it was auditioning for a soap opera. The architecture was mesmerizing, ancient and ornate, yet seamlessly blending with the modern.

I wanted to soak in every detail of the city I would now call home.

"Why are there so many people on the streets on a random Wednesday afternoon?" I wondered, watching groups of friends chatting animatedly outside cafés, their laughter ringing through the air like wind chimes. Didn't these people have jobs? Responsibilities? A mild sense of urgency?

Apparently not.

Even more puzzling, everyone looked effortlessly stylish. I had assumed that the cold would force everyone into purely practical, marshmallow-like attire, but no. The women strolled down the streets in effortlessly chic coats and heeled boots, scarves draped over their shoulders like a carefully curated accessory rather than a necessity. The men were just as polished with tailored peacoats, leather shoes, hair styled in that *I woke up like this but clearly I spent 20 minutes on it* way.

Then I caught my reflection in the taxi window: hoodie, travel pillow crease still stamped across my cheek. I wanted to apologize to the entire country.

And then, I saw it. The moment that officially screamed, *"Welcome to Spain, sweetheart."*

A street vendor selling roasted chestnuts stood on a corner, smoke rising from his makeshift cart. Children, their faces flushed from the cold, ran circles around him, catching hot chestnuts in their mittened hands before yelping and tossing them between their palms to cool.

I blinked, genuinely unsure if I had just hallucinated the opening scene of a Christmas movie. A movie that I so badly wanted to be in.

Meanwhile, my tropical blood was staging a full rebellion.

Singapore doesn't have winter. We have "hot," "slightly less hot," and "why do I even bother wearing makeup."

I was utterly unprepared for the relentless chill seeping into my bones. My fingers felt stiff, almost brittle, as if they might snap right off if I moved them too quickly. My nose had gone completely numb. The thin jacket I had brought from home, laughably inadequate, felt like little more than a decorative layer. I cursed myself for underestimating European winters.

"Guess I'll be investing in gloves," I muttered, hugging myself tighter as the taxi driver side-eyed me through the rearview mirror, probably wondering why this woman was talking to herself.

But none of it mattered. The discomfort, the freezing wind slicing through my clothes, the unfamiliar weight of my own breath hanging in the cold air. None of it could dull the exhilaration thrumming through me.

I had arrived. Alone in Barcelona.
No script. No expectations. No idea what the heck I was doing.

The first few days passed in a haze of small victories and minor disasters.

Finding my apartment? Victory.
Navigating the elevator the size of a broom closet? Disaster.
Buying groceries without accidentally purchasing cat food? Let's call that a draw.

The truth was, everything about Barcelona sparkled, but none of it felt like mine yet.

There was an awkwardness that lingered, a feeling that I was floating between two worlds but didn't belong to either. The city had its rhythm, its dance steps, and I was the awkward girl at the school dance pretending she knew the moves.

One evening, as I sat in the dimly lit kitchen of my apartment, poking at my half-eaten dinner, my flatmate, Douglas, walked in. He was a tall Scottish guy with an easygoing presence, the kind of person who could probably make friends with a tree if given enough time.

"You're quiet tonight," he noted, pulling out a chair across from me. "Missing home?"

I poked at my half-eaten dinner, debating how honest to be. "Sometimes," I said. Then, with a crooked smile, "Though if I'm being honest… home didn't exactly roll out a welcome mat before I left."

He tilted his head. "What do you mean?"

I swallowed, the memory sharp and unwelcome. "Let's just say my family doesn't do subtle."

And suddenly I was back there.

"You smell like an ashtray," my mother had said the moment I walked into the kitchen, no hello, no good morning. Just judgment, hot and steaming like the soup in her bowl.

Roselyn didn't even look up from her rice. "You came home at 3 a.m. again."

"3:45," Kyra corrected, eyes glued to her phone. "If you're going to scold her, at least be precise."

The thing about living with your parents in an Asian household is that privacy isn't a concept, it's a myth. You don't get secrets. You get community surveillance. You get group judgements over breakfast and emotional autopsies before your coffee's even brewed.

The three of them were a firing squad, and I was hungover and guilty, still wearing yesterday's eyeliner.

I tried to brush it off. "Glad my schedule's a group project now."

But my mother's spoon clattered down, broth steaming like it had joined the intervention. "You think we don't know what you're doing? Drinking, smoking... living like a delinquent."

"An embarrassment," Kyra added.

"Wasting her life," Roselyn piled on.

I'd tried to bite my tongue. Really, I had. But something brittle inside me snapped. "Maybe I like being a drama. Maybe I'm tired of living by your boring scripts."

Silence. The kind that doesn't just land, it drops.

My mother's lips thinned. Roselyn finally looked up. Kyra raised one brow in that smug, older-sister way that meant I was about to lose the argument before I knew I was in one.

"Stop acting like you're the only person who's ever been dumped," Kyra said. "Do you know how pathetic this looks?"

"I don't care how it looks!"

"You should," my mother hissed. "You are not just Nadia Harris. You are part of this family. Everything you do reflects on us."

"That's not my problem anymore."

That did it.

Roselyn's eyes finally lifted, cold as steel. "If you're going to live like this, you don't get to live under this roof."

I remember staring at her, heart pounding. "You're kicking me out?"

Kyra didn't blink. "We're giving you a choice. Shape up, or ship out."

There was no warmth. No wiggle room.

And that was it. The final blow.

I swallowed down the lump rising in my throat, the ache blooming in my chest. I refused to let them see me break.

Not here. Not now.

Fine. If they wanted me gone, I'd go.

So I went upstairs, shoved clothes into a duffel with shaking hands, vision blurred by hot tears. T-shirts, jeans, shoes, but none of it mattered. My mother and sisters stood like a jury as I walked back out, chin trembling, bag over my shoulder. Not one of them moved.

As I stepped outside and pulled the door shut behind me, I felt something inside me fracture.

Something final.
Something that would never be put back together.

For a moment, I stood there on the porch, my bag slung over my shoulder, my eyes burning with unshed tears.

I blinked, dragging myself back to the tiny Barcelona kitchen.

Douglas was staring at me, his expression somewhere between horrified and soft. "Bloody hell, Nadia."

I laughed weakly. "Yeah. Not exactly the tearful, supportive goodbye scene you'd expect in a movie."

He leaned forward on his elbows. "No wonder you left. That would've cracked anyone open."

I let out a long breath, tracing the rim of my glass. "They told

me to shape up or ship out. So I shipped out. And now..."
I gestured vaguely toward the window, where Barcelona
glowed in the night. "Now I have to figure out what shaping
up looks like on my terms."

Douglas was quiet for a moment, then gave me one of his easy
smiles. "Well. If you ever need reminding, you've already
done the hardest part. You got on the plane."

I forced a smile. "Yeah."

And that's the thing about planes and new beginnings, no
one tells you about the middle part. The waiting. The lonely
in-between where nothing fits yet.

You think all you need is bravery and a suitcase full of hope,
but no. Turns out you also need patience, the ability to sit
through the awkward silence of your own reinvention.

And patience wasn't something I'd packed.

The loneliness just showed up, no knock, no warning. I
missed Singapore. Not the questions about when I'd get
married, but the chaos, the late-night food stalls, the comfort
of knowing the language and the rules without having
to think. Mostly, I missed the connection. Casual texts.
Impromptu plans. People who knew my history without me
having to explain it.

Here, in Barcelona?

I sat in cafés where the only conversation was in Spanish or Catalan. I smiled at strangers who smiled back politely, then went back to their lives. I was nobody. Just another face in the crowd.

Barcelona was a beautiful stranger who hadn't invited me in yet.

Still, going home wasn't an option. I hadn't crossed an ocean just to quit at the first pang of homesickness.

"Grow up, get out, and just go, Nadia," I told myself on repeat like a very aggressive life coach.

And yet, even in that sadness, there was something else... something small, but persistent.
Hope.

A flicker of determination. A quiet voice reminding me: *You can find your place here. Just hold on a little longer.*

I was going to make this work. Somehow.

But sitting there in my room, watching people strolling and laughing through my window like they belonged here, I couldn't help wondering how it all started.

How did a girl like me, burnt out, heartbroken, and hiding in Singapore cafés with too much caffeine and not enough hope, end up here, on the other side of the world, trying to convince herself that possibility tasted better than fear?

CHAPTER 2 - No Gloves, No Script, No Clue

The answer, oddly enough, began with a food expo.

CHAPTER 3 – One Wink, One Way Ticket

"Tell me again why I'm doing this?" I asked, already sweating through my T-shirt as Kat, my friend of 13 years, shoved a lanyard around my neck.

"Because it pays," she said, waving her phone like gospel. "And because you told me, and I quote, 'I will literally sell my soul for rent money.'"

"Sounds like me," I muttered, tugging at the badge that read Event Staff like it was a scarlet letter.

The convention hall buzzed around us, hundreds of chefs, bakers, and food bloggers all trying to out-gesture each other while balancing trays of samples. It smelled like butter, espresso, and chaos.

The truth was, I didn't even care about food expos. What I cared about was escape. Singapore had started to feel claustrophobic, like a sweater two sizes too small—tight, itchy, impossible to breathe in. My dream job at the radio station had turned into background noise, my friends were scattered across the globe, and I was stuck replaying heartbreak like it was my favorite sad song on repeat.

So here I was. Temporary gig. Temporary distraction.

Kat elbowed me as an influencer with a ring light nearly mowed me down. "Cheer up. Free cheese."

Fair.

The job wasn't glamorous. I was basically a glorified food traffic controller; wrangling schedules, redirecting lost sous-chefs, and occasionally shielding the panna cotta from people with too much lip gloss and not enough boundaries.

And then, right in the middle of the madness, Spain happened.
More specifically, Barcelona happened.

A delegation of chefs and bakers arrived like a hurricane dressed in linen shirts—loud, laughing, and gesticulating like their hands had their own Wi-Fi connection. They unloaded crates of olive oil, towers of *cava* (champagne) bottles, and so much Iberico ham it could've qualified as an architectural structure.

I watched them from behind my clipboard, fascinated and mildly offended by how shiny their hair was.

One of them, Quique, according to the cheerful name tag slapped onto his flour-dusted apron, caught me staring.

He grinned. And winked.
And I dropped my clipboard.

"*¡Ven aquí, pequeña Singapur!*" he called out, waving me over with hands that had no business being that charming.

I hesitated just long enough to pretend I had dignity, then crossed the aisle like I wasn't internally screaming.

"What does that mean?" I asked.

He smiled like I'd just asked how to breathe. "It means 'Little Singapore.' You're our little Singapore girl, fast and curious. Like a sparrow."

"Not sure how I feel about being compared to a bird," I mumbled.

"You should love it! Sparrows are underestimated. But they always know where the good food is."

Honestly?
Sounds exactly like me.

And just like that, I was absorbed into the Barcelona crew.

They fed me cubes of manchego cheese drizzled with honey between shifts. They argued passionately about olive oil while handing me little glasses of *cava* behind the booth. They bickered like siblings and danced like no one had ever told them they weren't at a wedding.

"Have you ever had a proper *tortilla?*" Camila asked, already slicing into a warm, golden round of egg and potato.

I opened my mouth to answer, but was silenced by a bite being shoved into it. I chewed. I blinked.

"This is witchcraft," I whispered.

Camila threw her head back and laughed, a big, open, glorious sound that made the entire booth feel like the sun had come out just for us.

"No, *amiga*. That's Spain."

Then she leaned in conspiratorially and added, "Now, you have to say it the right way. Repeat after me: *¡Qué rico!*"

"Kay... ree... what?"

She grinned. "No no, like this: *¡qué rico!*" She dragged the rico out with such exaggerated joy that I was pretty sure she'd once been in a telenovela.

I tried again. "*¿Qué ricooo?*"

"Better! But with more drama. Like the food just proposed to you and you're saying yes."

I took another bite and gave it my all. *"¡Qué rico!"*

Camila gasped, delighted. "There! You're officially one of us now."

And for the first time in forever, I believed it. Something cracked open in me. Somewhere between the anchovies I swore I wouldn't like and the *cava* I nearly snorted out my nose, I realized I could breathe again.

Emily noticed. Of course she did.

She was the one who had opened her doors for me when I left home, the one who didn't flinch at my duffel bag and tear-streaked face. "Stay as long as you need," she'd said, already clearing space on her couch like it was no big deal, even though it was the biggest deal in the world to me.

So it made sense that here, too, she was the first to catch the shift in me. The way I laughed easier. The way my shoulders finally unclenched.

"So, Barcelona, huh?" she teased one night, catching me scrolling through photos of my new *tortilla* cult.

"Maybe," I shrugged, feigning casual. "Maybe Spain. Maybe... I don't know. Rome?"

Still, the idea lodged in my chest and wouldn't let go.

That night, sprawled across Emily's couch with her cat purring at my feet, I opened my laptop and started searching.

Living in Spain as a foreigner.
Moving to Barcelona alone.
Can you survive in Barcelona without speaking Spanish?

The results were a messy swirl of expat blogs, bureaucratic horror stories, and photos of sun-drenched plazas that felt like postcards from someone else's life. But I couldn't stop scrolling.

"Don't you think this is too much? Are you really trying to move overseas?" Kat asked me one afternoon over tea.

"Yeah," I admitted, blowing on my matcha. "But it's harder than I thought. Nobody wants to hire someone who isn't already there."

She tilted her head, skepticism clear in her eyes. "Why don't you just stay here? It's safe. Comfortable."

That's exactly why I need to go," I said with a sigh.

"Do you even speak Spanish? What's the backup plan?"

I laughed nervously. "Nope, no Spanish and no backup plan."

"Okay, you're crazy," she said, shaking her head.

And it was at that moment, when it suddenly hit me.

"I could teach English," I thought.

I had the qualifications. With a Cambridge diploma, I was considered a native-English speaker and could get certified to teach English as a second language.

With a newfound determination, I started looking for TEFL (Teaching English as a Foreign Language) courses in Barcelona.

Within a few months, I had enrolled myself into a one-month TEFL program in Barcelona, a city I'd only ever seen on social media and daydreams.

Was it all too easy? Was I in for a scam?

Maybe... but at the time, I didn't care. The allure of starting over in a continent I had never even visited was too intoxicating to let fear hold me back.

With my course secured, I faced my next challenge: apartment hunting. After weeks of combing through online listings, I found a place through a Facebook group.

"You're just going to send the deposit without seeing it?" Kat asked, her tone equal parts disbelief and exasperation.

"I mean, yeah," I said. "What choice do I have? It's now or never."

"Good luck, then," she said, her tone dripping with skepticism.

Thankfully, luck was on my side. The man I sent the deposit to turned out to be honest, though to this day, I still don't know if he was the owner or just the primary tenant. He did, however, tell me months later that he thought I was far too trusting.

"Too naive", were the exact words he used.

And maybe I was. But at that point, I had already burned my bridges.

After what felt like an eternity of preparation, I was finally ready. A strange sense of relief washed over me, knowing that I was about to step into the unknown and embark on a journey all by myself.

The plan was, shall we say, loosely constructed.

Was it risky? Absolutely.
Did I tell my family I was leaving? Nope. We were already on thin ice. No need to speed skate across it.
Was I sad? Tremendously.

But staying felt like slow suffocation.

So I threw myself into saving, every paycheck funnelled into the escape fund. I knew I needed a cushion because, for the first time in my life, I was stepping into a future without a safety net. Without any familiar faces to turn to in moments of crisis; just me, my savings, and the hope that I could make it work.

The night before my flight, I sat on the floor of my room, staring at my packed bags. My whole life, condensed into two suitcases.

"Am I really doing this?" I whispered, staring at my one-way ticket.
Yes.

The next day, I walked through the airport alone, heart pounding with fear and exhilaration. As the plane took off and Singapore shrank beneath me, a strange calm washed over me.

I didn't know what waited on the other side.

I only knew one thing: There was no turning back.

And now, a month later, I sometimes sit on the floor in my Barcelona apartment with my back pressed against the wall, suitcase shoved under the bed, and think about that girl in Singapore. The one with shaky hands and a one-way ticket.

She had no idea how hard it would be. No idea how lonely. No idea how many *tortillas* it would take to feel human again.

But she also had no idea that one day she'd be here. Alive, breathing, and daring to believe that maybe, just maybe,

Barcelona could be hers.

CHAPTER 4 - Who's Calling? Oh, Just My New Life

Luckily, I had something to look forward to—the TEFL course. If excitement were a sport, I would have been an Olympic gold medalist the morning of my TEFL course.

New life? New friends? A new purpose?
Sign. Me. Up.

"Maybe… just maybe, I can form a friendship with some of them," I whispered to myself as I carefully packed my pens, notebook, and highlighters like I was prepping for an academic expedition into the Amazon. If I couldn't control anything else about my life right now, at least my stationery situation would be flawless.

Naturally, I showed up 30 minutes early on the first day.

Because nothing says cool world traveler like loitering awkwardly outside a building before it even opens.

I adjusted my bag strap, checking my phone for the fifth time.

"Does this make me look too eager?" I wondered, shifting my weight from one foot to the other.

Probably, but I didn't care. I was just ready to start this new chapter of my life.

The school itself looked… well, rustic.
Wedged between a tiny café and a boutique so expensive I swear the mannequins were judging me, it had a heavy old door layered with so many coats of paint it could have survived a small war.

When I finally pushed it open, it creaked dramatically, as if deciding whether I was entering a charming language school or a haunted library. Jury was still out.

Inside, the classroom smelled like a perfect blend of white-board markers, old textbooks, and mild despair. Posters of outdated world maps and grammar rules hung askew on the walls, doing their best to inspire.

I picked a seat dead-center, the universal position for "I'm serious but not desperate."

Then came the introductions.

One by one, my classmates shared their names and where they were from, tossing out places like Australia, the US, the UK, and Canada. Easy breezy.

When my turn came, I said "Singapore" with my best confident smile.

Cue the blank stares.

"Singapore?" one guy asked, tilting his head. "That's in China, right?"

My left eyelid twitched slightly and I forced a laugh, though internally, I was sighing in five different languages

"Nope. Southeast Asia. Tiny, loud country. We specialize in food, shopping malls, and complaining about the weather."

He nodded slowly, as if I had just explained an abstract concept like time travel. Some nodded in understanding, but a few continued to look puzzled, as if I had just described an imaginary land. A few exchanged glances when I spoke, and I couldn't shake the feeling that some of them assumed I was less capable.

"Is it my accent?" I mused later that evening as I replayed the day in my head. "Or maybe my darker skin tone?"

To their credit, most of my classmates were friendly.

But it was impossible not to notice that I was the only Asian in the room.

It wasn't hostile. Just… isolating.
Like being the one person at a party who didn't get the inside jokes.

Still, I rallied. I cracked jokes. I smiled. I told myself this was part of the adventure.

Then there was Maddy.

Loud. Confident. American. The human version of a double espresso shot.

She commanded attention the way a general commands an army. She wasn't obnoxious, just unapologetically vocal.

"I just think English teaching should be about practicality, not stupid grammar rules no one actually uses!" she declared passionately, slamming her hand on the desk for emphasis.

Her confidence radiated through the room. Some of our classmates nodded in agreement, others exchanged amused glances, and a few shrank back, as if unsure whether to admire or fear her.

Me?

I shrank back, unsure of how to navigate her forceful opinions. In Singapore, I had been taught that keeping quiet was a sign of respect, that drawing too much attention to myself was unnecessary. Speaking up wasn't discouraged exactly, but it was something you did when necessary, not just for the sake of hearing your own voice. Meanwhile, my classmates had zero hesitation jumping into debates like it was an Olympic sport.

Part of me wanted to challenge her, to offer my own perspective. But the other part, the part shaped by years of cultural conditioning, held me back.

I just wanted to survive the day without bursting into culturally repressed tears.

So, I stayed quiet.

The rest of the class, thankfully, was easier to connect with. Most were new to the city, just like me, and we bonded over our collective confusion about life in Barcelona. We swapped stories about getting lost in El Raval, the inexplicable supermarket hours (why were they closed exactly when you needed them?), and the sheer impossibility of adjusting to a world where lunch started at 3 p.m.

Friends, though? Not quite.

We were more like friendly strangers thrown together on the same unpredictable journey.

Outside of class, things weren't much easier.

While the TEFL course consumed my days, my nights were

spent tirelessly searching for a job. I went on so many interviews that I started to feel like a contestant on a never-ending talent show, except instead of singing, I was just repeating "I'm a fast learner!" in various levels of desperation. My confidence grew, but the rejections still stung.

One school liked me, right up until the owner asked if I spoke Spanish.

"We're looking for someone who can understand some Spanish, as the classes are a combination of adults and kids," Daniela told me during one interview. "Do you speak the language?"

Do I just flat out lie and say yes? How hard could Spanish really be?

But something told me that getting caught would be far worse.

"I have some basic knowledge, but I'm already enrolled in Spanish classes," I replied, hoping my enthusiasm would make up for my zero percent fluency. "I believe I'll pick up the language soon enough."

Daniela offered a polite but noncommittal smile.

As I walked out of the school, I couldn't help but feel deflated. The pressure was mounting. I was three weeks into the TEFL course, and my savings were bleeding out faster than I wanted to admit.

I had about three months before I'd have to start considering very drastic life choices, like learning how to survive solely on bread, olive oil, and sheer delusion.

Then, in the final week of the course, my phone vibrated in my pocket mid-class. I sneaked a peek at the screen, and my heart nearly stopped.

A local number.

That could only mean one thing: it HAD to be one of the places that I had interviewed at.

I practically levitated out of my seat, muttering a hurried "Sorry!" as I made a beeline for the hallway.

The voice on the other end was Daniela's.

"One of my teachers resigned suddenly. Are you still interested in the position? Can you start immediately?"

I almost dropped my phone.

Struggling to keep my voice steady, I replied, "I'm definitely interested! However, I'm still doing my TEFL course, and there's one week left. How soon do you need me?"

"Today, if possible," she said, as if hiring a desperate, underqualified foreigner with questionable Spanish skills was the most casual thing in the world.

Today.
As in, right now.

I glanced back at the classroom, where my half-finished grammar notes sat mocking me.

Technically, I still had classes until 5 p.m., but desperation outranks academic punctuality.

"I can start after my TEFL class today," I said, forcing my voice to stay calm.

And just like that, I had a job.
A real, actual job.
In Barcelona.
In teaching.
Without fully speaking the language.

That week was a whirlwind of long hours and overwhelming excitement. My days stretched from 9 a.m. to 9:30 p.m., bouncing between TEFL class and teaching, but I thrived on the adrenaline.

Sleep? Optional.
Exhausting? Absolutely.
But I was too excited to care.

To celebrate the end of the TEFL course, our teacher took us out for dinner at a little restaurant tucked away in a Barcelona alley.

The place looked like something out of a movie—walls lined with dusty wine bottles, black-and-white photos, and a lingering scent of garlic and adventure.

I arrived late, slightly embarrassed, but instantly distracted by the chaos of the table. Plates of tapas scattered everywhere, people reaching over one another, eating straight from shared plates like it was a medieval feast.

A far cry from how we ate in Singapore, where meals were a well-organized, communal affair. Dishes were placed in the center, and everyone took their fair share. No one touched anything until all the food had arrived.

Here? It was a lawless land of "whoever stabs the last piece first, wins." It was chaotic, messy, and utterly charming.

I finally tried the famous *patatas bravas*, golden fried potatoes with a smoky, spicy sauce that made me wonder why fries back home weren't this exciting.

Then there was *pulpo a la gallega*: tender octopus, seasoned with olive oil, sea salt, and paprika, served on a bed of sliced potatoes.

And then, when I thought the food couldn't get any better, I tried what was to me the star dish—*bomba*. A crispy, breaded ball of mashed potatoes stuffed with spiced meat and fried to perfection. Somehow, this goofy little potato-meat grenade cracked something open in me, a tiny, wobbly certainty that Barcelona might not just swallow me whole... it might actually let me stay.

By dessert, I was full, slightly tipsy, and riding a high that maybe, just maybe, this whole moving-across-the-world thing might actually work out.

Then my phone buzzed. Another local number. My heart raced.

I excused myself and stepped outside into the cool Barcelona evening.

"Hello?" I answered hesitantly, unsure what to expect.

The voice on the other end was friendly, my flatmate Douglas.

"Are you done with dinner? I need you to come meet me when you're done."

My stomach clenched. Had I done something wrong? Was he about to tell me I needed to move out?

"Did I do something?" I asked, my voice laced with unease.

"We'll talk later," he replied mysteriously.

I stared at my phone, my heart pounding.

Whatever it was, my new life wasn't done surprising me yet.

CHAPTER 5 – Shots of Courage and Calling a Stranger Horny

"Why am I at a bar?" I muttered to myself, pacing in front of the entrance like I was about to commit a felony instead of, you know, meet my flatmate.

Do I go in and look for him?
Do I text and pretend I just got here, like a chill, sophisticated woman who doesn't panic about walking into bars alone?

I took a deep breath, smoothing down my shirt. "Get it together, Nadia. It can't be all that bad if he wanted to meet at a bar."

But the idea of meeting him in a crowded bar filled with strangers felt daunting.

Nope. Liquid courage first.

With a determined nod to absolutely no one, I pushed open the door. The low hum of conversation and bursts of laughter hit me like a wall of noise—laughter, clinking glasses, and the unmistakable smell of hope and bad decisions. A bartender, built like a rugby player but with the patience of a saint, wiped down the counter as I approached, feigning confidence.

"*¿Cuánto por un...* shot?" I ventured, my voice wobbling like an off-key violin string as I asked how much for a shot while gesturing toward the row of neatly lined-up shot glasses.

The bartender grinned. *"Dos euros"*.

"*¿Dos?*" I stared at him. Two euros?! Surely, I had misheard. Where I was from, two euros wouldn't even get me a sip of something questionable in a plastic cup.

He nodded, still smiling, as I scrambled for coins, sliding them across the counter like I had just won a bet. I watched in awe as he poured the golden liquid into a small glass.

"*Gracias,*" I mumbled, tossing it back in one swift motion. It burned in all the right ways.

By then, I was so nervous about meeting Douglas that I thought it might do me good to butter him up with some drinks.

More. Definitely more.

I turned to the bartender, this time with more resolve. "*Seis más, por favor.*"

The bartender gave me a look that said, "You're either heartbroken or insane," but lined up six shots without a word. "Enjoy," he said as he placed them on a tray.

"*Gracias,*" I said again, though this time, I sounded way more confident because, you know, tequila. Grabbing the tray, I wove through the crowd, dodging arms, coats, and the occasional overenthusiastic dancer. The pulsating lights made everyone look like blurry mannequins, but then I spotted Douglas.

Tall, auburn-haired, laughing easily with a group of strangers who somehow already seemed to love him.

"Nadia!" he called out, his Scottish accent slicing through the music. "You made it!" His grin was wide as he waved me over.

I shoved the tray of shots into his hands like a peace offering. "Just in case you're going to give me bad news," I joked.

His eyes sparkled with laughter as he passed the drinks around. "You guys, this is my new flatmate," he announced to the group of strangers around him. "She's been in Barcelona a month but has only just agreed to leave her cave and join us for drinks," he teased with a wink.

I rolled my eyes, but his teasing felt warm, not mocking.

Leaning closer, he added under his breath, "Thought you might be lonely."

And just like that, the knot in my stomach loosened.

So this wasn't a prelude to eviction. Just... kindness.

I let myself relax into the warmth of the group's welcome. They peppered me with questions about my move to Spain, my job, and my favorite local dishes. One girl with blue-tipped hair offered to take me on a tapas crawl. Someone else taught me a Catalan curse word, which I immediately forgot. Everyone was loud, messy, and welcoming.

As the night went on, I couldn't help but notice something unsettling happening all around me.

Everywhere I turned, walls, booths, the freaking dance floor, people were pressed together like Velcro, practically devouring each other. Couples were making out against walls, by the bar, in booths. Hell, I think I even saw one person sitting on their partner's lap, completely absorbed in a public lip-lock that looked like it had no plans of stopping.

All happening ten feet away from where I was sipping my drink like a prude.

In Singapore, kissing in public was practically scandalous. Passionate full-on makeouts in a crowded bar? Unheard of.

And yet, here in Spain, no one batted an eye. It was normal.

45

Expected. Encouraged, even.

I could feel the blush creeping up my face as I clutched my drink tighter, trying not to stare. Failing.

I tried to focus on my conversation, but my gaze kept darting unintentionally back to the shameless couples wrapped around each other like human pretzels. It was like an accidental cultural immersion, one that I wasn't prepared for but couldn't stop looking at.

Part of me was scandalized.
Part of me was fascinated.

The absolute audacity of these people to just be so openly affectionate. It was liberating. It was overwhelming. It was... a lot.

And a tiny, rebellious part of me kind of loved the reckless freedom of it. Not that I wanted to partake in a full-blown PDA marathon myself, but it was intoxicating.

Barcelona didn't care if you were seen, if you were messy, if you were loud.

Barcelona just was.
And I was beginning to realize just how much I liked that.

The night blurred into a haze of laughter, clinking glasses, and some questionable karaoke. At one point, I found myself swaying on a sticky dance floor, belting out an off-key rendition of Livin' on a Prayer with a guy named Jacobo who, for reasons unknown, was wearing sunglasses indoors.

By the time I stumbled home, I was riding a tequila-fueled high, blissfully untethered, drunk on freedom as much as alcohol.

Until the next morning.

The sun streaming through my window was unforgiving. It was too bright, too judgmental, and far too loud.

I groaned, peeling myself off the bed, my limbs feeling like they had been tied to bricks. My body was sluggish, my mind foggy, and every small movement felt like lifting a mountain.

Still, I got dressed because adulthood, apparently, doesn't take hangovers as an excuse, and dragged my half-functioning self to the sandwich shop around the corner.

The menu, however, was a cruel, merciless wall of confusion. No pictures, no English, just words that may as well have been an elaborate code meant to keep the unworthy from eating. My brain, still soaked in tequila from the night before, struggled to decipher the Spanish words in front of me.

Focus.

Pollo. Pollo means chicken. Chicken is safe.

I pointed at the only word I recognized. *"Polla,"* I croaked, hoping the man behind the counter would understand my desperate need for survival.

His eyebrows shot up so fast I thought they might take flight.

"*¿...Perdón?*" he asked carefully, like he was giving me a chance to save myself.

"*Polla,*" I repeated, louder this time, because apparently my survival instincts were on strike.

He pressed his lips together, clearly fighting a smile. "*¿Está segura?*"

Why wouldn't I be sure? I nodded with hungover confidence. "*Sí. Polla.*"

Behind the counter, a guy with dark curls and dimples actually choked on a laugh, covering it badly with a cough.

The man taking my order leaned forward and said gently, "*Señorita... pollo* is chicken." He paused, eyes twinkling. "*Polla...* is penis."

My soul left my body, collected its things, and boarded the next flight back to Singapore.

"I... chicken. I meant chicken," I sputtered, cheeks flaming hotter than the industrial oven behind him. "*Pollo.* Definitely *pollo.* No penises, please."

The dimples guy was grinning openly now, shaking his head in amusement as he sliced bread like this was the best entertainment he'd had all week.

I slumped against the counter, groaning. "Great. Of course I would order a penis sandwich."

The cashier, bless his heroic professionalism, just nodded solemnly. *"Pollo. Uno."*

While I waited, trying not to keel over, I absentmindedly glanced around, and that's when I realized it.

Dimples guy was effortlessly handsome, moving behind the counter with a kind of casual confidence that made even restocking bread rolls look attractive.

Was it possible for someone to look THIS attractive?

Apparently, yes.

He flashed a polite smile, and I perked up slightly. Maybe this was my chance to practice my Spanish. And flirt. In that order. Probably.

When he walked past my table, I cleared my throat. *"Perdón...* Excuse me."

He turned, eyebrows raised, and naturally, my brain evacuated the building. I forgot every Spanish word I had ever learned.

I panicked. "Uh… *¿Cómo se dice* 'hot' *en español?*" Was that the best I could do - asking him how to say hot in Spanish?

He smirked. *"Caliente."*

I nodded, trying to appear like a sophisticated bilingual queen instead of a hungover disaster. "Right. And… how do you say 'very hot'?"

His smirk widened. *"Muy caliente."*

I hesitated for a split second before raising an eyebrow, feigning innocence. "And… how do you say you are very hot?"

His laugh was low and amused. He leaned closer, eyes glinting with mischief. *"¿Me estás diciendo que soy muy caliente?"*

My brain short-circuited. Was I flirting successfully? Was I about to pass out? More importantly, did he just call me out and ask if I thought he was very hot?

Before I could respond, he continued, "Although… just so you know… in Spanish, *'caliente'* doesn't really mean temperature when you're talking about a person."

I blinked, still smiling. "It doesn't?"

He leaned in a little, lowering his voice conspiratorially.

"It means… horny."

"Oh my God," I whispered, already dying inside. "I meant the sandwich. Obviously. The sandwich."

He grinned like he'd just been handed the best part of his shift. "Of course. The sandwich is very horny."

"I'M LEAVING," I said, mostly to myself.

A minute later, another waiter brought out my order. I unwrapped it eagerly because I knew that Spanish food would never fail me, even if it was just a sandwich.

My excitement soon fizzled out like a deflated balloon. The sandwich was cold.

"C-Cold?" I muttered, poking at it. "Is this a mistake?"

I stared at it in disbelief. Where was the warmth? The toasty, golden perfection?

I looked up at Mr. *Muy Caliente*, who was watching me with amusement.

I groaned, burying my face in my hands. "This country is testing me."

He laughed, shaking his head. "Come back tomorrow. I'll help you order something *caliente*."

I looked up, narrowing my eyes. "Are you offering menu advice or are you flirting with me?"

He grinned. "Both."

Touché.

I left the shop clutching my cold sandwich of regret, half-horrified and half-proud.

On one hand, I had just successfully (or disastrously) flirted in Spanish. A milestone. A moment of personal growth. A scene straight out of a soap opera, minus the dramatic music and jealous ex-lovers lurking in the background.

On the other hand, I was clutching a cold sandwich, the single most disappointing meal of my life. The weight of my food-related misfortune was almost too much to bear.

I sighed, hugging the sandwich to my chest like it was the last shred of dignity I had left.

The waiter's words echoed in my head. *Come back tomorrow. I'll help you order something caliente.*

Was that... a date? A friendly gesture? A subtle attempt to prevent me from embarrassing myself in another food-related incident?

I didn't know.

But I did know one thing, I was not about to eat this sad, lifeless excuse of a meal.

By the time I got home, my appetite had vanished, leaving me alone with my sandwich of regret. I placed it on the counter like an artifact, a relic from a battle I had lost.

It was a Saturday afternoon, and I was both hungry and mildly annoyed at myself. There had to be a better way to spend the day.

Flopping onto my bed, I opened Facebook, scrolling mindlessly through updates until something caught my eye.

CHAPTER 6 – Nerves, Numbers, and Newfound Hope

The Facebook post read: ***Meet people and practice speaking multiple languages!***

I stared at the screen, my thumb hovering over the RSVP button as if it were a self-destruct switch. A language exchange? Hmm. It could be interesting. At the very least, I might meet people who spoke English. And, if nothing else, it was a perfectly good excuse to get out of the sweatpants of shame I had been wearing all day.

I exhaled and clicked Going.

An hour later, I stood in front of my mirror, staring at myself like I was about to walk into a battlefield.

Barcelona had effortlessly stylish people. I had... questionable fashion instincts and a deep personal relationship with hoodies.

I settled on a casual-but-not-too-casual look—jeans, a fitted top, and boots that said I was confident but screamed I had blisters incoming.

"You're going to be social," I told my reflection firmly. "You're going to meet people. You will not, I repeat, you will not stand in a corner pretending to check nonexistent emails."

My reflection did not look convinced.

Cuatro Gatos, the bar where the event was being held, wasn't far from my apartment, so I decided to walk. The streets were alive with their usual Barcelona energy; bars spilling over with people, lively conversations floating through the air, and the occasional scent of grilled meat drifting from hidden tapas joints.

As I passed one bar after another, I noticed something I hadn't before. These weren't just places for drinking; they were living rooms that happened to serve alcohol. In the mornings, they poured coffee and served breakfast; by afternoon, they dished out sandwiches and gossip; and by night, they were full-blown watering holes where entire families gathered like it was the most normal thing in the world.

It was all so different from Singapore, where bars belonged to the night, reserved for the stressed and the heartbroken. Here, they seemed to belong to *everyone*.

"A bar that serves croissants in the morning and sangria at night?" I mused. "Efficient."

When I finally reached Cuatro Gatos, I hesitated outside the door.

Every time it swung open, it released a blast of sound that included laughter, clinking glasses, and the kind of body heat usually reserved for subways and poor decisions.

My hand hovered over the door handle as a wave of nerves hit me.

"Am I really doing this?" I fidgeted with my bag strap, considering my options. I could still turn around. Go home. Eat my leftover cold sandwich of regret—

"Are you also gathering the courage to go in for the language exchange?" a voice broke my reverie.

I jumped.

Standing beside me was a guy around my age with slightly messy hair and a phone in his hand. His expression was sheepish, like we'd both been caught trying to sneak into a party we weren't cool enough for.

He flashed a hesitant smile. "I've been standing here for, like, five minutes pretending I'm checking messages." He held up his phone as proof.

I let out a relieved laugh. "Same. I was just about to fake an urgent email."

His American accent gave him away immediately.

"I'm Joshua, by the way," he said, sticking out a hand.

I shook it. "Nadia. Fellow overthinker."

Joshua grinned. "Nice. So, shall we socially flail together?"

I nodded, feeling slightly better about the night ahead. "Let's do it."

The bar was cozy, dimly lit, with walls lined with bookshelves that made it look like a cross between a library and a secret drinking hideout. Small groups clustered around tables, deep in conversation, languages switching mid-sentence.

Joshua and I made a beeline for the bar first, because let's be honest, nothing lubricates awkward small talk like a glass of cheap wine.

Armed with wine, we joined a table where a mix of locals and expats were talking animatedly in at least three different languages. It was like a live-action Duolingo app.

I immediately clicked with Laura, a Spanish woman with red lipstick, a contagious laugh, and the uncanny ability to make dirty jokes sound classy.

She had this way of switching between Spanish and English mid-sentence, like both languages belonged to her and were lucky to be there. It was a skill I found both impressive and enviable.

Naturally, I overshared.

"I've had two engagements," I said after one drink too many, "which I think means I either have excellent taste or terrible timing."

"Maybe you just need a Spanish boyfriend," Laura quipped.

"Oh God," I laughed. "Maybe."

Her eyes lit up and she leaned in conspiratorially.. "No, say it! Say, '*Estoy buscando un novio.*'"

I repeated hesitantly. "*¿Est... estoy buscando... un novio?*"

"Perfect!" she beamed. "Again! Like you mean it!"

And like a complete idiot, I said it louder. Like. I. Meant. It.

The words had barely left my mouth when a guy walking past our table stopped dead in his tracks and raised an eyebrow.

"You're looking for a boyfriend?"

I turned bright red.

He smirked.

Joshua nearly choked on his wine.

I opened my mouth to explain, to clarify that I was NOT in fact auditioning potential boyfriends in the middle of a bar, but my brain froze.

"Uh…" I stammered. "I… I mean technically, Laura made me say it…"

The guy murmured with a playful smile. "Well… good luck."

And with that, he gave me a wink and walked away, leaving me to question every single life choice I had ever made.

Joshua, now laughing hysterically, wiped at his eyes. "That was the best moment of my night. Hands down."

I buried my face in my hands. "I'm deleting myself from this country."

Despite the mortification, the night only got better.

Joshua and I ended up circling the room, occasionally chatting with others, but always drifting back to each other like orbiting planets of mild introversion.

There was an effortless connection between us - we laughed at the same jokes, found the same quirks about the event amusing, and kept each other grounded in the chaos of new faces and languages.

Later in the night, as the background noise softened into cozy chatter, he leaned in slightly and said, "Just so you know... I'm gay."

I blinked, momentarily caught off guard. "Oh. Cool! Uh... thanks for telling me?"

He chuckled. "You were being really nice. I didn't want to send the wrong idea."

I blinked again. Had I been accidentally flirting this entire time?!

Was this a new, accidental skill I had acquired??

"Well," I said, sipping my drink, "I was just about to propose, so I really appreciate the clarification."

He grinned. "Yeah, I figured I should tell you before you started shopping for wedding venues."

With that, we clinked glasses, our friendship now officially cemented. Instant besties.

We spent the rest of the night people-watching and gossiping about some of the more eccentric characters at the exchange, including a guy who was clearly using the event as his own personal dating service, shamelessly hitting on every single woman at the bar.

By the time I checked the time, it was well past midnight, and the crowd had started to thin.

As I hugged Laura goodbye and exchanged numbers with several others, I felt a warmth that had nothing to do with the alcohol.

"What a great night," I thought.

I walked home with five new numbers in my phone, a feeling of accomplishment, and a growing hope that maybe this new city wouldn't be so lonely after all.

The next day, I texted Joshua. He replied instantly, and we made plans to meet the following week.

When we did, he was full of wild stories.

"I went to a dog-friendly poetry reading last night," he said. "There was a guy reading a love poem to his beagle."

"How do you even find these people?" I asked, half-amused, half-intrigued.

He grinned. "You're going to laugh."

"Try me."

"Dating apps," he said, holding up his phone. "But not for, you know, dating. Most of them have an option where you can just look for friends. You'd be surprised how many people are in the same boat—new city, no friends, just looking to connect."

"A dating app?" I repeated, raising an eyebrow. I had always associated them with romance and, frankly, desperation. While I was far from conservative, the idea of meeting people online still carried a stigma for me. But Joshua was living proof it worked.

"Isn't that... for desperate people?"

Joshua snorted. "Desperate people or people who are too lazy to make friends the traditional way. And guess what? It works."

I crossed my arms. "I remain skeptical."

He shrugged and tapped his screen. "Suit yourself. But I've made five friends, two salsa partners, and one extremely good cake connection."

That night, after way too much deliberation, I downloaded Tinder.

The concept was easy enough: swipe right if you like someone, swipe left if you didn't.

At first, it was fun swiping into the abyss of questionable selfies and bios like "I lift weights and women's spirits."

But let's be real, I wasn't on Tinder for love. Or even fun.

I was still wrecked from two failed engagements. Their betrayals felt like a bruise I couldn't stop poking, and every time I did, it hurt all over again. I didn't know how to deal with the mess of it, anger, humiliation, the sinking fear that maybe I was just fundamentally unlovable.

So naturally, instead of processing those Very Big Feelings like a healthy adult, I decided to… not.

Tinder was the perfect emotional noise machine. A bottomless buffet of strangers who didn't know me, didn't know my history, and definitely didn't look at me like I was "the girl with two broken engagements."

Here, I could be anyone. Flirty, breezy, totally-not-a-disaster me. It was easier to drown in bad bios and gym selfies than sit alone with the ache of what had actually happened.

Basically, I was using thirst traps as therapy.

For ten minutes, I swiped like my life depended on it. But then the panic set in. What if no one swipes on me?

The next morning, I woke up to a dozen notifications.

Apparently, someone had. Several someones.

As I sifted through them, it became painfully clear why dating apps had such a mixed reputation.

Half the messages were outright obscene. A few couldn't

speak English, leaving me with a small group of men who seemed genuinely interested in conversation.

No women, though. So much for expanding my female friend group.

Just as I was about to delete the app entirely, one message caught my eye.

Intrigued, I decided to reply.

This could be the start of something… interesting.

CHAPTER 7 – Short Skirts and Shorter Relationships

⸻ ❦ ⸻

Gerardo was the first person I officially dated in Barcelona, which made him the proud recipient of my expat dating virginity, an honor I'm sure he'll never fully appreciate.

I had agonized over this date. What to wear, how to act, whether I should play it cool or lean into the excitement. Was I supposed to kiss him at the end? What if he was one of those guys who thought Asian girls were submissive? What if he expected me to giggle and say things like *Oh my god, your Spanish is so good* like I was auditioning for a role in a romcom movie?

The spiral of doubt nearly made me cancel.

But I had moved across the world to be bold. To live larger. I was not about to let an overactive imagination (and two ex-fiancés' worth of trust issues) ruin a free drink and the possibility of good banter.

So I went. In a short skirt and leggings, in the middle of winter. Because questionable fashion decisions are my love language.

I got to the bar early, because nothing screams "foreign girl alone in a new country" like someone wandering in circles, clutching Google Maps like it holds the secrets of the universe.

I stood outside with a drink in one hand and a cigarette in the other, attempting that casually disheveled just-flew-in-from-Paris look. I mostly resembled a very cold raccoon.

"I can't believe I'm wearing a short skirt in this weather," I muttered to myself. "He better be worth it."

"*Hola!* Are you Nadia?"

The voice came from behind me, smooth and accented, and when I turned, I nearly dropped my drink and cigarette.

His photos had been criminally humble.

Gerardo was tall, intimidatingly tall. The kind of tall that made me instinctively straighten my spine like I was suddenly auditioning for a shampoo ad. Dark hair. Ridiculous cheekbones. A sweater that clung to him in all the right ways. He had that dangerous combination of easy confidence and warm eyes that made you forget your last name.

I summoned a flirtatious smile, even as my brain turned into mashed potatoes. *"Hola*! Yes, I'm Nadia. Gerardo?"

He flashed a devastating smile, eyes twinkling with mischief, and leaned in to greet me the Spanish way—two kisses, one on each cheek.

No warning. No easing into it. Just straight-up face-to-face skin contact with an absurdly handsome man.

My brain promptly shut down.

I had no idea where to put my hands. One arm flailed awkwardly in the air before I decided to just clutch my drink like it was my emotional support animal.

He stepped back, amused. "Shall we?"

Shall we? SHALL WE?? What kind of girl was I supposed to be here? The charming, flirty one or the disaster who somehow still gets the guy?

I nodded. Big mistake. My frozen limbs failed me, and I stumbled slightly in my ridiculous heels.

His hand shot out to steady me, warm against my waist. "Cold?"

"Nope," I said too quickly, trying to salvage my dignity. "Just making sure you have an excuse to keep holding me."

Oh. My. God.

Gerardo chuckled, clearly enjoying my internal suffering, and guided me inside before I could embarrass myself further.

At the bar, I tried to play it cool. "I'll get the first round," I declared, confident, sexy, independent.

Then I saw the menu. A glass of wine? €2.50. A beer? €2.

Excuse me??

I blinked at the prices. Was Spain some kind of magical alternate universe where drinks were actually affordable?

Gerardo watched my reaction, amusement dancing in his eyes. "Something wrong?"

"No," I said, waving a hand. "It's just where I come from, drinks this cheap usually mean you'll wake up blind."

He laughed and ordered for us, and I was suddenly painfully aware of how attractive confidence was when paired with an accent.

As we settled at a small table, he studied me like I was a puzzle he was excited to solve. "So, why did you come to Barcelona?"

I realised this was a question I had to be ready to answer if I were to live here.

I twirled my straw, trying to find the right words. "I wanted a change. Something different from Singapore, less strict, more… freedom."

He tilted his head. "And have you found it?"

I sipped my drink, pretending to consider it. "Well, I did just let a handsome Spanish man buy me a drink, so I'd say I'm off to a good start."

His eyes flashed with amusement. "Handsome, huh?"

Crap. Did I say that out loud?

I took another sip to hide my blunder. "I meant… objectively speaking. Like, statistically, you're probably in the top… I don't know, 15%?"

He laughed. "Only 15? You wound me, Nadia."

I shrugged. "Barcelona has high standards."

The banter continued, a playful and flirty rhythm forming between us, like two people pretending they weren't already imagining what the other looked like in a shared Netflix account.

At one point, he leaned in slightly, his gaze locking onto mine.

69

"So tell me, what's the most spontaneous thing you've ever done?"

I considered this. "Does moving here count? It wasn't exactly planned."

He raised his glass to me. "That counts. But next time, you should jump into something with no plan at all. That's where the fun begins."

I teased. "Is that how you live your life? No plans, just vibes?"

He shrugged, his grin widening. "It's worked for me so far."

The night flew by. He was engaging, funny, and flirty in a way that should have been illegal. And against all odds, I was actually enjoying myself.

As we walked outside into the crisp night air, I felt an unexpected butterfly situation happening in my stomach as he took my hand into his.

His expression softened and I felt the weight of his gaze. "You're interesting, Nadia," he murmured. "Barcelona suits you."

I opened my mouth to say something clever, but before I could, he leaned down, brushing his lips against mine.

Not a maybe-I-like-you peck. A full, warm kiss that belonged in a movie.

My brain promptly restarted like an old computer that hadn't been shut down properly.

By the time we pulled apart, I was lightheaded... either from the kiss or the sheer audacity of my life choices.

Gerardo grinned. "You're blushing."

"I'm not."

I was.

He laughed, and I hated how much I liked it.

For a moment, I let myself believe in the fantasy.

At first, everything with Gerardo felt exhilarating. He was attentive, charming, and had an uncanny ability to make every moment feel like it was lifted straight out of a romantic film. Our dates were indulgences: late-night walks by the beach, candlelight flickering over tapas, laughter echoing in hidden speakeasies I never would've found on my own. With him, the world seemed to hum at a higher frequency.

But fantasies had a way of unraveling, and as the weeks passed, cracks began to appear.

It started subtly. His replies became shorter, less playful. Our plans became more sporadic. The Gerardo who once eagerly set up the next date before the current one even ended was now harder to pin down. He felt like a guest star in my life, appearing at random intervals.

The final straw? I suggested we meet one weekend, and he hit me with: *"Let's see, I might be busy."*

Busy doing what? Being attractive somewhere else with someone else?

We met one last time on a chilly evening, and I could already feel it in my bones: this was going to be the conversation. The one where we pretended everything was fine while both of us knew it wasn't.

I had suggested meeting at a café, hoping that being in public would force us to act like rational adults rather than two people awkwardly dancing around the fact that one of us was more invested than the other.

Gerardo arrived looking effortlessly handsome as usual, messy dark hair, that stupidly perfect jawline, and a wool coat that probably cost more than my rent. I, on the other hand, had spent an unhealthy amount of time trying to look casually unbothered, which ironically made me look very bothered.

He smiled like this wasn't about to be The Talk. "Hola, Nadia."

I stirred my coffee aggressively and tried to smile back, but it probably came out more like a grimace. "Hey."

We launched into mindless small talk… work, the weather,

something about the new tapas place down the street that he had totally meant to take me to but never did. But even through the filler conversation, the distance between us was undeniable.

I decided to just rip the Band-Aid off.

"Gerardo," I said, setting my cup down. "Be honest. Are you looking for something serious, or…?"

He exhaled, running a hand through his hair, a classic stalling tactic. "Nadia, you're amazing. Truly. But I think I'm just not in the right place for anything serious right now."

Ah. There it was. The internationally recognized "It's not you, it's me" speech.

I nodded, swallowing down the petty urge to respond with *Oh really? Because two months ago, you were in the right place to flirt over croquetas and tell me I was 'different from other girls'* but I refrained. Growth.

Instead, I let out an annoyingly understanding laugh. "Oh, of course! No worries. I mean, I totally get it."

We lingered for a second, neither of us quite sure whether to go for a hug, a handshake, or a dramatic movie-style goodbye.

I settled for stepping back before he could lean in for a cheek kiss.

"Goodbye, Gerardo."

And just like that, it was done.

As I walked home, I realized I wasn't even heartbroken, just... mildly annoyed that I had ignored the signs.

Still, Gerardo had been the perfect introduction to dating in Barcelona, handsome, passionate, and a walking, talking warning label.

Later that week, I flopped onto Joshua's couch with a dramatic groan, swiping half-heartedly through Tinder like it was a boring grocery list.

"Gerardo's old news," I announced. "Now it's all about... Alejandro-who-looks-like-he's-smoldering-in-a-wind-tunnel."

Joshua peered over his wine glass, unimpressed. "You do realize you're not actually dating, right? You're just... using these poor men like human Band-Aids for your feelings."

I gasped. "That is a terrible analogy. But also, pass me the wine."

He ignored me. "Seriously, Nads. Maybe you don't need another guy right now. Maybe what you need is to just... be alone. Figure yourself out without a distraction."

I waved him off, thumb still swiping. "Wow, thank you,

Buddha. Should I meditate on a mountaintop while I'm at it?"

Joshua arched a brow. "Or you could just, I don't know, sit with your feelings for once instead of flirting your way out of them."

I winced because ouch. Then I grinned, because denial is my favorite sport. "I'll sit with my feelings... right after tapas with Alejandro."

Joshua groaned, flopping back into the couch like he'd been personally victimized. "You're impossible."

"Impossible," I agreed cheerfully, holding up my phone. "But also getting drinks on Thursday."

I didn't listen to him. Not even a little.

Barcelona still had so much left to offer, and I was determined to swipe my way through it.

CHAPTER 8 – Dating Abroad: One Swipe at a Time

~ංමං~

The months that followed Gerardo felt like I was speed-dating my way through Europe, one glass of vermouth at a time. Tapas, terrazas, and a revolving door of romantic "possibilities."

I hadn't planned to become a serial dater. I really hadn't. But somehow, I went from mock-gasping at Joshua for suggesting dating apps to becoming his main competition.

"You," he declared one night, pointing at me over our drinks like I'd committed a felony, "were skeptical. I remember the dramatic eye roll. The judgment. And now look at you, out here collecting dates like loyalty points."

I narrowed my eyes. "Excuse me for embracing the local culture."

"Local culture?" he snorted. "At this rate, YOU are the local culture. If Barcelona had a trophy for 'Most Romantic Enthusiasm in a Calendar Year,' you'd have it. Etched. In gold."

I threw a sugar packet at him. "Stop making me sound like the female Casanova. I'm just… open to new experiences."

"Open?" Joshua raised an eyebrow. "Nadia, you've gone on more dates than me this month. And I've been here longer."

"Maybe you should step up your game." I sipped my wine smugly.

Joshua sighed dramatically. "Unbelievable. I created a monster, and now the student has surpassed the master."

But he wasn't wrong. My dating app history looked like a European tourism brochure.

First, there was Luca. An Italian architect with an easy laugh, an impressive jawline, and a talent for making even the simplest plate of pasta sound like poetry.

Our first date was at a rooftop bar overlooking the Sagrada Familia, where he gestured wildly, explaining how Gaudí's work was a revolution of movement and natural form.

"It's incredible, no?" he asked, his expressive hands painting shapes in the air.

"It is," I admitted, sipping my wine. "But you talk about buildings the way people talk about their children."

He placed a dramatic hand on his chest. "That's because they are my children."

Charming as he was, Luca soon became too intense for what I was ready for. Was this an Italian thing? By the third date, he was already planning vacations together, and I was just trying to decide whether I even liked his cologne.

Next up was Chris. A British expat in finance who had the uncanny ability to make taxes sound interesting.

"You know," he mused over tapas one afternoon, "if you were a financial strategy, you'd be a high-risk, high-reward investment."

I blinked. "Is that… a compliment or a red flag?"

"Both," he admitted with a smirk.

Chris was fun, but his tendency to analyze everything, including my personality, like it was a case study for a business merger made me feel like I was being assessed rather than wooed.

And then there was Pierre, a brooding French photographer who carried his camera everywhere and took himself far too seriously.

Our first date? A gallery in El Raval where he monologued about haunting black-and-white portraits from his travels while I tried to decode a photo of a pigeon.

"You see?" he murmured, pointing at an image of an old man with deeply etched lines in his face. "This is what life looks like. Not the filtered Instagram version."

I admired his passion, but Pierre had a dark side that felt too heavy for me.

When he suggested a spontaneous trip to Paris "to feel the cold, raw truth of winter," I realized I was out of my depth.

Each date was an adventure, a lesson in culture and chemistry, or the lack thereof. But none of them felt quite right.

But if I was honest, somewhere between Luca the poetic architect, Chris the finance bro, and Pierre the tortured French photographer, it all started to blur together. First kisses, first "so where are you from?" questions, first glasses of wine. It was like being stuck on a merry-go-round. Fun at first, but after a while, you just feel dizzy and wonder why you thought spinning in circles would fix your life.

It wasn't that any of them were terrible. They weren't. They were nice. Charming, even. But nice and charming started to feel like recycled material, like I was starring in the same pilot episode over and over with different guest stars.

The excitement dulled. The sparkle faded. And the truth

slipped in during the in-between moments. Walking home after a date that should've made me giddy but instead left me hollow. Sitting across from a man who was perfectly nice and interesting, but made me feel like I was interviewing for the role of Girlfriend instead of actually… being one.

I should've been buzzing. Instead, I felt… hollow.

Because here's the thing: the carousel kept spinning, but deep down I was terrified of what would happen if it stopped. If I stepped off, there'd be no dates, no distractions, no clever banter to keep me entertained. Just me. Alone with all the messy feelings I'd been duct-taping together since Singapore.

And honestly? That was a much scarier date than any stranger with good hair and a questionable bio.

So I kept swiping. Kept dressing up and pretending the next one might feel different.

Then, almost a year after my first date in Barcelona, I met Diego.

It wasn't supposed to be a big deal… just another date arranged through an app. He was from León, a city in the northwest of Spain, and he was a biologist.

A scientist. The first scientist I had ever dated. I was initially hesitant to meet him. Would he start talking about migration patterns of storks over drinks?

But the moment he walked into the bar, something in my chest rearranged itself.

And just like that, I was in trouble. The fun kind. The please-don't-let-me-embarrass-myself-in-the-first-five-minutes kind.

He had that slow-burn kind of sexy. The kind you don't clock at first because your brain is still booting up, and then BAM. Ten seconds later, you're wondering if your lipstick is still intact and whether now's a good time to start emotionally preparing for marriage.

Dark, wavy hair, forearms rolled into full display, and eyes that said "I've read at least one emotionally intelligent book this year." He wasn't flashy, but he had presence, the kind that made the air around him feel warmer. Or maybe that was just me overheating.

And then he smiled—lazy, crooked, unfairly attractive—and my ovaries filed an official complaint.

He hadn't even spoken yet, and I already needed a drink, a fan, and possibly divine intervention.

"Hi, Nadia?" he asked, his voice low and warm, a soft Spanish lilt curling around my name like a ribbon.

"That's me," I said, standing like I was being called in for a job interview.

He smiled playfully. "We don't do handshakes in Spain." Before I could react, he leaned in for a kiss on each cheek, and I couldn't help but laugh.

We sat down, and before I knew it, two hours had passed.

Diego had a way of making even the smallest things sound magical. He asked thoughtful questions, not the standard *so what do you do for work?* nonsense. And his stories of growing up in a small city were laced with humor and just the right amount of nostalgia.

He was funny in an unintentional, nerdy way, the kind of funny that sneaks up on you when you least expect it.

"You moved here alone?" he asked at one point, his dark eyes studying me.

"Yeah," I said. "I needed a clean start. Singapore was starting to feel like a pair of shoes that didn't fit anymore."

He nodded, his expression softening. "I get that. Sometimes you have to take a leap to find where you're meant to be.

I paused, caught off guard. Not just by what he said, but how he said it... like he really understood.

The date with Diego had been light and easy, just the kind of evening I hadn't realized I needed.

When we left the bar, the air was crisp but not unkind, a

typical Barcelona autumn evening. We walked side by side, weaving through narrow streets toward the train station.

My brain was already composing imaginary wedding vows.

"So," he said, breaking the comfortable silence, "did the bar live up to your expectations, or should I feel personally offended?"

I laughed. "It was good, but I'll admit, I was distracted. The company was a bit more interesting."

Diego tilted his head, feigning surprise. "Is that so? I'll take that as a compliment, though I think you're just buttering me up so I'll let you pick the spot next time."

I was about to fire back a teasing comeback when a sudden bark sliced through the air.

Before I could think, I instinctively grabbed Diego's arm.

From around the corner, a scruffy brown dog darted toward us, barking furiously. It wasn't large, but it had that chaotic, unhinged energy that made my heart race.

"Diego…"

"It's okay," he said calmly, stepping slightly in front of me. His hand found mine, firm but gentle, as he shielded me from the dog.

The owner appeared moments later, shouting apologies in rapid Spanish as they secured the leash. *"¡Lo siento!* He's harmless, really!"

I nodded quickly, forcing a smile, but my pulse was still pounding. Diego didn't let go of my hand until the dog and its owner disappeared into the crowd.

"Are you okay?" he asked, turning to face me. His expression was full of concern, the teasing from earlier replaced by genuine care.

"Yeah," I said, exhaling a shaky breath. "I'm just… not great with dogs."

He smiled, still holding my hand. "You didn't need to tell me that. I figured it out when you nearly climbed onto my shoulders."

I laughed despite myself, the tension easing. "Well, you were in the way."

He squeezed my hand. "I'll be in the way again if you ever need me to be."

And then, as if it was the most natural thing in the world, he leaned in and kissed me.

Right there, in the middle of the sidewalk. Slow. Sweet. Like we'd known each other in a past life and this was just us picking up where we left off.

It wasn't hurried or awkward. It was slow and deliberate, like he was giving me the chance to pull away. But I didn't. My chest tightened, my pulse spiking as his lips met mine, warm and steady. The world around us, including the chatter from the street, the flicker of passing headlights, melted into the background.

When we pulled back, our hands still intertwined, Diego's smile returned. This time it was small, bashful, like even he hadn't expected the electricity between us. I could feel the faint tremor in his fingers, and it mirrored my own.

"I hope that was okay," he said, his voice quieter now, like he was afraid to break the moment.

I nodded, feeling the heat creep up my cheeks. "More than okay."

We continued walking toward the metro station, our hands still entwined, like it was the most natural thing in the world. Every few steps, one of us would steal a glance at the other, only to be met with an equally ridiculous smile. It was embarrassing. It was perfect.

For the first time in a long time, I felt like I wasn't just taking a leap into the unknown. I was landing somewhere I actually wanted to be.

He texted me later that night:
   "I had a great time. Let's do this again soon?"

And we did.

One date turned into two. Then three. Then Sunday afternoon strolls. Midweek coffees. Long chats about jellyfish reproduction that somehow felt flirty.

With Diego, everything felt effortless.

No strategic texting gaps, no second-guessing what he meant... just easy, uncomplicated joy. He didn't try to impress me with grand gestures or deep existential theories.

He just showed up. Consistently.
And it turns out? Showing up might be the most romantic thing of all.

I stared at my phone one night, smiling like a fool at another thoughtful message.

Maybe, just maybe, I'd found someone who was more than a chapter. Maybe Diego was the beginning of something whole.

CHAPTER 9 – Not All Heroes Wear Capes—Some Wear Cozy Sweaters

"Are you sure he's going to like me?" Diego asked, his tone light but with a hint of nerves as we walked hand in hand toward the metro station.

I squeezed his hand, shooting him a reassuring smile. "Joshua? Oh, he's going to love you. You're funny, charming, and most importantly, you know your way around good wine. That's basically his holy trinity."

Diego chuckled, dimples appearing the way they always did when he was genuinely amused. "Well, I'll do my best not to embarrass you."

"You couldn't even if you tried," I teased, nudging him lightly with my shoulder.

It had been months since our first date, and things between us had grown steadily, naturally. Diego wasn't just my boyfriend; he was becoming my best friend, my constant in a city that had once felt so foreign.

Which was precisely why I was nervous as hell about introducing him to Joshua.

Joshua wasn't just any friend. He was my first friend in Barcelona. My accidental emotional support American. And the one person whose opinion I actually cared about.

The restaurant, a cozy Greek spot tucked into a corner of El Raval, had been Joshua's choice. He had been raving about it for weeks, and if he had a religious devotion to anything, it was food recommendations.

As soon as we stepped inside, the low hum of conversation and the rich aroma of grilled meats, warm pita, and garlic-heavy tzatziki enveloped us. Diego held the door open for me, his hand resting lightly on the small of my back, a gesture that shouldn't have made me feel like melting, but here we were.

"Nadia!" Joshua's voice rang out from a table near the back. His face lit up as soon as he spotted me. He shot up from his chair and practically lunged for a hug before turning his attention to Diego.

"And you must be the famous Diego. Finally, I get to meet the guy who's been monopolizing all of her free time."

Diego extended a hand, but Joshua waved it off completely, pulling him into a full-body hug instead.

"We don't do formalities here," Joshua said with a wink.

Diego laughed, clearly relieved. "Good to know. I've heard a lot about you."

"All good things, I hope," Joshua said, his eyes twinkling as he ushered us to the table.

The dinner started seamlessly, with Diego fitting into the group as though he'd been part of it all along. He listened intently to Joshua's stories, interjecting with the perfect amount of humor and making the entire table laugh with his quick wit. Then, he asked Joshua about his strong, borderline-militant opinions on food.

"You don't understand," Joshua said, gesturing wildly with his fork as he launched into a very serious discussion about Greek cuisine. "The best souvlaki I've ever had was from a tiny street stall in Thessaloniki. I still have dreams about it."

Diego nodded, pretending to take mental notes. "And how do I, a mere mortal, get on your level?"

Joshua smirked. "Oh, you don't. But I do accept applications for my elite foodie club."

I groaned. "Oh god, please don't encourage him. He's impossible when he gets like this."

89

Diego shot me an amused glance. "I don't know. I think I like this guy."

Joshua dramatically placed a hand over his heart. "Finally, someone with taste."

Halfway through the meal, as I reached for my glass of wine, Joshua leaned over and whispered in my ear.

"He's a keeper. Seriously."

I beamed, my heart swelling with a ridiculous amount of joy.

Then, just as the dessert platters arrived—honey-drizzled baklava, thick, creamy yogurt with figs—I reached for my bag to grab my phone.

My hand met empty air.

"Where's my bag?" I muttered, frowning as I peeked under the table.

Joshua paused mid-bite, his brow furrowing. "You had it when you sat down, right?"

"Yeah…" My stomach dropped. I scanned the restaurant, panic creeping in.

That's when Diego's entire demeanor shifted. His eyes sharpened as he pointed toward the door.

"That guy," he said, his voice low but urgent.

I turned just in time to see a man slipping out of the restaurant, my bag tucked under his arm, a glimpse of it flashing before he pulled his oversized jacket tight around himself.

Diego didn't hesitate. He shot out of his seat and took off like a man on a mission.

"Diego!" I yelped after him, but he was already weaving through tables, dodging a waiter, and bolting out the door.

For a few agonizing seconds, the entire restaurant seemed to hold its breath. Joshua placed a reassuring hand on my shoulder, but I could barely hear him over the pounding of my heart.

"He'll get it," he murmured. "He's got that mild-mannered biologist, but secretly an action hero vibe."

I would have laughed, except my entire body was locked in panic.

Then, through the front window, Diego reappeared, walking briskly beside the man who had taken my bag. Except he wasn't dragging him back or starting a brawl. No, Diego looked calm, controlled, but his presence was commanding. His hand hovered near the thief's arm, ensuring he didn't bolt as they stepped back into the restaurant.

The thief, scruffy and visibly uncomfortable, muttered under his breath while nervously shifting on his feet.

Diego stopped in the middle of the restaurant, crossed his arms, and gave the man a look so unimpressed it could have been patented by an exasperated teacher.

"Where is it?" Diego's voice was calm but firm, his Spanish accent sharpening the edges of his words. "The bag. Did you take it?"

The man shook his head vehemently. "No, no. I didn't take anything," he said in Spanish, his voice rising in pitch. "You've got the wrong person!"

Diego raised an eyebrow. "Really?" His tone was all skepticism, zero patience. "Because you were running, and she..." he gestured toward me "just noticed her bag was gone."

The man took a step back, but Diego didn't move, his eyes locked on the thief.

"Listen," Diego continued, lowering his voice but keeping it steady. "You're not leaving here until we sort this out. So, do you want to tell the truth now, or wait for the police to do it for you?"

The thief visibly calculated his options, his eyes darting between the exit and Diego's broad-shouldered, no-nonsense stance. Then, in the most anticlimactic move imaginable, he reached into his oversized jacket and pulled out his phone while at the same time letting my bag drop to the floor with a dull thud.

It was so absurdly casual, I almost laughed. It was like watching a chicken lay an egg.

"There," the man mumbled, holding up his hands in mock surrender. "I didn't take it. It was just there on the floor."

Joshua whispered next to me, "That was the most dramatic anti-climax I've ever seen."

At that moment, two uniformed police officers stepped inside, alerted by the commotion. Their sharp eyes swept over the scene before settling on Diego and the thief.

One of the officers stepped forward, and addressed Diego in Spanish. "What's going on here?"

Diego gestured to the man and then to my bag on the floor. "He stole her bag. She can confirm it," he said, glancing back at me.

The officer turned to me. "Miss, is this your bag?"

I nodded quickly, my voice steady despite the adrenaline still coursing through me. "Yes, it is."

The officer bent down to pick up the bag and handed it to me before turning back to the thief, who was now looking more nervous by the second. He spoke to me in Spanish, but

I was too frazzled to do any translation in my head.

Diego helped me out, "Do you want to press charges? It would involve going to the police station and giving a statement."

I hesitated, glancing between Diego and the thief. Diego's expression was unreadable, but his hand found mine, giving it a slight, reassuring squeeze.

"It's up to you," he said softly, his voice steady and without judgment.

I swallowed hard, my mind racing. Barcelona was notorious for pickpockets, and part of me wanted to make an example of him. But another part of me, a bigger part, couldn't ignore the look in his eyes.

"No," I said finally, shaking my head. "I just want my things back."

The officer nodded, his expression neutral but firm. "Understood." He turned to the thief and issued a warning, his tone sharp enough to make the man flinch.

As the police escorted the thief out, the tension in the room dissipated. Diego turned to me, his expression softening. "Are you okay?"

I nodded, clutching my bag tightly. "I am now, thanks to you. You didn't have to do all that, you know."

He smiled softly, brushing a stray strand of hair from my face. "Of course I did. You're important to me, Nadia."

As I sank back into my chair, bag clutched tightly in my lap like a lifeline, I exhaled the last remnants of panic. Diego, ever steady, gave my hand a reassuring squeeze under the table. Joshua, never one to let a moment pass without commentary, stabbed his fork into the baklava and said, "Okay, hero, you're making the rest of us look bad."

Laughter rippled through the group, and something in me finally relaxed.

I looked around at the people sitting with me—Joshua, who had become my accidental rock in a foreign land. Diego, who had somehow walked into my life and made me feel like I belonged. Laura, always ready with jokes and a good time. The warmth of the restaurant, the sounds of clinking glasses, and the mix of English and Spanish floating through the air.

And just like that, I realized I had done it.
I had built a life here.

More than a year ago, I was alone in a new city, unsure if I had made a terrible mistake. I second-guessed every decision, wrestled with loneliness, and wondered if I would ever feel at home. And yet, here I was, surrounded by people who mattered, in a city that finally felt like mine.

The realization settled deep in my chest, warm and undeniably real.

And then my eyes landed on my bag, and my contentment was immediately interrupted by indignation.

Because seriously, a pickpocket?!

This would never happen in Singapore. Never.
I could leave my laptop in a café, go for a casual 10-minute walk, and come back to find it untouched, possibly even charged by a helpful barista. A literal dream.

But Barcelona?
Oh, Barcelona had other plans. I was too busy floating through life like some wide-eyed optimist who thought the universe was basically a giant hug.

Spoiler: it's not. Sometimes it's a guy in an oversized jacket making off with your bag.

Joshua, as if plucking the sarcasm straight out of my head, smirked. "Welcome to Barcelona. Pickpockets love an easy target."

I groaned. "Perfect. I've officially been initiated. Do I get a badge for 'Naive Tourist of the Year' or just a missing credit card?"

Diego, bless him, stayed calm. "It's not naivety. You just felt safe here. That's a compliment to the city."

Joshua snorted. "Until she ends up wallet-less in the middle of La Rambla."

I shot him my best glare, but Diego's words stuck. Maybe he was right. Maybe it wasn't about being careless. Maybe it meant that between tapas, questionable metro rides, and one very stolen bag, I'd already started to belong.

And wasn't that something?

I picked up my fork and took a bite of the baklava, the honey-soaked layers sticky on my fingers, the flaky pastry melting against my tongue. Sweet, nutty, perfect, and somehow, impossibly, it tasted like *home* here, in the middle of Barcelona, with Diego's hand brushing mine under the table.

The night continued, with Diego firmly at my side and Joshua throwing not-so-subtle approving glances our way, but all I could focus on was the quiet rhythm between us, the ease, the warmth, and the tiny sparks that made my chest feel like it was both full and light at the same time.

As we walked home later, the city's lights glittering around us, a strange, wonderful calm settled over me. With Diego, every laugh, every brush of his fingers against mine, felt steady, safe, and just a little bit magical, like I had stumbled into a place where I didn't need to guard myself, where I could just be.

CHAPTER 10 – Accidental Violence and Sweet Misunderstandings

The pickpocket incident had been humbling. A splash of cold sangria right to the ego.

Sure, Diego had swooped in like a sexy, Spanish-speaking Marvel hero, but the whole situation made one thing painfully clear: I was nowhere near fluent enough to survive without him. What if he hadn't been there? Would I have been able to explain the situation to the police? I probably would've ended up miming "thief" like a budget charades act, while butchering every verb conjugation in the Spanish language.

The realization hit even harder a few days later, when I found myself in yet another ridiculous situation, but this time, in the middle of a kickboxing class.

CHAPTER 10 – *Accidental Violence and Sweet Misunderstandings*

"*¡Izquierda! ¡Izquierda!*" the instructor barked, his voice slicing through the air like we were training for the Hunger Games.

Oh no. Left or right?

I froze, trying to remember if that was left or right. My brain scrambled, the other word for either left or right refused to come to me, and in my panic, I threw a punch to the right... directly into the poor guy next to me.

"¡Ay!" he yelped, clutching his arm like I'd dislocated his soul.

"Oh my god, I'm so sorry!" I gasped, horrified, my cheeks going up in flames.

The instructor turned, his hands on his hips as he rattled off a stern lecture. I caught words like 'pay attention' and 'focus,' but the rest of his sentence blurred into a mix of frustration and incomprehension.

I stood there like a toddler caught drawing on the walls, mumbling a hundred apologies to the poor man I'd assaulted while wondering if it was too late to switch to yoga.

The embarrassment was enough to solidify one thing in my mind: I needed to take this language barrier seriously.

Later that day, I met up with Laura and Joshua, who were already in stitches before I could even finish telling them what had happened in kickboxing.

"You punched someone?!" Laura shrieked, practically spitting out her sangria. "God, I wish I had been there. That poor man!"

Joshua, ever the instigator, leaned in with a wicked grin. "Did you at least knock him out? Maybe you've got a future in underground street fighting."

I groaned, hiding my face in my hands. "It was so embarrassing. The instructor looked at me like I had personally ruined his entire career."

Laura took a dramatic sip of her drink, then gasped loudly, eyes locking onto something, or rather, someone, across the bar.

"Oh my god," she whispered, her face lighting up like she'd just found buried treasure.

Joshua followed her gaze and immediately grinned. "Oh, yes. This is happening."

Before I could react, Laura was already standing up and making a beeline for a very tall, very attractive man who looked like he had just wanted a quiet beer.

"Oh no," I groaned, reaching for Joshua's arm. "Stop her. Stop her right now."

Joshua, looking way too entertained, casually leaned back in his chair. "Nope. This is your circus now."

I turned just in time to see Laura talking animatedly to the guy, pointing at me with the enthusiasm of a game show host revealing a grand prize.

"She's telling him, isn't she?" I muttered.

Joshua grinned. "Oh, absolutely."

Seconds later, Laura returned, dragging said attractive but very confused man along with her.

"Meet Miguel!" she announced triumphantly, plopping him into the empty chair at our table. "He would love to hear about how you broke someone's arm today."

Miguel, bless him, looked both intrigued and slightly concerned. "*¿Uh... hola?*"

"*Hola*, Miguel," Joshua said, leaning in conspiratorially. "You're in for a treat. Our dear friend Nadia here is Barcelona's newest accidental menace."

Miguel raised an eyebrow, his lips twitching into an amused smile. "Oh?"

I was fairly sure I'd never been more mortified in my life. "I didn't break anything," I hissed. "I just... slightly traumatized a stranger."

"She's a kickboxing queen," Joshua added. "You're lucky she didn't punch you just now."

Miguel laughed, surprisingly not running for the exit. "Should I be scared?"

"Yes," I said, deadpan

He grinned and pulled out a chair. "Well, now I have to hear the story."

And just like that, he joined our table, listening with amusement as Joshua and Laura narrated the saga like it was a Netflix special.

"Oh, it gets better," Joshua added, scooting closer like he was about to spill the world's juiciest gossip. "Then she got yelled at in Spanish and just nodded along like she was being knighted."

Miguel laughed, and I wanted to die right then and there.

I buried my face in my hands, groaning. "Why do I hang out with you people?"

"Because we make your life more interesting," Laura said smugly, clinking her glass against mine.

Miguel leaned an elbow on the table, grinning at me. "So... is this a regular thing for you, or was today special?"

"Special," I mumbled, giving Joshua and Laura the stink eye.

Somewhere between the second glass of wine and Laura

suggesting I make punching people part of my brand, I started to laugh too.

This was my life now, ridiculous, unpredictable, and occasionally violent, but with really great company.

Diego, of course, would never let me live this down once he heard about it.

But for now, sitting at a table with my ridiculous, chaotic friends and a total stranger who had somehow been roped into my public shaming, I couldn't help but feel... content.

I had felt so alone in this city. Now?
I had people. And apparently, a reputation as Barcelona's most charming disaster.

That night, fueled by embarrassment and a slightly bruised ego, I started researching intensive Spanish classes. Enough was enough.

Diego, ever perceptive, leaned over. "What are you looking at?"

"Spanish classes," I said. "I'm tired of feeling like I'm playing charades in daily life. I want to actually know what's going on instead of guessing."

He smiled, squeezing my hand. "That's a great idea. And honestly? You're already doing better than you think."

For one blissful second, I basked in the support. And then, because apparently my boyfriend's mouth had a death wish, he added, almost casually, "It'll be nice not having to translate everything for you anymore."

…Excuse me?

I whipped my head around. "Wow. Okay. So I'm basically your full-time job?"

His smile faltered. "No, no. That's not what I meant." He dragged a hand through his hair, clearly regretting every choice that had led him to this moment. "I just… sometimes it's a lot. Always stepping in."

I swallowed, heat prickling the back of my neck. "Cool, cool. So I'm the helpless foreign girlfriend. Love that for me."

He sighed, rubbing his face. "Nadia. That's not it. I like helping you. But I want you to feel confident here, too. I don't want you to always need me to step in."

My chest pinched because okay, maybe he had a point. But also? Ouch. I crossed my arms and gave him my best death glare. "Well, congratulations. You've officially lit a fire under me. I'm taking classes. Intensive ones. Five days a week, two hours a day. By the end of it, you won't even recognize me."

The silence stretched. Finally, he leaned closer, voice softer. "Nadia, I didn't mean it as an insult. I just want you to feel like you belong here, without relying on me."

I exhaled, but the sting lingered, sitting in my ribs like a splinter. So I smiled sweetly and pulled my laptop closer. "Great. Then watch me belong so hard they'll think I'm Spanish."

The next morning, I signed up. Fueled by equal parts determination, hot chocolate, and the tiniest bit of spite.

By the end of it, I was either going to be bilingual... or they'd find me buried under a pile of flashcards.

Fast forward a week, and I was already questioning all my life choices. The first week was brutal.

Everyone else in class looked like they'd been whispering sweet nothings to Duolingo, a language app, for years. Meanwhile, the teacher would call on me, and suddenly my brain would shriek *Evacuate!* My throat locked up, my verbs fled the scene, and what came out of my mouth was... well, let's just say I accidentally told the class that my uncle was pregnant. The teacher corrected me with a smile so kind it almost made it worse.

But by the second week, something shifted. I started catching onto patterns. Grammar rules began making sense. I even began enjoying the challenge, finding little victories in correctly ordering at a cafe or understanding Diego's jokes without him having to slow down and repeat them three times.

I even corrected someone else's grammar once and immediately texted Diego in triumph.

"Who are you?" he replied.

"A legend," I wrote back.

A month into the course, I had a breakthrough moment, one of those "I am thriving in this country" moments.

That day in class, our teacher introduced us to *porras*, a variation of *churros* I had never heard of.

"They're thicker and fluffier than *churros*," she explained, "less sweet, and often paired with hot chocolate for breakfast."

I scribbled down notes eagerly, mentally planning my next café visit.

When I got home that evening, Diego was lounging on the couch, a book in hand.

"Diego!" I called out, dropping my bag by the door. "Did you know there's a different kind of *churro*? They're called *porros!*"

His head snapped up so fast I thought he might get whiplash. His eyebrows shot toward his hairline.

"Wait, what?"

"*Porros!*" I repeated, beaming. "They're thicker and fluffier—"

106

CHAPTER 10 – Accidental Violence and Sweet Misunderstandings

Diego's laughter erupted before I could finish my sentence. Like, full-body laughter. Clutching-his-stomach, wiping-tears-from-his-eyes kind of laughter.

I blinked, completely confused. "What? Why are you laughing?"

Diego said between breaths. "Nadia..." He leaned back, shaking his head. "*Porros* means... joints."

I froze.

"You mean..."

"Yes." He nodded solemnly, still grinning like an idiot. "Marijuana."

My soul left my body.

"Oh my god. I was telling everyone at the café about them! I even said I couldn't wait to dip them in chocolate!"

Diego lost it again, his laughter bouncing off the walls. "Well, I'm sure they got a good laugh out of it too." He reached for me, pulling me into a hug. "You're doing amazing, by the way. Just... careful with those words, okay?"

I groaned, collapsing onto the couch and burying my face in his shoulders. "Why is this language so tricky?"

"Because it's Spanish," he teased, brushing a strand of hair out of my face. "But seriously, you're doing great. And I, for one, think it's hilarious that you accidentally told a bunch of strangers you were excited to try chocolate-dipped joints."

I groaned louder, but even I couldn't help but laugh.

Then Diego pulled me closer, his lips brushing against my temple. "I'm proud of you, you know," he murmured.

My stomach did an embarrassing flip.

I turned my head to look at him, our faces just inches apart. "Yeah?"

"Yeah," he said softly, his fingers trailing down my arm, his touch light but deliberate. "Watching you throw yourself into learning Spanish, putting yourself out there... It's kind of amazing."

I smiled, my breath hitching slightly. "You know, you could always reward me for my efforts."

His lips curved into a slow grin. "Oh? And what kind of reward are we talking about?"

I leaned in, pretending to think. "Maybe... a kiss?"

Diego chuckled, his nose brushing against mine. "Well, since you've been working so hard..."

And then, he kissed me. Soft at first, teasing, before

deepening with a warmth that made my toes curl.

Moments like these, as mortifying as they were, reminded me of how far I'd come. And how much further I still had to go.

But no amount of preparation could have prepared me for what happened a week later in one of my classes.

CHAPTER 11 - I Accidentally Sang a Sexy Song to My Students

"Alright, everyone," I said, clapping my hands to get the class's attention. "Let's focus. We're going to start with our writing exercises."

My class of teenagers groaned in unison. It was a familiar sound by now, one I'd come to accept as part of the deal when teaching English to a room full of restless Spanish-speaking teenagers.

"But *profe*, it's Monday!" Pedro whined dramatically, dropping his head onto his desk.

"Monday is the perfect day for writing," I chirped, ignoring the protests. "It's like starting with a blank page. Full of possibilities!"

"Or full of suffering," Carla muttered under her breath, earning snickers from the others.

I rolled my eyes playfully. "Come on. Just twenty minutes. Then you can tell me all about your weekends."

This was our unspoken agreement: they worked hard for most of the lesson, and in return, we spent the last part of class chatting. My students loved to fill me in on their lives, weekend parties, football matches, family drama. In turn, I'd tell them stories from my own week. It was our way of making the classroom feel less formal, more like a place where we all belonged.

Today, as I glanced at the clock and saw that the twenty minutes were up, I set my pen down. "Alright, you've earned it. What did everyone get up to this weekend?

Carla, as usual, jumped in first. "I went to my cousin's birthday party. It was chaos. A *piñata* almost hit my uncle in the head."

The class erupted in laughter, and I grinned. "Sounds like a success to me."

Pedro followed up with a story about a disastrous football game, mimicking the goalkeeper's flailing attempts to stop the ball. One by one, the students shared snippets of their weekends until, inevitably, they turned the spotlight on me.

"What about you, *profe*?" Carla asked, leaning forward. "What did you do?"

I hesitated, already feeling a blush creeping up my neck as I remembered my *porras* versus *porros* disaster with Diego. I had a feeling they'd enjoy this one.

"Well," I began, trying to keep a straight face, "I learned something new about *churros* this weekend."

"*Churros*?" Pedro perked up. "What about them?"

"I assume you know what *porras* are. They're like *churros* but thicker, fluffier, and not as sweet," I explained. "I was so excited to tell Diego about them when I got home... except instead of saying *porras*, I said *porros*."

The room went dead silent for about two seconds. Then, chaos.

"¡*Profe*!" Pedro cried, practically falling out of his chair. "You asked for joints instead of *churros*?!"

The other students laughed hysterically and Carla gasped, clutching her stomach as she laughed.

I held my hands up defensively, though I couldn't stop laughing along with them. "I didn't ask for them! I just said the wrong word to Diego, and he hasn't let me live it down."

"Oh, *profe*, you're a disaster," Carla teased, wiping tears of laughter from her eyes.

"I know," I said dramatically, placing a hand over my heart. "That's why I need help. Clearly, I can't be trusted with this language."

Pedro raised his hand like he was making an official announcement. "We'll teach you, *profe*."

"Teach me what?"

"Spanish. But with music," Carla chimed in. "Songs are the best way to learn. Everyone knows that."

I considered it for a moment, then smiled. "Alright, I have a deal for you. If you behave during class, do all the work, and don't drive me insane, you get the last ten minutes to teach me Spanish. Deal?"

"¡*Sí*!" they chorused excitedly, already buzzing with ideas.

From that day on, our arrangement began. The first day of "Spanish song time" was chaotic but endearing. Pedro chose *Vivir Mi Vida* by Marc Anthony, declaring it "easy" and "impossible to mess up."

"Famous last words," I muttered as they started playing the song from someone's phone.

"*¡Voy a reír, voy a bailar!*" Lucas sang loudly, throwing his arms out for dramatic effect.

I copied him, repeating line by line as they laughed, corrected my pronunciation, and cheered me on when I got it right. I wasn't exactly a natural, but I was getting better. They even started teaching me slang, giving me tips on how to "sound cooler" in conversations.

"Stop saying '*lo siento*' all the time when you want to apologise or say excuse me," Pedro said one day. "Say '*perdona*' instead. It's more natural."

"And don't call everything *bonito*," Carla added. "Use *guay* or *chulo* if something's cool."

I scribbled everything down in a small notebook I'd jokingly titled "Nadia's Survival Spanish." My students were relentless, but their energy and encouragement made me feel like I was finally making progress.

But, of course, Spanish still found ways to trip me up.

One afternoon, during class, I decided to compliment one of my students, Alejandro, on how well he'd done on his latest test. Smiling brightly, I said, "¡*Tienes mucho éxito!*"

The class froze. Alejandro's eyes widened as his friends started snickering.

"What?" I asked, already feeling a sense of doom.

"*Profe*," Carla said, biting back laughter, "do you know what you just said?"

114

I frowned. "Yes! I said he's very successful!"

Pedro clapped a hand over his mouth, shaking with laughter. "Well, yes, *éxito* means success. But... saying it like that can sound like you're saying he's 'good in bed.'"

My stomach dropped. "Oh no. Oh no, no, no. That's not what I meant!"

Alejandro, now blushing furiously, buried his face in his hands as the class erupted into laughter. I groaned, covering my face as well.

"Class dismissed!" I said, waving them out of the room in mock defeat.

As they filed out, still laughing, Carla called back, "Don't worry, *profe*! We'll fix this in song time next class!"

I slumped into my chair, shaking my head with a laugh. Spanish, it seemed, still had a way of keeping me humble.

And I had a feeling my students wouldn't let me forget this mistake anytime soon.

The following week, I walked into class, prepared for the usual mix of grammar exercises and teenage antics. But as soon as I set my bag down, Pedro was already grinning like a Cheshire cat, a mischievous look I'd come to know well.

"*Profe*, today we have the perfect song for you," he announced, dramatically holding up his phone as if it were a golden trophy.

Carla leaned in with an innocent smile that immediately made me suspicious. "It's a classic. One that every Spanish learner needs to master."

"Alright," I said warily, already sensing a setup. "What's the song?"

Pedro hit play, and the unmistakable opening notes of *Despacito* filled the room.

"Really? *Despacito?*" I said, shooting them a skeptical look as Luis Fonsi's smooth voice drifted through the speakers.

"Yes!" Carla said, clearly delighted. "It's perfect. Everyone knows it, and it'll help you with pronunciation."

"And flirting," Pedro added, winking dramatically.

"Pedro!" I shot back, though I couldn't help but laugh.

They insisted, and soon, my attempts to repeat the lyrics became the highlight of the day.

"*Des-pa-cito…*" I sang, carefully enunciating every syllable.

The entire class groaned. "No, no, no!" Carla interrupted, holding her hands up as if stopping a crime scene. "You sound like a robot. It's *despacito*, not *des-paaaaa-ci-to*. Feel

116

the flow!"

I sighed. "Okay, let's try again."

Pedro grinned, standing up and demonstrating with an exaggerated sway of his hips. "Like this, *profe: 'Quiero respirar tu cuello despacito...'"*

The class dissolved into laughter, and I buried my face in my hands. "Why do I feel like this is less about learning and more about torturing me?"

"It's both," Carla said cheerfully. "We're helping you and having fun. Win-win."

By the time we got to the infamous *"Pasito a pasito, suave suavecito"* line, I was gasping for air from laughing so hard. My students were delighted by my attempts, cheering me on with exaggerated encouragement.

"¡Muy bien, profe! Very good!" Pedro called, clapping dramatically. "You're basically Spanish now!"

"Yeah, sure," I replied, wiping tears of laughter from my eyes. "Because nothing says fluency like me butchering reggaeton lyrics."

"Just wait," Carla teased. "Next week, we'll bring *La Gasolina.*"

"Oh no," I groaned, shaking my head as the bell rang.

Later at home that evening, I sat on the couch, still shaking my head over the day's events. Diego was in the kitchen, pouring us two glasses of wine. When he came over and handed me one, I couldn't hold it in anymore.

"You won't believe what my students made me do today," I said, taking a sip.

He raised an eyebrow as he sat down beside me, draping his arm over the back of the couch. "Go on."

"They taught me *Despacito*," I said flatly. "The full thing. Line by line. They called it 'pronunciation practice.'"

Diego's grin appeared instantly, those dimples making their usual appearance. "*Despacito*? Seriously?"

"Yes! They said it's a 'classic' that every Spanish learner needs to know."

He let out a low chuckle and leaned closer. "They're being cheeky. You do know what that song is about, right?"

I blinked. "What do you mean? It's just about dancing... slowly, right? *Des-pa-ci-to*," I enunciated, mimicking the way my students had teased me earlier.

Diego nearly spit out his wine as he laughed. "Oh, Nadia, no. It's not about dancing. Well, not only dancing. It's..." He paused, clearly trying to choose his words carefully. "It's... let's say... very suggestive."

118

"Suggestive?" I repeated, narrowing my eyes at him. "What kind of suggestive?"

"Let's break it down," he said, a mischievous glint in his eye as he set his wine glass on the table. "Take the first line, for example: '*Quiero respirar tu cuello despacito.*' That means, 'I want to breathe on your neck, slowly.'"

I nearly choked on my wine. "Wait, what?"

He continued, enjoying himself far too much. "Or '*Déjame decirte cosas al oído.*' That's, 'Let me whisper things in your ear.'"

My eyes widened. "You're kidding me."

"I'm not," he said, grinning as he leaned in, dropping his voice into an exaggerated sultry tone. "The whole song is basically about seduction. Slow, passionate seduction."

I groaned, covering my face with my hands. "Oh my god. And here I was, singing it in front of a class full of teenagers, trying to 'feel the flow' like they told me."

Diego burst into laughter, falling back against the couch cushions. "They tricked you! Those little devils knew exactly what they were doing."

"I'm never trusting them again," I mumbled, still mortified. "I was out there singing about whispering sweet nothings in someone's ear, and they were probably dying inside."

119

Diego pulled me closer, still laughing. "Well, to be fair, it is great pronunciation practice. Plus, now you know a very useful song for your next karaoke night."

I shot him a look. "You're not helping."

"No?" he teased, pressing a kiss to my forehead. "I think you're adorable when you're embarrassed. And honestly, it's kind of impressive that you got through the whole thing without realizing."

I groaned again, though I couldn't help but laugh. "I'm blaming you for this. You should have warned me about reggaeton lyrics."

He held up his hands in defense. "Don't look at me. Your students are the masterminds here."

"I swear," I muttered, sipping my wine again, "next class, they're conjugating verbs for an hour. No songs."

Diego chuckled. "Sure, sure. Until they bring out another classic."

I rolled my eyes but couldn't help laughing, because he wasn't wrong. My students had a way of winning me over.

But sometimes, I needed a break from all that teenage energy. That's why I like to go to familiar places, where I won't be overwhelmed.

CHAPTER 12 – Pitch-Perfect Chaos

───❦───

Joshua and I were at our usual spot, a cozy Irish pub nestled in the Gothic Quarter, the kind of place you'd walk right past if you didn't know it was there. Dim lighting, wooden booths, and the comforting smell of Guinness, old books, and questionable life choices.

It was our midweek refuge, a place to catch up, people-watch, and complain about life.

We'd claimed our usual booth and were deep in the art of semi-dramatic life complaints—me about a student who kept calling me "Miss *Churro*" and Joshua about his latest dating app disaster with a guy who claimed to be "emotionally available" but also "between apartments and currently living in his ex's storage unit."

Then it happened.

The bartender tapped the mic, his voice booming through the pub.

"Ladies and gentlemen, it's that time again… karaoke night!"

The crowd erupted into cheers while I nearly choked on my beer.

"Karaoke? Here?"

Joshua was already glowing like a child who'd just been given a puppy and a lifetime supply of glitter. "Oh my god. YES. We're doing this."

"Nope." I shook my head so hard I might've given myself whiplash. "Absolutely not."

"Why not?"

"Because!" I gestured toward the stage, eyes wide with horror. "It's out in the open! Back home, you get a private room to embarrass yourself in. This? This is public humiliation."

Joshua, completely unbothered, grinned. "That's the whole point. Come on, Nad. You've got a great voice."

"Nope," I said firmly, taking another sip of my cocktail. "Not happening."

But Joshua gave me The Look. The one that said, "I know where your emotional landmines are and I'm going to joyfully dance on them anyway."

"Come on. It'll be fun. You've been working too hard. You need to let loose."

I hesitated.

The first singer who got up was a tipsy dude who absolutely butchered Sweet Caroline. The crowd cheered him on anyway, completely forgiving his lack of talent. The atmosphere was electric, and I felt a tug of curiosity.

Maybe Joshua was right. Maybe I did need to let loose.

"Fine," I sighed. "One song."

Joshua clapped his hands in triumph. "Yes! But first, shots."

We grabbed more drinks and signed up for songs. Joshua chose Livin' on a Prayer (predictable), while I picked Like a Prayer (Madonna supremacy).

As we waited, he returned from the bar carrying what looked like a small swimming pool of alcohol.

"What is that?" I asked, horrified.

"The Blackout Tray," he announced proudly. "Eight shots, four cocktails, and a jug of vodka Red Bull."

I stared at him. "Joshua. That is a cry for help."

Joshua just shrugged. "Look, if we're going down in flames, we might as well burn spectacularly."

We took it as a personal challenge. The shots disappeared quickly, followed by the cocktails. The jug of vodka Red Bull? A mistake. But at that point, we were far beyond making good decisions.

As we waited for our songs, we approached the bar yet again. The bartender, a tall, ridiculously handsome guy with a ponytail and an earring that suggested he had traveled Europe by motorcycle, gave us a conspiratorial grin.

"This round's on me," he said, placing two shots in front of us.

Joshua raised an eyebrow. "Wow, thanks! What's the occasion?"

The bartender shrugged, his lips curving into a sly grin. "You two seem fun."

We clinked our glasses together. Free alcohol? This was a good omen.

As the night went on, the free drinks kept coming. A round of shots here, a cocktail there.

"Damn," I said to Joshua. "I think the bartender really likes

CHAPTER 12 - Pitch-Perfect Chaos

us."

Joshua grinned proudly, swirling his whiskey. "Yeah, we do have great energy." Then, after our third free round, I noticed something.

The bartender wasn't looking at us. He was only looking at Joshua.

It suddenly clicked.

I turned to Joshua, barely holding back laughter. "Dude. He's flirting with you."

Joshua blinked. "What? No way. He's just being nice."

Right on cue, the bartender reappeared, sliding yet another round of drinks toward us. This time, he leaned onto the bar, resting his chin on his hand as he stared at Joshua like he was a Renaissance painting.

"So, Joshua," he said smoothly. "Are you... seeing anyone?"

I spit out my drink.

Joshua, finally catching on, nearly choked on his whiskey. "Oh! Uh... wow. That's, uh, flattering."

The bartender leaned in slightly, amusement dancing in his eyes as he clearly enjoyed Joshua's reaction. "I get off in an hour."

Joshua turned to me, wide-eyed. "Help."

I, being the supportive friend that I am, took a slow sip of my drink and said absolutely nothing.

"Come on," the bartender pressed, still devouring Joshua with his eyes. "Let me take you out sometime."

Joshua, still in shock, let out a nervous laugh. "I... uh actually, I'm—"

"Straight?" The bartender guessed, completely unfazed.

Joshua nodded aggressively.

The bartender sighed dramatically. "A shame." Then, after a brief pause, he smirked. "But you never know, maybe one drink could change your mind."

I howled with laughter.

Joshua hesitated for a second before scribbling something on a napkin and sliding it across the bar.

The bartender raised an eyebrow. "Is this—"

Joshua gave a wicked grin. "My number. You did give me, like, six free drinks, after all."

The bartender beamed like he had just won the lottery.

"Joshua, are you actually flirting?" I whispered in shock.

He shrugged, taking a smug sip of his drink. "Hey, free drinks, Nad. Free drinks."

I cackled. "You absolute menace."

The bartender tucked the napkin into his pocket, winked at Joshua, and sauntered off.

Joshua turned to me, still grinning like a little shit. "I feel so powerful right now."

After processing Joshua's new admirer, it was finally my turn to sing. I stepped onto the stage, gripping the microphone tightly. The lights were bright, the crowd was loud, but as the music started, something shifted.

The nerves melted away, replaced by a rush of adrenaline.

I didn't just karaoke, I performed. Full dramatic arm gestures, hair flips, power stances. The crowd was into it. People clapped along, cheered during the chorus, and by the end of it, I felt invincible.

As I hopped off the stage, Joshua, still riding the high of free drinks and flirty bartenders, was waiting for me.

"That. Was. Everything," he shouted, pulling me into a hug.

"That was amazing," I gasped, still buzzing from excitement.

"I want to do another one."

And we did.

We sang more songs, cheered for other performers, and made new friends with people who shared our love of music. It felt like we'd found a secret club where everyone was welcome, no matter how good—or bad—you were at singing.

At some undetermined point, we stumbled out of the pub, still singing loudly.

"WE'RE HALFWAY THERE"

"OOOOOOHHH LIVIN' ON A PRAYER!"

We were so loud that a woman walking her dog crossed the street to avoid us. Fair.

By the time we flagged down a cab, we had the coordination of newborn giraffes.

"We need… a taxi," Joshua slurred.

The cab driver eyed us warily. "*¿Dónde?*"

Where?

I blinked. "Uhhh… My place," I told the driver, giving him my address.

But by the time we arrived, both Joshua and I were too tipsy to figure out which key opened the building's front door.

"I'm calling Diego," I muttered, fumbling with my phone.

He picked up after two rings. "Nadia? What's going on?"

"Um… we're outside. Can you come help?"

Diego sighed, but he wasn't annoyed. "Stay there. I'm on my way."

A few minutes later, Diego appeared, looking far too put-together compared to our disheveled state. He wore a hoodie and jeans, his hair slightly tousled, and he had that calm, steady presence that could calm a stampede.

"Okay," he said, eyeing us both. "Let's get you inside."

Joshua stumbled toward him, throwing an arm around his shoulders. "Diego! You're a saint."

Diego smiled, steadying him. "I know."

As he helped Joshua with the keys, Diego glanced over his shoulder at me. "You okay?"

I nodded, suddenly feeling the night catch up with me. "Yeah… just tired."

He unlocked the door and held it open, motioning for me to

go first. As I passed, he gently pressed a kiss to my temple. Like a gentleman. Like the human version of hot chocolate.

"So," he said, crossing his arms, "karaoke?"

I grinned, still buzzing from the night. "Magical."

Diego shook his head, laughing softly. "You're ridiculous."

"I'm serious!" I said, sitting up. "It was one of the best nights ever. You have to come with us next time."

Diego raised an eyebrow. "Next time?"

"Oh, there will definitely be a next time," Joshua called from the floor, where he was sprawled out, scrolling through his phone.

Diego chuckled, shaking his head. "Fine. But no blackout trays."

"No promises," I said with a wink.

Diego sat next to me, resting his hand on my knee, his thumb drawing lazy circles through the fabric of my jeans. "You really had fun, huh?"

"More than I expected," I admitted.

He leaned closer, pressing a soft kiss to my cheek. "I like seeing you like this. Happy."

I turned to face him, our eyes meeting for a quiet moment. "It's because of you, you know."

His hand lifted, brushing a strand of hair from my face, fingers lingering against my cheek. Then, almost like he couldn't hold it in anymore, he said softly, *"Te quiero."*

I froze. My heart did a dramatic leap worthy of Olympic gymnastics. "Wait. Did you just…? Because either you told me you love me or you said you want me, and honestly, both are working for me right now."

He chuckled, eyes warm. "I meant it the way you think I meant it."

"Oh." My face went hot. My heart was pounding harder than the drunk guy screaming Sweet Caroline earlier. "Well, in that case…" I blurted, "I love you too."

Smooth. Zero chill. But the way his grin spread, like I'd just handed him the winning lottery ticket, I didn't care.

We'd been dating a little over six months, and somehow, this felt both terrifying and inevitable. Like karaoke, I didn't want to do it. I was sure I'd make a fool of myself, and then once I finally opened my mouth… It was magic.

As I lay in bed that night, head spinning from vodka Red Bull and Diego's words, I couldn't stop smiling.

CHAPTER 13 – A Breath of Fresh Air... Kind Of

Why don't you just stay here?" Diego asked the next morning, pouring coffee like he was suggesting we buy more milk.

I blinked at him from across the kitchen table. "Stay here... like, for breakfast?"

He shook his head, amused. "No, Nadia. I mean stay here. Move in with me."

The mug nearly slipped out of my hands. Move in? With him? My heart did a cartwheel, followed immediately by a nervous collapse.

Part of me wanted to squeal yes, to start mentally measuring closet space and alphabetizing our spice rack. But another part whispered: six months. Was it too soon? What would my mom say? (She wouldn't say anything, because she'd be too busy fainting.) Would my sisters think I'd lost my mind? Or worse, that I was losing my roots?

Back in Singapore, moving in with a man without a ring on my finger was basically the cultural equivalent of running naked through a hawker center.

And yet, sitting there in his kitchen with the smell of coffee in the air and Diego smiling at me like he already knew my answer, I felt it: freedom. Messy, terrifying, wonderful freedom. The kind I'd crossed continents to find, even if it meant bending a few unspoken rules.

And Barcelona had always smelled like freedom to me... at least when I first arrived.

The scent of freshly baked bread from corner bakeries, the salty sea breeze drifting in from the Mediterranean, and the faint citrusy aroma of the orange trees lining the streets made me feel like I was living inside a sun-drenched postcard.

But after a while, that romanticized scent was replaced by something else entirely.

Weed.

And not just sometimes. Weed was basically the neighborhood's unofficial perfume.

At first, I couldn't place the smell. It was stale, earthy,

pungent, like someone had overcooked a batch of herbal tea and left it out to rot in the sun. It clung to the narrow alleyways, floated out of apartment windows, and lingered in the parks, merging seamlessly with the scent of espresso and grilled meat.

One evening, as Diego and I walked home, I wrinkled my nose. "Does anyone else smell that?"

Diego turned to me with an amused grin. "What, the weed?"

My eyes went full cartoon-character-wide. "That's weed?" I did a dramatic spin, pointing toward no one in particular. "It's everywhere!"

Diego chuckled. "Welcome to Raval."

It amazed me how casual it all was. In Singapore, weed wasn't something you smelled. Or saw. Or joked about. Or accidentally agreed to buy in the middle of a club line (but we'll get to that). No, weed in Singapore was the Voldemort of substances—it shall not be named. You could be arrested, heavily fined, or worse, even executed for certain drug offenses. The idea of someone just walking down the street, puffing on a joint without a care in the world, was unthinkable.

But in Barcelona? It was basically a personality trait.

And it wasn't just the people I expected, teenagers or guys with Bob Marley t-shirts and commitment issues.

No.

One day, I walked past a fancy little shop selling artisanal cheese, and the owner stood outside, casually smoking a joint like he was pairing it with a nice Manchego.

Another time, at a language exchange, one of the organizers who was a university professor told me he loved unwinding with a joint after a long day of teaching.

But the moment that truly broke me?

An elderly woman, sitting peacefully on her balcony, knitting with a joint casually tucked between her fingers like it was just another needle.

It was the most wholesome drug use I'd ever witnessed.

Despite my curiosity, I never tried it. I was too chicken.

"You've never smoked weed?" Joshua asked one night over drinks.

"Nope."

"Not even once?"

"Nope."

He stared at me like I'd just confessed I'd never eaten pizza. "But you've lived in Barcelona for how long?"

"I know, I know," I said, laughing. "I'm curious, but... I don't know. I'm scared."

"Scared of what?"

"Getting caught. Getting in trouble. I don't know... old habits from Singapore, I guess."

Joshua rolled his eyes. "Nad, you're in Spain. Nobody cares."

"I know," I groaned. "It's like I'm failing at being a local."

"You are," he said solemnly. "But we still love you."

Things hit a new level of chaos the night Laura and I went to a club in the Gothic Quarter. It was one of those places that didn't even open until midnight, because apparently Spain runs on vampire hours.

We were waiting in line, Laura in her sparkly crop top, me in a jacket I instantly regretted wearing, and suddenly, a man approached.

Slick smile. Casual swagger. He leaned in like we were all in on a secret.

"*¿Queréis algo?*" he asked, his voice low.

Now, at this point, I had learned just enough Spanish to think I understood basic questions. Do you want something?

I glanced at Laura, who was already shaking her head, but I, in my infinite wisdom, decided to be polite.

"*Sí*," I answered with a cheerful nod.

Laura's head snapped toward me so fast I thought she might get whiplash. "Nadia, NO."

But it was too late.

The guy grinned and pulled a small baggie out of his pocket. "*¿Cocaína?* MDMA? Weed?" he offered, listing the drugs like they were items on a menu.

I stared at it. Blinked. Then stared at it some more. He was openly offering everything.

"Oh my god," I whispered. "That's not tapas."

Laura groaned. "Of course it's not tapas! Did you think he was offering you a free *croqueta*?!"

My entire soul left my body. "I… how was I supposed to know? He was so vague! *Do you want something?* Something what? Something fun? Something edible? Something deeply illegal?!"

The dealer, now very confused about why I wasn't enthusiastically handing him money, chuckled and backed away. "Ok, ok," he muttered before moving on to his next potential customer, clearly unbothered by my sheer incompetence.

Laura grabbed my arm and shook me. "Nadia, you literally just agreed to buy drugs."

"I panicked!"

"No, you just lack common sense!"

I groaned, burying my face in my hands. "This city is going to get me arrested."

That night, after recounting my near-criminal moment to Joshua (who almost fell off his chair from laughing), I decided to tell Diego.

And because he is a menace disguised as a biologist, he laughed for five straight minutes.

"You agreed?" he wheezed. "You just… just said yes?!"

I crossed my arms. "I was trying to be polite."

He shook his head, still laughing, and pulled me into his arms. "You are too precious for this city."

I huffed, but it was hard to stay mad when he was kissing my forehead like I was some small, delicate animal that had accidentally wandered into the wilderness.

That's when he got a glint in his eye. That glint. The one that always meant he was about to test my limits.

"So... since you already almost bought some," he murmured, his lips dangerously close to my ear, "why not try a puff with me?"

I immediately pulled back. "Diego."

"Nadia."

"You know I don't do that."

He grinned, reaching out to tuck a strand of hair behind my ear. "One puff. Just one. No pressure. No peer pressure. Just... cultural immersion."

I squinted. "This is definitely peer pressure."

"Is it working?"

I groaned, covering my face. "Maybe."

Somehow, Diego wore me down.

It wasn't immediate, but after two weeks of his teasing ("You wanted freedom and independence, aren't you supposed to be open to new experiences?"), I found myself sitting on the balcony, holding a joint like it was a live grenade.

Diego, looking far too amused for someone who had just convinced his girlfriend to try weed for the first time, lit it and took a slow drag before passing it to me.

I stared at it.

He raised an eyebrow. "You're not going to sniff it, are you?"

"I don't know how this works!"

"Just inhale."

I took the tiniest, most cautious puff imaginable. It barely counted. It was like sipping air.

Diego laughed. "No, no, no. Actually inhale."

I tried again. This time, I inhaled.

And immediately started choking like I was dying.

Diego lost it. I mean, full-body shaking, can't-breathe laughter. Meanwhile, I was coughing so hard I was convinced my lungs had declared war on me.

"Oh my god," cough "I hate you" wheeze "why is this legal?!"

Diego wiped away a tear. "You are, by far, the worst stoner I have ever seen."

"I AM NOT A STONER," I croaked.

The high didn't even hit properly before my stomach suddenly decided that it hated everything about this decision.

"I think I'm gonna be sick," I muttered.

Diego's laughter stopped instantly. "Oh, shit."

Cue me dramatically running to the bathroom, flinging myself over the toilet, and vomiting like I had just been poisoned.

Diego, to his credit, held my hair back and rubbed soothing circles on my back. "Okay, maybe weed isn't your thing," he admitted, chuckling.

"You think?!" I gasped.

Diego tucked me into bed like I was a small child who had just suffered an emotional trauma. He brought me water. He spoon-fed me tiny bites of chocolate like I was a wounded war hero.

The worst part? He was so smug about it.

The next morning, as I lay dramatically draped across his couch, groaning about my ruined dignity, Diego leaned down and kissed my forehead.

"You tried," he said, grinning. "I'm proud of you."

I glared. "You are never allowed to be in charge of my life choices again."

He laughed, pressing another kiss to my cheek. "Fair enough."

But later, as we sat on his balcony, Diego stretched his arms behind his head and said, "So… what about edibles?"

I paused. Edibles.

No smoking. No inhaling. No death.

"…Maybe a brownie."

He grinned. "I knew you had a rebel somewhere in there."

And that's how I went from accidentally agreeing to buy drugs to planning my first pot brownie experience.

Because apparently, this was my life now.

For all the cultural shocks I had endured between Singapore and Spain, the late dinners, the non-existent personal space, the way people casually ignored traffic laws, this one took the cake. Or, more accurately, the brownie.

Barcelona was like a chaotic fever dream. It was wild, unpredictable, and constantly toeing the line between genius and disaster.

And then… there was the beach.

CHAPTER 14 – When Your Summer Fling is a Donut Man

Barcelona's beach scene wasn't quite what I expected.

Back in Singapore, a trip to the beach meant careful planning, including packing snacks, applying sunscreen with the precision of a scientist handling hazardous materials, and bringing a book to quietly read under a perfectly positioned umbrella. It was a calm, organized affair. A peaceful communion with nature.

But Barcelona's beaches? Oh, they were a whole different beast.

For starters, there wasn't just one beach. There were many, each with its own distinct personality.
Barceloneta was the flashy, chaotic older sibling—crowded, loud, and teeming with tourists who vastly underestimated

the Mediterranean sun. Bogatell was a little calmer, drawing more locals and fewer sunburnt backpackers. Nova Icària was the family-friendly spot, full of picnic setups and toddlers flinging sand into their parents' faces. And then there was Mar Bella, home of the unofficial nudist section, where I made the rookie mistake of wandering in unprepared and got an eyeful of an elderly man doing lunges in the sand. You can't unsee that.

But no matter which beach you ended up at, there was one sacred constant: the *chiringuitos*.

The first time I heard the word *chiringuito*, I assumed it meant something exotic. Maybe a type of dance? A rare sea creature? Nope. It was just a beach bar. But these weren't just any bars; they were the cultural hubs of the beach experience.

Some were laid-back with reggae music and straw umbrellas, while others were practically mini nightclubs, with DJs spinning electronic beats at 3 p.m. and people dancing like it was already midnight.

Diego and I became *chiringuito* connoisseurs.

"Where are we going today?" I asked one Saturday morning, already stuffing a towel and sunglasses into my bag.

He pretended to think. "Nova Icària. I heard one of their *chiringuito* has great calamari."

"You just made that up."

"I did not," he said, pressing a dramatic hand to his chest. "I take my beach snacks very seriously."

We spent whole weekends bouncing from one *chiringuito* to the next, tasting everything from grilled sardines to *patatas bravas*, and, to my new addiction, *tinto de verano* (which was essentially red wine mixed with lemon soda and the reason I kept agreeing to things like volleyball with strangers). It was the closest I'd come to living inside a Spanish postcard.

It felt like a dream. Sun, sea, cold drinks, and good food. And then, of course, there was Diego.

At some point, as we lay sprawled on the sand at Bogatell, Diego leaned over, brushing a strand of hair from my face. His touch lingered, warm against my sun-kissed skin.

"Relaxing yet?" he murmured, his voice teasing.

"Getting there," I replied, closing my eyes as his fingers lazily traced patterns on my arm.

It was moments like these that made me forget everything else—the city, the stress, the fact that I still occasionally got my lefts and rights mixed up in Spanish.

But as I grew more familiar with the beach culture, I started noticing something bizarre.

At first, it was just one guy walking up and down the sand with a cooler bag.

"*Cerveza*, beer, cold beer!" he called out, weaving effortlessly through the crowd like some sort of beer-delivering magician.

I thought it was clever to bring the drinks to the people rather than make them get up.

Then, more vendors appeared.

"¿*Cerveza*? Beer?"
"¿*Agua*? Water?"
"Mojitos?"

The mojitos caught my attention. Unlike the beers, which were at least factory-sealed, the mojitos were homemade. The men selling them carried large jars filled with green liquid, ladling the drink into plastic cups for anyone willing to pay a couple of euros.

I squinted at them. "People actually buy that?"

Diego shrugged. "Of course. It's cheap, it's convenient."

"But…" I wrinkled my nose. "Where do they make them?"

"Honestly? You don't want to know." He laced his fingers through mine, squeezing gently as if to say, Relax. This is Barcelona.

I very much did want to know, but I also did not want to know.

146

And it wasn't just the drinks.

As we dozed in the sun one afternoon, a woman appeared at the edge of our towels, carrying a small bottle of lotion. She smiled at Diego like he was her next paycheck.

"*¿Masaje?*" she asked softly, her voice like honey.

My eyes popped open. "What did she say?"

"She's offering a massage," Diego said easily, not even looking up.

The woman crouched slightly, her hand already reaching toward his shoulder as if testing the waters. "*¿Masaje?*" she repeated, slower this time, her eyes locked on Diego like I was invisible.

I sat up so fast my sunglasses nearly flew off. "No, *gracias*," I blurted, a little too loudly, clutching Diego's arm.

The woman blinked, surprised, then gave me a polite shrug and moved on to the next sunburned victim.

But the damage was done.

Diego chuckled. "Nadia, she was just offering. Relax."

Relax? RELAX? My brain chest tightened, my fingers tingling like tiny electric shocks. Was I about to compete with some random stranger on a sun-drenched beach for a man who was supposed to be mine? Because honestly, it wouldn't be the first time.

Both my failed engagements had started with little things. Tiny, innocent sparks that snowballed into chaos. Someone smiled too long. A message arrived at the wrong time. An interaction I hadn't meant to read *into*. And suddenly, everything I thought was safe unraveled.

Now, on this perfectly sunny afternoon in Barcelona, I was doing it again... Overanalyzing the way Diego said *"masaje,"* heart hammering, pulse jangling like wind chimes in a storm.

He noticed my silence and nudged me gently. "Hey. You okay?"

I forced my mouth to move. "Yeah." I fiddled with the corner of my towel, fingernails digging little grooves into the fabric.

The truth? No. Not okay. Not even close. The paranoia I thought I'd left in Singapore had apparently packed itself in my suitcase and followed me across continents. Every laugh he shared with someone else and every smile that lingered too long felt like a subtle betrayal, a tiny avalanche threatening to tumble over everything.

I hated it. Hated the smallness, the raw, pulsing fear. What if he woke up one day and realized I was just a temporary chapter?

I forced a smile and reached for his hand. "I'm fine. Just... still getting used to Barcelona being so… friendly."

He squeezed my fingers, oblivious to the storm in my chest. "That's all it is, *cariño*. Just friendly."

I nodded, trying to believe him, but the pit in my stomach wasn't so easily convinced. Maybe I was being ridiculous. But paranoia doesn't check your passport when you cross borders; it follows you, settling into your beach bag like unwanted sand.

I tilted my sunglasses down, scanning the stretch of sun-bathers and vendors, suddenly hyper-aware of every glance, every exchange. Was Diego smiling too easily at strangers? Was I setting myself up for another heartbreak? Again?

I took a deep breath, trying to shove the paranoia back into the messy mental drawer labeled **Singapore Baggage: Do Not Open**. Easier said than done.

And then, like divine intervention, I heard it.

"Donuts, €1!"

I shot up from my towel. "Did he just say donuts?"

Diego nodded. "You haven't met the donut man yet?"

"No!" I gasped, my paranoia temporarily forgotten. "There's a donut man?"

A few minutes later, he appeared.

Balancing a massive wooden tray on his head, the donut man strutted down the beach like a snack-bearing deity. His golden treasures—fresh, warm, sugar-coated donuts—were stacked high, ready for anyone who flagged him down.

I watched, fascinated, as people waved him down. He'd lower the tray with expert precision, pulling out donuts wrapped in paper napkins and collecting coins with a grin.

"He only comes in the evenings," Diego explained. "And he sells out fast."

I was immediately intrigued. Fresh donuts on the beach? It sounded too good to be true.

That evening, as the sun dipped lower in the sky, I spotted him again.

"There he is!" I practically jumped up from my towel, grabbing Diego's arm.

He laughed, holding onto me to keep me from falling. "Easy, tiger."

I waved frantically, practically launching myself off my towel. The donut man made his way over and lowered his tray with expert precision.

"One, please," I said, handing him a euro.

He handed me a donut. Soft, golden, and still warm. I took a bite and nearly melted on the spot.

"Oh my god," I moaned through a mouthful of fried perfection.

Diego laughed. "Good?"

"Amazing. I need another one."

From that moment on, I was obsessed. The donut man was my white whale.

But he was elusive. Some days, he'd sell out before I could get to him. Other days, he simply wouldn't show up. It soon became a game. Would I get my donut today or not?

"Do you really need another donut?" Diego teased one afternoon as we packed our beach bag.

"Yes," I said firmly. "It's tradition now."

"Tradition?" He raised an eyebrow. "You've only had one."

"Exactly. And I've been chasing him ever since."

Diego chuckled, shaking his head. "You're obsessed."

"Maybe," I admitted, grinning.

We arrived at Bogatell Beach around midday, and as usual, it was buzzing with life. Families set up picnic spots, kids built sandcastles, and groups of friends lounged under umbrellas, sipping cocktails from the nearby chiringuito.

I kept an eye out for the donut man as we spread out our towels.

"Donuts, €1!"

I sat up immediately, scanning the beach.

"Relax," Diego said, laughing as he rubbed sunscreen on my shoulders. "He'll make it over here eventually."

The warmth of his hands against my skin made me forget about the donuts for a moment.

"Still obsessed?" he teased, leaning down to kiss my shoulder.

"Completely," I replied, my voice softer now.

But as the afternoon passed, there was no sign of him.

We ordered drinks from the *chiringuito*, dipped our toes in the water, and people-watched as hawkers made their rounds, offering everything from mojitos to fake Ray-Bans.

Still no donut man.

By the time the sun started to set, I was getting restless.

"Maybe he's taking the day off," Diego suggested.

"Or maybe he's already sold out," I sighed, disappointed.

As we packed up to leave, I spotted a familiar figure in the distance. A man balancing a large wooden tray on his head, making his way down the beach.

"There he is!" I gasped, grabbing Diego's hand and tugging him along.

The donut man was here!

I practically ran across the sand, dragging Diego with me.

"You're ridiculous," he said, laughing as I waved the donut man down.

"One, please," I said breathlessly, handing over a euro.

He smiled and handed me a donut wrapped in a paper napkin.

The first bite was everything I remembered... soft, sweet, and just the right amount of indulgent.

"Worth it?" Diego asked as I returned to our spot.

"Absolutely," I said, savoring every bite.

Barcelona's beaches weren't the peaceful sanctuaries I'd imagined. They were lively, chaotic, and full of surprises.

Between the *chiringuitos*, the hawkers, the massage ladies, and the ever-elusive donut man, every beach trip felt like an adventure.

As we walked back to our apartment that evening, the scent of sea salt and sunscreen still lingering on my skin, I thought about how different life here was from the one I'd left behind.

In Singapore, life was structured, predictable. But in Barcelona, the days unfolded like improvised music. I was learning the tempo of the city, noticing the tiny contradictions that made it feel alive: the cafés that spilled laughter onto cobblestone streets, the sudden breeze carrying the scent of grilled meat, the way sunlight danced across the facades of buildings that had stood for centuries.

Each corner held a possibility. A bakery tucked away behind a narrow alley. A street musician playing a song I didn't know but somehow recognized. A random conversation with a stranger that left me smiling for hours. It wasn't what I had expected. It was chaotic, unpredictable, and sometimes overwhelming, but it was *mine* to explore.

And every time I bit into a €1 donut, I knew I wouldn't trade it for anything.

CHAPTER 15 – Barcelona's Traffic Is Out to Get Me

꩜

After a year of living in Barcelona, you'd think I'd have mastered the basic life skill of crossing the street. It sounds like a minor thing, but no. Despite everything I'd survived, from Spanish bureaucracy to flaky landlords and to accidentally ordering intestines at a tapas bar, the one thing I couldn't seem to nail?

Traffic direction.

Blame it on being raised in Singapore, where cars drive on the left and jaywalking feels like a capital offense. Every time I crossed the street, my body betrayed me, instinctively looking the wrong way like it had been programmed by years of Singaporean traffic laws.

And Barcelona's traffic wasn't exactly forgiving. Scooters

zipped past like they had a death wish, cyclists appeared out of nowhere, and cars parked wherever they could squeeze in. Crossing the street wasn't just about following traffic lights; it was about survival.

Joshua, ever the supportive friend, had made peace with the idea that my demise would be traffic-related.

"One day, you're going to get hit," he warned as we walked toward the beach with Laura one weekend.

"Relax," I scoffed, waving him off. "I've got it under control."

Apparently, I did not.

Later that day, as we stood at a crosswalk, I was distracted, laughing at something Laura said, while Joshua scrolled through his phone a few steps behind us. The light turned red for cars, but the pedestrian signal hadn't turned green yet. I stepped forward anyway, standing a little too close to the curb, completely oblivious to the bus pulling up behind me.

Joshua glanced up just in time to see my impending doom.

"Nadia, move!" he shouted.

Too late.

The bus mirror clipped the side of my head with a firm thunk, sending me stumbling backward.

"*¡Dios mío!*" Laura gasped, grabbing my arm to steady me.

I stood there in shock, clutching my head. The hit wasn't hard enough to knock me down, but it hurt. Tears welled up in my eyes from the sting, more from surprise than actual pain.

Joshua ran over, wide-eyed. "Are you okay?"

I nodded slowly, still processing what had happened. "I... I just got hit by a bus mirror?"

That's when the laughter started.

Joshua doubled over, hands on his knees, laughing so hard he could barely breathe. Laura bit her lip, trying to keep a straight face, but the moment I met her eyes, I lost it too.

This was absurd. Who gets hit by a bus mirror? Me. That's who.

"This is exactly what I meant!" Joshua wheezed, wiping his eyes. "I told you this would happen!"

We decided there was only one way to recover from such an incident: vermouth. We found a little bar nearby, ordered a round, and sat in the sun, nursing my bruised dignity.

Laura shook her head, raising her glass. "Only you, Nadia. Only you would get hit by a bus and laugh about it."

I raised mine. "To public transport violence."

But Barcelona wasn't finished with me yet.

A few weeks later, I was on my way to the academy, in my usual "power walk but still semi-late" mode. I approached a zebra crossing and glanced quickly in both directions—wrong directions, of course—and stepped onto the road.

That's when I noticed a car… slowly backing up toward me.

I froze, my brain lagging behind reality. The car kept rolling backward, and before I could react, one of the rear wheels rolled over my foot. Not hard enough to break anything, but firm enough that I felt every excruciating second of it.

I yelped, more out of surprise than pain.

The driver noticed way too late. His window rolled down, his face filled with panic.

"*¿Estás bien?*" he asked if I was ok, his voice high-pitched with guilt.

I waved him off, trying to laugh. "I'm fine! *¡Todo bien!*" I called out, still standing in the middle of the road, shaking my head at my own carelessness.

The truth was, I wasn't hurt, but I was definitely embarrassed.

When I got home that evening, Diego was waiting for me in

the kitchen, flipping through a magazine. He looked up as I walked in, and his brow furrowed at the sight of me limping slightly.

"What happened?" he asked, setting the magazine down.

"Uh… a car ran over my foot," I said casually, kicking off my shoes.

Diego's jaw tightened. He was across the room in seconds, his hands on my waist, his eyes scanning me like I had just told him I'd been shot.

"A car ran over your foot?" he repeated, his voice dangerously calm.

"It wasn't that bad!" I said quickly, trying to downplay it. "The guy was going really slowly."

Diego pulled me toward the couch, his hands warm and steady as he guided me to sit down. "Let me see."

"It's fine, really—"

"Nadia." His voice had that firm, no-arguments tone, and I sighed, plopping down.

I sighed and stretched out my leg. He crouched in front of me, gently lifting my foot onto his lap. His fingers traced lightly along my ankle and the top of my foot, pressing just enough to check for swelling.

"No bruising," he muttered. "And you can walk?"

"Of course. See?" I stood up, giving him a playful twirl. "Good as new."

Diego was not amused.

"Nadia, you have to be more careful," he scolded, running a hand through his hair. "You've been here long enough to know which way to look."

I tried to hold back a laugh. "I know, I know. But you have to admit, it's kind of funny. First a bus mirror, now a car?"

"It's not funny," he said, his jaw tightening. "You could've been hurt."

I reached for his hand, squeezing it gently. "Hey. I'm okay."

Diego sighed, some of the tension leaving his shoulders. He pulled me into a hug, his arms wrapping tightly around me. "I just don't want anything to happen to you."

I buried my face in his chest, enjoying the warmth of his embrace. "Nothing's going to happen to me. I'm indestructible."

Diego pulled back slightly, tilting my chin up so I'd meet his gaze. His eyes softened, a hint of a smile tugging at the corner of his lips. "Indestructible, huh?"

"Completely."

"Let's hope the traffic agrees." He leaned down, pressing a soft kiss to my forehead, lingering just long enough to make my heart flutter.

For the next few weeks, Diego went into full protective boyfriend mode.

Every time we crossed the street, he'd reach for my hand like a human seatbelt. "Right first. Then left," he'd say solemnly, as if he were training a small, easily distracted child. Or a confused puppy.

"Diego," I'd groan. "I am a grown woman."

"Mm-hmm," he replied, pulling me back onto the curb just as a Vespa screamed past us. "A grown woman who nearly died. Twice."

"Clipped. I got clipped."

Diego narrowed his eyes. "Your definition of 'clipped' is suspiciously close to 'injured by a moving vehicle.'"

One morning, we were walking to the market, hand-in-hand, me proudly not limping. I was feeling good. Confident. Independent. I looked left, then right, then stepped into the street like a boss.

And immediately got yanked backward as a bike whizzed

past.

Diego didn't even say anything. He just gave me a Look.

"Oops," I mumbled, squeezing his hand.

Diego sighed, shaking his head. "You're going to be the death of me."

I grinned up at him, squeezing his hand tighter. "Impossible. You're stuck with me."

Diego laughed, pulling me closer as we continued walking. "Lucky me."

Barcelona may have been trying to teach me a lesson, but I wasn't going to let it win.

I just needed to actually look the right way before crossing the street. And maybe stay a safe distance away from bus stops.

But as long as Diego was beside me, shaking his head and laughing at my near-death experiences, I figured I'd be okay.

CHAPTER 16 – Next Stop: Nowhere I Meant to Be

Getting lost isn't something I do often, but when I do, I like to make it the theatrical kind that's complete with rising panic, a cast of confused bystanders, and a dramatic phone call or two.

That morning, I was feeling confident. Bold, even. I'd woken up early-ish (which in Barcelona counts as an achievement), had my morning cup of tea, and decided to squeeze in a few errands before work. To save time, I took what I believed to be a shortcut via a different train station.

Bold of me to assume I had mastered public transport.

What began as *"Look at me being efficient!"* quickly spiraled into *"Why is this train moving through rolling fields instead of city blocks?"*

45 minutes in, I was no longer cruising through Barcelona. I was halfway to Narnia.

I frantically checked my phone and confirmed what my stomach had already suspected. I had taken the right train line… just in the completely wrong direction.

Brilliant.

I jumped off at the next stop: Castellbisbal.

Now, I don't know what I expected from a town with a name like that, but silence wasn't it. The platform was almost comically deserted, save for a single wooden bench, a faded station sign, and the occasional bird looking at me like I was its next form of entertainment.

I thought I had accidentally wandered into a low-budget indie film about small-town isolation.

I took a deep breath and did what any rational person would do. I called Diego.

He picked up after a few rings. "Nadia? Where are you?"

"Castellbisbal," I replied, pacing the platform and squinting at the station sign like it might offer a portal back to Barcelona.

There was a pause. Then, a chuckle. "What?"

"I took the train the wrong way. I swear I followed the map, but apparently, I have the navigational skills of a potato."

He chuckled again, and for a second, it soothed me. Then I heard it, a voice in the background. A female voice. Clear as day. "I'll wait for you."

Something cold pinched the back of my neck.

"Diego?" I asked, trying to sound casual. "Where are you?"

"In a meeting," he said quickly. "I'd come get you if I could, but I can't leave."

A meeting. With who? Another scientist who actually understood the nerdy papers he read for fun? Someone who didn't need Google Translate to understand half his jokes?

My chest tightened. My fingers curled into fists around the phone. Heat rose to my cheeks. I could *feel* my heartbeat in my throat.

"Right," I said, my voice tighter than I meant. "Of course. No problem."

We hung up, but my brain was already in panic mode. My stomach churned, my hands trembled, and every rational thought I tried to force in got shoved aside by a torrent of *what ifs*:
What if he finds someone more interesting? Someone who gets him? Someone I'll never even meet until it's too late?

I tried not to think about it and called a taxi service, but the dispatcher wasn't optimistic. Castellbisbal, it seemed, was far enough from Barcelona to be inconvenient but not far enough to warrant urgency. It would take too long for a taxi to get there.

So, I swallowed my pride and called the one person I was dreading having to explain this to… my boss.

I braced myself for the fallout. The long sigh. The disappointed silence. The "we need to talk when you get here."

Daniela picked up almost instantly. "Nadia?"

I sighed. "So… I may have taken the wrong train and now I'm stranded in Castellbisbal, waiting for the next train. I'll get there as soon as I can."

There was a pause. Then, to my surprise, she laughed.

"Oh, don't worry about it," she said. "It's the holiday season. Your students probably won't even show up. Just come in when you can."

"Really? No one showed up?"

"Nope. In fact, once you get here, we might just go for drinks."

Wait, what? Daniela offering cava instead of consequences?

"Did you say… drinks?"

166

Daniela chuckled. "Well, if no one's coming in, might as well enjoy ourselves."

Her understanding tone eased my anxiety a little, but the hour-long wait still felt like an eternity. I paced the platform, scrolling aimlessly on my phone and mentally kicking myself for being so careless. I rehearsed apologies in my head, preparing for the awkwardness of walking into the academy embarrassingly late.

Finally, the train arrived, and I practically collapsed into the nearest seat, the stress and frustration of the morning weighing me down as paranoia gnawed at me. Maybe I was just projecting old wounds—Remy, Henry, all the lies I hadn't seen until it was too late. Or maybe this was exactly how it started: with one little voice in the background that meant nothing… until it meant everything.

By the time I finally made it to the academy, Daniela was waiting at the reception desk, arms crossed and a playful smile on her face.

"Ah, the prodigal teacher returns," she teased.

I groaned. "This is never leaving the staff room, right?"

"No promises."

I let myself laugh with her, pretending the unease hadn't burrowed in. But it was still there, sharp and insistent.

We joined a handful of teachers in the break room, where *cava* flowed and someone had pulled out a tray of *jamón* and olives. Apparently, when no students showed up, the teachers went rogue and started celebrating like it was New Year's Eve.

Daniela grabbed two glasses and handed one to me. "To surviving Castellbisbal."

I clinked my glass against hers. "And to never stepping foot in that place again."

As the drinks flowed, Daniela, who was normally all business, loosened up, sharing stories about her own disasters with public transport.

"I once got on a train to Girona instead of Tarragona," she confessed. "Ended up accidentally crashing a wedding."

"How do you accidentally crash a wedding?" I asked.

"There was a buffet," she said simply. "And I was hungry."

We laughed, and I had to admit, this was turning out to be one of my better accidental days.

At some point, after a couple of glasses, Daniela leaned in conspiratorially. "So, tell me the truth, how's Diego?"

I nearly choked on my drink. "What?"

"Oh, come on," she said, rolling her eyes. "The way you talk about him. He's cute, right?"

I narrowed my eyes. "Are you asking as a boss... or as a woman in the market?"

Daniela raised an eyebrow. "Listen, I am a single woman, and you have a boyfriend who, from what I hear, is tall, Spanish, and romantic."

I sipped my *cava*. "I mean, I could ask Diego if he has single friends..."

Daniela's eyes sparkled. "See? That's what I like to hear."

I giggled like a teenager. "So... what's your type?"

"Someone who doesn't take the wrong train to Castellbisbal."

"Wow," I muttered. "Okay."

A few minutes later, one of the male teachers walked into the break room, tall, dark-haired, and objectively attractive.

Daniela elbowed me. "Okay, what about him?"

I choked on a piece of *jamón*. "Daniela!"

"What? I'm trying to be efficient!"

I pressed my fingers to my temples. "You want me to set you

up with a coworker?"

She took a sip of her drink and gave me an unapologetic smile. "If you get me a date, I'll delete the Castellbisbal Incident from all records."

I sighed dramatically. "Fine. But I want a raise."

"No."

"Worth a shot."

As the day wrapped up, Daniela was still on the hunt, scanning the break room like a woman on a mission.

I shook my head, amused. "I'm going home before this turns into The Bachelor: English Teacher Edition."

She grinned. "Let me know if Diego has any friends."

I walked out laughing. This had been one hell of a day.

When I finally dragged myself home, Diego was at the stove, stirring something that smelled like garlic heaven. He looked calm, collected, like the human embodiment of "everything's fine." Meanwhile, my insides were still staging a one-woman panic concert.

He turned, flashing that easy smile. "You survived Castell-bisbal."

"Barely," I muttered, dropping my bag with all the drama of a Shakespearean heroine.

We ate. We joked. I laughed in all the right places, even teased him about his obsessive seasoning habits. But the whole time, a single question gnawed at me like a squirrel with a death wish. Finally, I couldn't take it anymore.

"So... who was she?"

His fork stilled midair. "Who?"

"The woman," I said, stabbing my pasta like it had personally wronged me. "In the background. When you said you were in a meeting."

Diego blinked, clearly blindsided. "Nadia, she's a colleague. We were in the lab. She said she'd wait for me to finish before starting her part."

"Uh-huh." My fork jabbed again, faster this time, as if stabbing the plate could puncture the rising panic in my chest. *She's just a colleague. She's just a colleague. Just a colleague.* My thoughts ran in a loop, but the voice in my head refused to quiet: *Maybe not. Maybe he wants her. Maybe I'm always one step behind.*

"And you didn't think that was worth mentioning?" I pressed, my jaw tight.

His brows pulled together. "Because it wasn't important.

What is important is you getting lost in random towns and calling me like it's a sitcom plot. Do you realize how reckless that was?"

The words hit sharper than I expected. My cheeks burned. "I got on the wrong train, Diego. I'm not twelve."

"Then stop acting like it!" His voice was louder now, edged with frustration I hadn't heard before. "First the traffic, now this. Do you ever actually pay attention to where you are? To what's happening around you?"

I swallowed hard, the lump in my throat blocking air. "I'm trying. But maybe I'm just not good at being... normal. At being an adult like everyone else." Every syllable echoed in my head, reminding me of years spent feeling inadequate, unworthy, unseen.

The silence after that was heavy. He sighed, dragging a hand through his curls, and for a moment he looked as exhausted as I felt.

Finally, softer. "I just... I need you safe. That's all."

I nodded, but inside, doubt gnawed at me. My chest tightened, stomach fluttered, and every instinct screamed *look out, he'll leave you for someone better, someone smarter, someone easier.* The jealousy and paranoia wrapped around me like tendrils of smoke from a fire I thought I'd extinguished.

I wanted to tell him that being safe wasn't the same as being

172

okay. That the fear wasn't about trains or lab meetings, and I'd heard versions of *it's nothing* before. The fear was about men who once swore I was the only one. And then... wasn't.

Diego turned back to the stove, humming like the world had steadied itself again. I smiled at his back, because that's what you do when you don't want someone to see you splintering.

But privately, I made myself a promise.

If he ever gave me reason to believe he was one of them... that he preferred someone else, someone who spoke his language better, someone who fit his world more easily, I'd be ready.

No begging. No collapsing on kitchen floors.

This time, I'd walk away before the ground caved in. Because loving him was terrifying enough. Losing myself again? That wasn't an option.

So instead, I leaned harder into distraction. Jokes. Stories. Anything that kept me from staring too long at the cracks I was afraid to see.

Which is why, as we sat at the kitchen table later, I launched into Daniela's unexpected matchmaking efforts like it was the funniest plot twist of my week.

"She literally tried to recruit me as her personal dating assistant."

Diego grinned. "Oh, really?"

"Yes, and now I have to set her up or she'll never let me live this down."

He tilted his head, mischief tugging at his mouth. "Well, I do have a cousin…"

I gasped. "Diego."

He flashed a teasing smile. "He's single."

For a split second, just a split second, I wondered if that smile was too easy. If it was the kind of smile he'd given someone else earlier that day. Paranoia, sharp and petty, fluttered in my chest before I forced it down.

"This is getting out of hand," I said, masking the thought with a laugh.

Diego leaned in, brushing his lips against mine. "But it's fun, isn't it?"

I sighed dramatically, but I couldn't stop smiling. "Fine. But if this turns into a disaster, you're taking responsibility."

Diego laughed, kissing me again. "Deal."

As I curled up next to him later that night, I couldn't help but think about how different this life was from the one I'd left behind.

Messier? Yes. A little chaotic? Absolutely.
But infinitely more fun.

The day had been a disaster, but it made for a story I wouldn't forget anytime soon. Living in Spain was nothing if not an adventure, and even when things went wrong, there was always something to laugh about.

"Just promise me you'll stick to walking next time," Diego said, brushing a kiss across my temple. "Fewer chances to end up in Castellbisbal."

I smiled, but a sliver of doubt pressed in. Did he say that because he really worried or because he was tired of cleaning up after me? I hated how quickly my brain could turn tenderness into suspicion, how fast it could spin an ordinary comment into a secret judgment.

Walking did feel like the safer bet, which says a lot, considering I'd already been clipped by a bus mirror and had my foot run over by a car. But compared to public transport? A stroll sounded practically life-insured. No wrong trains, no disappearing into towns with names that sounded like medieval battlefields.

Just me, my tragically accident-prone body, and the city streets daring me to survive another day.

But the next morning proved me wrong.

CHAPTER 17 – The Apple of Someone Else's Eye

Some mornings in Barcelona felt like they were ripped straight from a movie. The kind where the sunlight hit just right, golden and warm, with a slight breeze carrying the scent of fresh bread from the corner bakery.

It was one of those mornings. And because the universe has a wicked sense of humor, it was also the morning I became the target of what can only be described as a real-life low-budget thriller.

I'd arrived at the train station early for once, a rare achievement given my usual habit of cutting things too close. Inspired by the weather, I decided to take advantage of the extra time and walk to the academy instead of catching the bus. The route wasn't far, and I figured the exercise would do me good after too many mornings spent sitting on the train.

The streets were unusually quiet as I strolled along, my steps echoing faintly against the cobblestones. My mind wandered to my lesson plans for the day and the weekend ahead. I had nothing special planned, but maybe I'd finally get around to exploring that little café Diego had been raving about.

He kept mentioning it, hinting that we should go together. "They have the best *churros*," he'd told me one evening, pulling me close on the couch. "Crispy on the outside, soft on the inside, dipped in thick chocolate. Pure magic."

I smiled at the thought, imagining us sitting outside the café, the morning sun warming our faces as we shared pastries and coffee.

Lost in my daydream, I barely noticed the small car slowing down beside me until the hum of the engine caught my attention.

A small, nondescript car pulled up, its tires crunching softly against the edge of the curb. I hesitated, glancing toward the driver's side window, which was rolling down. The man behind the wheel looked to be in his late thirties or early forties, with dark hair and a calm expression that did little to ease my nerves.

"*Perdón,*" he said, leaning slightly out of the car. "*¿Puedes ayudarme? Estoy buscando la estación de tren.*"

Ah. Lost? Relatable. He needed directions to the train station.

I hesitated for a second because, you know, stranger danger, but he seemed harmless enough. I'd gotten pretty decent at giving directions in Spanish, so I smiled and did my best to explain the route.

"*Gracias,*" he replied, nodding with a warm smile as he thanked me.

Crisis averted. I gave a polite nod, ready to continue my morning stroll.

And then he reached for something.

I froze, my brain instantly spiraling into worst-case scenario mode. Was this the moment I got kidnapped? Would my disappearance end up as a dramatic documentary on Netflix?

But instead of pulling out something suspicious, he extended an apple. A... what?

"For you," he said in Spanish. "Thank you for helping."

An apple. A literal apple.

Not a granola bar, not money, not a thank you and a wave. Just a single apple. Like I was Snow White and he was testing my survival instincts.

I hesitated. What kind of person just… carries around apples to give away?

But he was still holding it out expectantly, and I didn't want to be rude, so I did the only thing that seemed appropriate. I took the apple.

"*Gracias*," I said, feeling ridiculous.

I was already turning to leave when he spoke again.

That's when he said it, almost casually. "*He notado que te gustan las manzanas.*"

I froze mid-step, brain buffering like bad Wi-Fi. Translation, please? Oh. Right. "I've noticed you like apples."

"What?" I spun back toward him.

He smiled, like he'd just shared a fun fact from my personal Wikipedia page. "*Sí, te he visto durante los últimos ocho meses.*"

Eight. Months.

He had seen me. For the last eight months.

My stomach dropped straight to my shoes. *Eight months.* My skin prickled like I'd just stepped into cold rain. Was this normal? Was he just being neighborly… or was I about to become the subject of a very dramatic newspaper headline? Should I be smiling politely, or sprinting?

179

The apple in my hand suddenly felt radioactive. *Put it down. Drop it.* I didn't. I just stood there, smiling like an idiot, every instinct screaming *run*.

"I... I need to go," I stammered, clutching my bag and the world's most suspicious fruit as I hurried away, heart pounding so loudly it could've echoed off the alley walls.

But then I heard it. The low hum of his car engine. Creeping forward. Matching my pace.

Oh hell no.

My mouth went dry. My hands were slick. Is this actually happening? *Don't look back. Don't run. Running makes it worse.* Every muscle in my body ignored reason and tensed anyway, ready to sprint.

I sped up. So did the car.

The world narrowed to sound—the engine, my heartbeat, the slap of my shoes against the pavement. It was like every crime story I'd ever read was replaying at once, all whispering the same thing: *this is how it starts.*

By the time I reached the academy, my vision was tunneling. I fumbled with the door, missed the handle twice, shoved it open with both hands. Inside, I was surrounded by light, voices, normalcy.

I practically collapsed against the counter. "Someone's

following me," I said, my voice shaky and rushed.

Daniela's head snapped up instantly, her eyes narrowing with concern. "What?"

I gestured frantically toward the street. "He's in a car. He stopped me, gave me an apple, and said he's been watching me for eight months."

To her credit, her expression barely flickered. Instead, she grabbed her coat with military precision and marched toward the door. "Stay here."

I didn't argue.

I watched her step outside, her head swiveling as she scanned the street. My heart pounded as I peered out the window, half-expecting the man to drive off the moment she appeared. But the car was still there, idling a little way down the road.

After what felt like an eternity, she came back inside, shaking her head. "I saw the car," she said, her tone even but her expression hard. "It was a dark sedan, wasn't it?"

I nodded, my throat too dry to speak.

"Well, it's gone now," she continued. "He must have seen me watching him and decided to leave. You did the right thing coming straight here."

"What if he comes back?" I asked, my voice barely above a

whisper.

Her expression softened slightly, but there was still a trace of steel in her gaze. "If you see him again, let me know immediately. And don't hesitate to call the police. You're not alone in this."

That evening, I told Diego everything.

He didn't take it well. At all.

"He's been watching you for eight months?" he repeated, pacing the living room. His voice wasn't calm or reassuring. It was sharp. Accusing. "And you didn't notice? Not once?"

I flinched. "How was I supposed to? I'm not out here doing background checks on every man with a piece of fruit!"

"This isn't about fruit, Nadia," he snapped, running a hand through his hair. "First it was the traffic thing, now this. Do you ever pay attention? You walk through life like nothing bad can touch you."

The words landed like stones in my chest. "I'm sorry I don't live in constant paranoia, Diego. Not all of us scan every license plate like we're in an action movie."

He stopped pacing, his jaw tight. "It's not paranoia when someone is following you. It's survival."

We stared at each other, the air between us heavy. For once,

I didn't feel safe in his anger. I felt small. Defensive. Like I'd failed some test I hadn't known I was taking.

"I didn't ask for this," I whispered, voice trembling, tears stinging my cheeks. "I didn't ask to be stalked. And I sure as hell don't need you making me feel stupid on top of being terrified."

His chest rose and fell rapidly, and I saw the flash of something raw in his eyes. Frustration, fear, maybe guilt. "I'm not saying you're stupid," he said, voice tight. "I'm saying you need to see what's happening around you. Because if you don't—" His tone cracked, fear bleeding in. "If you don't, one day I might not get to you in time."

The words sliced through me, sharper than I expected. My stomach lurched. He's scared. I'm scared. And somehow we're both hurting each other instead of fixing this. My throat tightened, my hands curled into fists at my sides.

He stepped closer, closer than necessary, and I instinctively stepped back, but his presence filled the space anyway. We were too close and too far at the same time.

We didn't resolve it that night. Not really. He kissed my temple eventually and murmured, "I just want you safe."

I whispered, "I know."

But the tension stayed, thick and unspoken, between us.

And maybe part of me hoped it was over—that the man, the car, the cursed apple—were just a fluke. That Diego's worry and my defensiveness would fade into background noise, like the hum of the fridge.

But then it happened again.

This time, I was walking with Gabriela, a colleague, after work. We'd stayed late preparing lesson plans for the upcoming term, and the sun was already beginning to set as we made our way toward the station.

"So, any plans for the weekend?" Gabriela asked, her tone light as we strolled side by side.

"Not really," I replied. "Probably just a quiet dinner with Diego. You?"

Before she could answer, the sound of an engine idling nearby caught my attention. My stomach twisted as I turned my head slightly, catching a glimpse of a dark sedan creeping along behind us.

I stiffened. "Gabriela."

She followed my gaze. Her face paled. "Is that—?"

"Yes," I whispered, trying to keep my voice steady. "Let's just keep walking. Don't stop."

We picked up our pace, our steps quick but deliberate as

we tried to act natural. The car didn't speed up but kept its slow, steady crawl behind us, like a shadow that refused to be shaken.

"What does he want?" Gabriela whispered, her voice tight with fear.

"I don't know," I whispered back, my pulse hammering in my ears.

By the time we reached the train station, the car had turned off down a side street and disappeared from view.

Gabriela let out a breath. "That was terrifying."

I nodded, gripping my bag tightly. "I need to tell Diego."

That evening, when I recounted the incident to Diego, he was furious.

"You didn't even think to write down the plate?" he barked after I told him.

"I was too busy trying not to die, Diego!" I shot back, my voice cracking. "I'm sorry my note-taking skills weren't at their peak while I was being hunted like a prey in a forest."

He shut his eyes, his fists clenched at his sides. And I realized we weren't just fighting the stalker. We were fighting each other, too.

185

Because fear doesn't just bring people close. Sometimes it drives a wedge, reminding you of the ways you see the world differently. He wanted vigilance, I wanted normalcy. He wanted control, I wanted air.

We didn't fix it that night. Not even close.

There were half-apologies mumbled into the dark, long silences where neither of us wanted to be the first to speak, and promises tossed out like lifelines we weren't sure either of us could actually grab.

From then on, he started escorting me to work every day, jaw tight, eyes scanning the streets.

And me? I let him. Even though a part of me hated the unspoken message in all of it, like I couldn't be trusted to see danger unless it came with flashing neon signs.

But I also knew one thing: this wasn't just about a stalker in a car.

This was about me, him, and the uncomfortable truth that sometimes love means seeing each other's blind spots and not liking what you see.

It settled between us like a third presence, heavy and uninvited. Some days we ignored it, filling the silence with small talk about weekend plans or what to make for dinner. Other days, it was louder, buzzing in the spaces between our words, reminding me that Diego wasn't just walking me to work;

he was guarding me. And I wasn't sure if that made me feel safer or smaller.

One afternoon, as we walked to his car after he'd come to pick me up, I tried to lighten the mood. "You know, the students probably think I've hired a bodyguard."

Diego cracked a small smile, though the tension in his posture remained. "Good. Let them think that. Maybe word will get back to your stalker, and he'll stay away for good."

While I appreciated Diego's vigilance, a part of me felt guilty for disrupting his routine. "You don't have to keep doing this, you know," I said one evening as we sat at the dinner table.

He reached over, taking my hand in his. "I want to. I need to know you're safe."

I squeezed his hand, a lump forming in my throat. "Thank you."

Diego smiled, his thumb brushing gently over my knuckles. "Anything for you, *mi amor.*"

Eventually, as the weeks passed without any sign of the stalker, Diego began to ease up, though not without hesitation. "I'll stop taking you," he said one morning, "but promise me you'll call if anything feels off. No hesitation."

I nodded, though I couldn't promise I'd stop looking over my shoulder. Because the truth was, Diego's watchful eyes did train me to be more aware, but also more afraid.

Even with his unwavering support and the apparent disappearance of the car, I couldn't shake the feeling that someone was still out there, seeing me in ways I didn't see myself.

And maybe that was the most challenging part, not the shadow of a man in a sedan, but the realization that no matter how much I wanted to be strong, some part of me would always be looking for danger too late.

It was a paranoia I carried now, stitched into me like another scar. And though I tried to move on, I couldn't shake the thought that maybe Diego was right. Maybe I really was too naive to see the danger until it was already at my door.

CHAPTER 18 – When the Train Becomes a Stage

I was on my way to work, lost in my usual morning haze, scrolling through my phone as the train rocked gently along the tracks. The hum of the metro, the soft chatter of commuters, and the occasional screech of brakes created the familiar soundtrack of my commute.

That morning, though, something unusual happened.

As the train stopped at the next station, a couple carrying instruments stepped inside, a man with a guitar and a woman with a violin. They set up near the doors, placing a small portable speaker on the floor.

I glanced up, curious. People carrying instruments weren't unusual in Barcelona, but the combination of a violin and a guitar on a train felt like something special.

The doors slid shut, and without any announcement, they began to play.

The woman's violin sang out first, a lilting, mournful melody that filled the carriage. The man followed, his guitar adding a gentle rhythm. Together, they created a beautiful harmony, their music transforming the dull, routine train ride into something magical.

I glanced around. Surely, everyone was as enchanted as I was.

But no.

Most people were aggressively committed to pretending nothing unusual was happening. Phones. Books. The window. Even their own shoes. Honestly, if someone had burst into flames in front of them, they would've nodded politely and gone back to whatever they were doing.

Why was everyone ignoring them? They were good.

I sat back, letting the music wash over me. The morning light filtering through the train windows, the gentle sway of the carriage, the unexpected beauty of live music… I couldn't help but smile.

When the song ended, the musicians exchanged a quick glance and a nod. Then the man bent down, picked up a hat, and started walking through the carriage.

Ah.

It hit me. This wasn't just a spontaneous performance; it was busking.

The man approached each passenger, holding out the hat. Most people ignored him, shaking their heads or keeping their gazes firmly fixed on the floor. But when he reached me, he lingered just a second longer, clearly having noticed that I'd been watching the performance.

I'd outed myself as the only one actually paying attention. Caught red-handed.

Crap.

I fumbled in my bag, pulling out a euro coin and dropping it into the hat.

"*Gracias,*" he said with a polite nod before moving on to the next passenger.

The woman with the violin followed, holding out her own hat. I quickly shook my head, avoiding eye contact. She moved past me without a word, continuing her circuit of the carriage.

As they left the train at the next stop, I sat there, replaying the moment in my head. It wasn't a big deal, just a euro. And honestly, the music had been worth it.

But also… how many coins did I need to carry to get through a week of metro buskers?

Over the next few weeks, I noticed the same pattern repeating more frequently.

One day, it was a saxophonist playing *Besame Mucho* with a flourish. The next day, a man with an accordion filled the carriage with lively folk tunes. Then there was the singer who performed an emotional version of Hallelujah while clutching a portable mic.

Some performers were incredibly talented, while others… well, let's just say they lacked the polish of the professionals. But they all followed the same routine: perform a few songs, then walk through the train with a hat, hoping for tips.

At first, I felt obligated to give every time. I didn't want to seem rude, and I assumed there might be consequences if I didn't contribute—an awkward confrontation, a dirty look, or worse, a public call-out. But the more it happened, the more uneasy I became.

Did I have to give money every time? Was it rude not to? I wasn't sure of the etiquette, and it was starting to bother me.

One evening, over dinner, I brought it up to Diego.

"Hey," I said, twirling my fork in a plate of pasta. "Do you ever give money to the buskers on the train?"

He raised an eyebrow, pausing mid-bite. "Buskers?"

"Yeah, you know. The people who play music on the metro and then walk around asking for money."

Diego chuckled. "Oh, them. Why? Did you give them money?"

I nodded, frowning. "Well, yeah. Isn't that what you're supposed to do?"

He laughed again, clearly amused. "No, you don't have to give them anything. Most people don't."

"But... they're playing music," I argued. "It feels wrong to just sit there and ignore them."

He reached across the table, squeezing my hand. "Nadia, trust me. Nothing happens if you don't give them money. They're not going to shout at you or make a scene. They just move on to the next person."

I sighed, feeling a little foolish. "I guess I've been overthinking it."

Diego shrugged. "It's just part of life on the metro here. You'll see the same performers over and over. Some are really good. Some..." He made a face. "Not so much."

I laughed. "I've definitely seen a few questionable ones."

The next morning, I was power-walking toward the station, matcha in one hand, my bag slipping off my shoulder, and Joshua trailing behind, not running but casually strolling like we weren't already three minutes behind schedule.

"Joshua, hurry up!"

"This is a you problem," he called back. "I operate on European time now."

"You're American."

"Details."

By some miracle, we caught the train, Joshua managing to wedge his way inside just before the doors slammed shut behind him. He turned to me, grinning. "See? Right on time."

I rolled my eyes, trying to catch my breath. "One day, you're going to miss the train."

"One day, you're going to relax."

I was about to argue when the sound of a violin filled the carriage. A woman and a man had stepped inside, instruments in hand. Without any announcement, they began to play.

The violinist led the melody, slow and sweet, while the guitarist accompanied her, adding soft, rhythmic chords.

Suddenly, the drab grey metro was a movie set and I was part of the cast, minus the hair and outfit budget.

I looked around, expecting at least a little awe.

Nope.

Most of the passengers remained entirely unbothered—heads down, scrolling through their phones, looking out the window, or pretending to be in deep thought about something very important (which was probably just what they were having for lunch).

Joshua leaned in. "I love how nobody cares."

I whispered back, "Are we the only ones who appreciate this?"

"We are the moment."

As we listened, I sat there thinking about how different busking in Singapore is.

Back home, busking is practically an Olympic sport of permits, auditions, and government approval. There, performers stand in carefully designated spots with laminated badges, singing like their rent depends on it because it does. Everything is neat, regulated, and polite. Even the rebellion has rules.

Here? Music feels unruly. Unplanned. A little messy. And somehow, so much more alive.

And just like that, I missed home.

It had been more than a year since I'd spoken to my family. A whole year of silence sitting heavy on my chest. I wondered if they ever lay awake at night, scrolling through their own memories of me and wondering if I was safe. Or if they were just angry. Maybe both.

The truth? I cycled through guilt, rage, relief, and terror daily like it was an emotional spin class I'd never signed up for. Sometimes I imagined my mom pacing the kitchen, muttering prayers under her breath. Sometimes I pictured my sisters rolling their eyes, writing me off as selfish. Other times, I let myself believe they'd moved on, their lives perfectly intact without me.

The not knowing was the worst.

And in moments like this—watching strangers sing on a train, thinking about the way my sisters and I used to belt out cheesy pop songs while washing dishes—I felt the ache of it so sharply it made my throat burn.

But then Joshua leaned in, whispering, "Do you think they'd play Stand by Me if I asked?" and just like that, the melancholy cracked into laughter.

Because Joshua did ask. Loudly. And shockingly? They said yes.

Just like that, the metro transformed into our own private

concert. The guitarist began strumming, the violinist adding a soft harmony. Then Joshua started singing.

Not just quietly humming. Full voice, committing to the bit.

I died. Like, soul-left-my-body kind of mortification.

People started looking. Some were smiling, a few were tapping their feet. One old man nodded approvingly, while a teenager recording on her phone was clearly about to turn us into a viral meme.

Joshua elbowed me. "Come on, Nad. Back me up."

"No."

"Come on."

I groaned, but against my better judgment, I joined in.

It was ridiculous. It was chaotic. It was perfect.

As we sang, more people joined in. A businessman at the far end mumbled the lyrics under his breath. A little girl clapped along. A woman wearing earbuds took them out, which, honestly, was the biggest compliment.

By the time the train pulled into the next station, half the carriage had joined in.

The song ended, and for a brief, perfect moment, the entire

carriage cheered. People clapped, laughing as they turned back to their phones and returned to their normal metro routine.

Joshua took an exaggerated bow. "Thank you, thank you! We'll be here all week!"

The guitarist laughed, giving him a thumbs-up. "You have a good voice."

I turned to the violinist. "You guys are amazing. Do you play outside the metro?"

She nodded. "*Sí*. We have a show this weekend. You should come."

She handed me a flyer with an address on it. Joshua took it before I could, studying it as if he was already RSVPing.

"We have to go," he whispered. "This is fate."

I sighed. "Fine."

The buskers packed up and left at the next stop.

That night, over dinner, I told Diego what happened.

"You sang?" he said, visibly trying to picture it.

"I was coerced."

"I'm shocked. And weirdly impressed."

"Joshua's fault."

"I bet he loved it."

"He did," I admitted. "But honestly? It was kind of... amazing."

Diego leaned back in his chair, arms crossed, watching me with an amused expression. "So when are you quitting your job to join your new band?"

I threw a piece of bread at him.

Later that night, as I lay in bed scrolling through my phone, I got a text from Joshua.
   Joshua: You're bringing Diego to the gig, right?
   Me: Maybe.
   Joshua: We could go viral. This could be our origin story.
   Me: It's a flyer for a metro concert, not a Netflix documentary.
   Joshua: Yet.

I couldn't help but laugh. As wild as it was, the whole day reminded me of something important. Maybe this was the point of Barcelona. Not perfection. Not approval. Just saying yes, even when you're terrified.

Even when part of your heart still aches for the family you left behind.

CHAPTER 19 – Teaching? Nah. Selling Chaos? Absolutely.

By June, Barcelona had transformed into tourist soup. The kind where the heat shimmered off the pavement and the streets were thick with visitors clutching oversized maps.

Locals? They rolled their eyes so hard I worried they'd get stuck that way.

At first, I was vibing. My students were buzzing about beach days and Nutella-stuffed croissants, and I was dreaming of slow mornings, salty hair, and maybe, just maybe, learning how to paddleboard without dying.

Then reality smacked me in the face.

The Spanish academic calendar wasn't like Singapore's. Here, schools shut down for almost three whole months. No students. No classes.

And for me? No income. Just me, my fridge whispering "feed me," and my landlord not-so-gently reminding me that rent is, in fact, a year-round commitment.

The tragic realization hit me during a casual conversation with my boss, Daniela, who chirped, "So what are your summer plans?" with the cheerfulness of someone who absolutely had money.

The answer? Apparently, starving.

My rent, utilities, and groceries didn't magically go on vacation. I'd spent the past year surviving just fine as an English teacher, but suddenly, I was staring at a long, empty summer with no paychecks on the horizon.

I needed a job. Fast.

That's how I found myself selling party packages on the beach and co-leading pub crawls in the Gothic Quarter.

The gig came via a friend of a friend who introduced me to Max, a sun-kissed Australian with a sleeve of tattoos, a beer in one hand, and the kind of laid-back confidence that screamed I've never paid rent late in my life.

"You sign people up for beach parties, booze cruises, pub crawls, whatever," Max explained, handing me a flyer and a wink. "Easy sell. Tourists are already halfway drunk and fully reckless."

I was desperate. "Sure," I said, ignoring the creeping anxiety in my gut. "I can do that."

The next day, I arrived at the beach, armed with flyers, optimism, and a T-shirt that quickly became a mistake.

Because here's the thing, I showed up looking like I was on my way to a casual brunch, while my colleagues looked like the cast of a Netflix travel docuseries: glowing, carefree, and suspiciously un-sweaty.

The women wore bikinis and breezy cover-ups that screamed effortless beach goddess. The men—tanned, chiseled, and permanently shirtless—were tossing frisbees, chatting up tourists, and generally looking cooler than I had ever been in my entire life.

And then there was me.

Standing awkwardly in my sweaty T-shirt and shorts, gripping my stack of flyers like they might save me from drowning in social anxiety. I felt like a flamingo among flamingos, except my feathers were ruffled, mismatched, and trying way too hard. I tugged at my T-shirt self-consciously, wishing I could disappear.

Max clapped me on the back. "You good?"

"Yeah, I'm fine," I lied.

"Just smile, be confident, and don't take it personally when people say no. They're tourists. They barely know what day it is."

I nodded. Then immediately took it very personally when the first three groups walked past me like I was an invisible lamppost. A sad lamppost.

By hour two, I was ready to fake an injury and limp away dramatically. I was sunburned, under-hydrated, and spiritually defeated by a French bachelorette party that laughed directly at me.

Meanwhile, my colleagues who were flirting, laughing, effortlessly charming were raking in sign-ups like it was nothing.

I wanted to crawl into the sand and hide. But rent wasn't going to pay itself, so I forced myself to push through. I found my rhythm, tweaking my pitch so I didn't sound like a malfunctioning robot.

"Hey guys, looking for a night you'll regret in all the right ways? Free shots, exclusive club entry, and at least one story you won't want your parents to hear."

To my surprise, they laughed. And signed up.

It wasn't glamorous, but by the end of the first week, I'd sold enough packages to buy real groceries and a bottle of shampoo that wasn't on clearance.

That night, I counted my crumpled euros like they were precious gold coins.

Okay, I reassured myself. *I can survive the summer.*

But then came the next phase of the gig, which was actually leading these drunk tourists around on pub crawls.

If selling was convincing drunk tourists to spend their money, pub crawling was herding drunk tourists through the chaotic streets of Barcelona while making sure nobody got lost, arrested, or scammed into buying a fake Rolex. I learned quickly that tourists have two goals: drink as much as possible and take embarrassing photos they'd later pretend never happened.

On my third night, I was co-leading with Sam, a ridiculously good-looking Canadian who looked like he'd stepped off the cover of Men's Health. Sam was in his element, effortlessly charming groups of tourists, leading drinking games, and exuding the kind of confidence that made him seem like he belonged in this chaotic world of summer parties.

He had charisma. I had a water bottle and a fanny pack full of bar maps.

I was still figuring out how to keep up, trying to find the balance between a responsible guide and someone who wasn't completely killing the vibe. I was doing okay... reminding people where the next bar was, pointing out bathrooms, and occasionally joining in for a laugh.

Halfway through the crawl, we arrived at a packed bar. Sam turned to the group and clapped his hands together. "Alright, everyone, it's time for body shots!"

The crowd erupted into cheers as if he had just handed out free money.

I blinked at him. "Body what?" I asked, leaning closer so I could be heard over the music.

Sam stared at me, his mouth slightly open in disbelief. "You've never seen one?"

"No," I admitted, feeling my face heat up.

His grin widened, delighted. "Oh, you're in for a treat. Watch and learn."

He handed a shot glass to a blonde girl in the group, who squealed with excitement. With zero hesitation, she climbed onto the bar and lay back like she was in a music video. Sam placed the shot glass in the hollow of her collarbone. One of her equally enthusiastic friends stepped forward, licked salt off the girl's stomach, took the shot straight off her chest, and finished with a wedge of lime held between her teeth.

I gawked, half shocked, half amused. "THAT'S a body shot?"

Sam laughed, clearly enjoying my reaction. "Welcome to the party life, Nadia. What do you think?"

I couldn't help but laugh. "I think it's ridiculous. But kind of… fun?"

"Fun is the whole point." He wiggled his eyebrows, grabbing another round of shots from the bartender. "You should try one."

"Me?" I stared at him, wide-eyed. "Absolutely not."

"Come on," he teased. "You're the new girl. Think of it as your initiation."

I hesitated, glancing around at the group of tourists who were now fully invested in whether I would surrender to peer pressure. The energy was infectious. Maybe it was the cocktails or the heat of the moment, but against my better judgment, I realized I wanted to try it.

"I'll do one," I said suddenly, surprising even myself.

Everyone in the group lost their minds. Sam's grin spread wider. "That's the spirit!"

"Wait, wait," I added quickly, pointing at him. "But I'm doing the drinking, not the lying-on-the-bar part."

"Fair enough," he said with a shrug, already setting it up.

Moments later, I stood in front of one of the pub crawl participants, an equally amused girl from Ireland who volunteered for the other half of the "shot partnership."

Sam handed me a glass of tequila and guided me through the process with a smug look of satisfaction.

"Salt, shot, lime," Sam instructed like a professional body shot coach. "And don't spill, or you're buying the next round."

"No pressure," I muttered under my breath, laughing nervously.

The group cheered as I leaned forward, licking salt off her stomach (dear god, what was my life?), grabbed the shot from its precarious spot on her chest (was this hygienic?), and finished with a lime wedge from her mouth (yep, it was happening).

It was over in seconds, but the crowd erupted into cheers as I swallowed the burning tequila, feeling equal parts exhilarated and ridiculous.

Sam patted me on the back, grinning like a proud mentor. "Look at you, fitting right in!"

"I can't believe I just did that," I said, laughing as I wiped tequila off my chin.

"I can't believe you didn't do it sooner," Sam shot back.

For the rest of the night, I was on a tequila-powered high. I danced with tourists from six countries, avoided stepping on something suspicious on the sidewalk, and may have given a motivational speech to a guy named Brad about finding his purpose.

It was ridiculous, silly, and something I'd never in a million years expected myself to do, but there I was, laughing, dancing, and embracing the chaos of the Barcelona summer.

But as much fun as I'd had that night, the reality of the job was still there in the morning, pressing down on me like a hangover I couldn't shake.

I woke up with zero dignity and a mild existential crisis, my feet aching from walking groups through cobblestone streets in shoes that definitely weren't meant for "pub crawl mode".

As I sat on my tiny balcony with a cup of tea, staring out at the Barcelona skyline, I thought about how far I'd drifted from what I imagined life here would be.

I came to Barcelona for culture and tapas and the romantic notion of *becoming*. What I got was salt-licking strangers, sticky nightclub floors, and a crash course in crowd control.

Sure, it was fun. But it wasn't sustainable.

The money was unpredictable, the hours were brutal, and every morning after a pub crawl felt like I had gone into battle without armor. Not to mention the endless parade of bronzed, beach-ready colleagues didn't help with my growing insecurity.

No matter how much I smiled or how hard I worked, I

couldn't help but feel like I didn't quite belong in this world of eternal summers and carefree party vibes.

This wild gig was exactly what I needed to survive right now, but it wasn't where I wanted to stay.

I exhaled, already trying to figure out what came next.

Maybe I'd find something better. Something easier. Something that didn't involve licking salt off strangers.

CHAPTER 20 – Rent Ain't on Vacation, But I Am

❦

"I still don't get it," I huffed, pacing around my tiny kitchen like a caffeinated hamster on the verge of a nervous breakdown. "Why would schools just stop for three months? No classes, no nothing? What are teachers supposed to do? Hibernate?"

Joshua, my best friend and occasional therapist-by-default, was leaning against my counter, unbothered, stirring sugar into his iced coffee. "This is Europe, babe. Teachers get summers off. But it's not the all-expenses-paid vacation you imagined, huh?"

I groaned dramatically, flopping onto the couch.

"It's not a vacation if you're broke," I grumbled into a throw pillow. "Vacations have cocktails and cabanas. Not unpaid bills and passive-aggressive reminders from landlords."

Joshua sipped his coffee with zero sympathy. "Why don't you do what you always do?"

I blinked up at him. "Cry in the shower and then Google how to become a pet psychic?"

He smirked. "No. Charm your way into something new. You're basically a walking LinkedIn recommendation. 'Nadia: excellent communicator, resourceful under pressure, once talked a teenager out of a panic attack using only Taylor Swift lyrics.'"

I snorted. "Sure, I'll just wander into an office and announce Hi, I'm great at wrangling hormonal teenagers and explaining the past participle, hire me."

Joshua tapped his chin, pretending to consider it. "Honestly, someone might be into that."

I threw a pillow at him.

"Okay, okay," he laughed, dodging it. "You need a distraction, so let's go to the beach. You're going to love it. Sun, gorgeous men, and absolutely zero chance of any straight guy creeping on you."

I narrowed my eyes. "You're really selling this. What's the catch?"

Joshua grinned. "No catch. Just lots of sunshine, hot men, and good vibes."

He wasn't wrong.

Mar Bella Beach was Barcelona's unofficially official gay beach. As soon as we arrived, I felt like I'd entered an alternate universe where joy was currency and abs were mandatory.

The sand glittered like something out of a skincare commercial. People lounged in curated chaos that involved rainbow towels, sequined fans, and music that felt like summer in sound form. There were men in tiny swim trunks laughing over mojitos, couples walking hand in hand with the ease of people who didn't have to look over their shoulders, and a general aura of effortless fabulousness.

The straight beaches had screaming kids and frisbee injuries; Mar Bella had cocktails and drag queens in platform heels.

"I feel like I should've moisturized more for this," I muttered, setting down my towel.

Joshua snorted. "It's fine, you're beach hot."

Joshua's friends were just as fabulous as he'd promised. Enrique, a charming man with a mischievous grin, introduced himself by handing me a cocktail he'd pre-mixed. "For you, darling," he said, raising his glass.

I took one sip and instantly knew I would follow this man into battle. "Enrique, we're going to get along just fine."

The day was a blur of laughter, music, and the kind of people-watching that made me question if everyone on this beach was legally required to be stunning. Everyone was friendly and open, and I quickly felt like part of the group.

At one point, Enrique nudged me, nodding toward a group of guys playing volleyball. "Which one's your favorite?"

I squinted at the group of gleaming shirtless men bouncing around like Greek gods on holiday. "Tall one. Curly hair. Distractingly symmetrical face."

He whistled low. "Good taste. Also, tragically out of your league."

"Thank you for that confidence boost, you magnificent menace," I replied, shoving him playfully.

But despite the friendly insult, I had never felt more at ease. The usual tension of being at a beach—who's looking, who's judging—was non-existent here. Everyone was having fun, and for the first time in weeks, I wasn't obsessing over money or my next career move or the weird smell in my apartment.

I was laughing. Relaxing. Feeling like I'd been accepted into a glittery, sun-drenched family I didn't know I needed.

As the sun began to set, we packed up and made plans to

meet up again soon. I left the beach feeling lighter, happier, and more connected than I had in weeks.

A few nights later, Enrique and I found ourselves wandering through the Gothic Quarter after a particularly wild night out.

"Josh bailed on us," I noted, finishing the last of my drink.

"Coward," Enrique deadpanned. "Guess it's just us."

We turned down a narrow alley, only to realize too late that this was not one of the charming, rustic ones. The street was lined with dimly lit clubs and questionable-looking women in tight dresses leaning against door frames, their eyes scanning for potential customers.

I instinctively moved closer to Enrique, my nerves kicking in.

"Don't worry, *guapa*," he said, slipping his arm around my shoulder. "I've got you."

Enrique's demeanor shifted instantly, transforming into the role of a doting boyfriend. Arm around my waist. Chin tilted down like he was whispering something flirty in my ear.

"Laugh," he murmured. "So it looks real."

I let out a forced giggle, and Enrique pulled me closer, his hand resting protectively on my waist. The groups of men loitering nearby barely gave us a second glance as we strolled past, and I realized how much safer I felt with him there.

Once we were out of the alley, I let out a breath I didn't realize I'd been holding. "That was… intense," I said, my heart still racing.

"Yeah, even a cool city like Barcelona has its seedier side," Enrique replied. "You owe me for that Oscar-worthy performance, by the way. I was very convincing."

I laughed, shaking my head. "You're the best fake boyfriend ever. Drinks on me."

Two weeks later, Barcelona exploded in color. Pride had arrived, and baby, she was loud.

I'd been to Pride before. But not like this. Not Barcelona Pride.

Rainbow floats rolled through the streets blasting everything from reggaeton to Lady Gaga. Drag queens vogued on balconies. Strangers danced like no one was watching and everyone was watching with absolute joy. It felt like the entire city had taken a deep breath and decided to live out loud.

"This," Joshua declared, spinning in a circle, "is what life is meant to be."

Enrique looped an arm around my shoulders. "How do we

feel?"

"I feel like I should permanently replace my wardrobe with sequins," I said, eyes wide.

I didn't know it yet, but I had a new job that day: Cupid in Platform Sandals.

As we wove through the crowd, I quickly realized my true purpose: gay matchmaking.

Every few minutes, one of Joshua or Enrique's friends would spot someone cute, and it was suddenly my job to make introductions.

"You," I said, shoving Enrique toward a tall guy in a pink crop top. "Go flirt."

"Nadia, I swear—"

"I'm paying you back for that fake boyfriend act in the alley. Go."

Enrique huffed but obeyed. Within minutes, they were exchanging numbers.

Joshua clutched my arm dramatically. "You're dangerously good at this."

"Some people have talents," I said modestly. "Mine just happens to be orchestrating gay love stories."

We danced through the crowd, cheers erupting every time I successfully set someone up. At some point, Joshua grabbed my face with both hands.

"I love you," he declared.

"I know. You're very clingy," I said, laughing.

And for the first time in months, maybe even years, my mind wasn't racing. I wasn't obsessing over deadlines, rent, or what came next. I was just here, laughing until my cheeks ached, swaying to music blasting from some unseen speaker, letting the rhythm carry me through streets I hadn't yet claimed as my own.

The more time I spent with Enrique, Joshua, and their friends, the more I realized I was falling not just for Barcelona, but for the life I never thought I'd let myself have. Drag shows that defied every rule I'd grown up with. Impromptu dancing in alleys lit by orange street lamps. Friends who could turn even the bleakest day into something that made my ribs ache with laughter.

It wasn't just fun. It was a reclamation. A quiet rebellion against the rigid life I'd left behind in Singapore. Against the girl who'd spent years doubting her own right to joy.

And in that whirl of color, noise, and warmth, I felt it. Something rare and fragile, yet undeniable. I belonged.

Not just in the city. Not just with them. But finally, in my own life.

One afternoon, as we lounged on the beach after another wild night out, Enrique turned to me.

"You know what you need?" he said.

"A six-hour nap?"

"A new apartment," he corrected.

I blinked. "What?"

"You've been in the same place since you got here. Time for something new."

I opened my mouth to protest, but stopped. Because he wasn't wrong.

I had been clinging to that apartment like it was an anchor. Same coffee shop. Same bakery. Same pothole that tripped me once a week. But maybe it was time to explore.

There was so much more to see, and I wanted to experience it all. I just wanted to know what it would be like to wake up in a different part of the city, to fall in love with another side of this city.

I'd fallen into Barcelona like a coin in a fountain—ungraceful, chaotic, but full of hope. And now, maybe it was time to make a wish. A new neighborhood. A new chapter.

So, I began the search. Full of excitement, but completely unaware of the strange twists that were about to come.

CHAPTER 21 – The Street Didn't Want Me And It Was Mutual

Apartment hunting in Barcelona was like speed dating with emotionally unavailable men.

Every listing was either out of your league, hiding something sinister, or offering something too tiny to be real.

I had spent hours scrolling through listings, circling neighborhoods that sounded promising: Gràcia, Eixample, Poble Sec. They all had their own charm, but every option fell into one of three categories:

1. Unreasonably expensive (Would you like to pay €1,500 for a shoebox? Comes with a shared bathroom and a cat you didn't sign up for.)
2. Suspiciously cheap (No photos. No details. Probably a front for a cult.)

3. Too small to exist (The only way to fit a bed is if you sleep vertically against the wall.)

One evening, as I was deep into my latest bout of real estate-induced despair, Diego leaned over my shoulder, his damp curls brushing against my cheek. He smelled of sandalwood soap and warmth, and his presence alone made the stress of the day slightly more tolerable.

"Any luck?" he murmured, pressing a slow, lazy kiss to my temple before settling into the chair beside me.

I sighed dramatically, tilting my screen toward him. "Nothing that doesn't require selling a kidney to afford rent."

Diego scanned the listings, his lips curving into a smile. "What about this one?" He pointed at a listing in the Gràcia neighborhood.

I squinted at the photos. "It's cute and I love the tile floors, but we'd have to fold ourselves like a yoga mat to fit a bed in there."

"Well," Diego said, leaning in closer, his breath warm against my ear, "it's not the size that matters."

I gave him a look. "You're banned from making real estate innuendos."

"Can't ban what's natural." He grinned, smug and perfect.

"You'll find the right place. Barcelona has a way of surprising you."

Oh, Barcelona would surprise me, alright. Just not in the way anyone wanted.

The next day, I finally landed a promising lead. The photos made the place look cozy, the rent was within my budget, and it was in a quiet residential neighborhood.

"Apartment viewing tomorrow at 5 PM," the message read, along with the address.

Hope fluttered in my chest. This could be it.

The next day, I arrived at the street a little early. It seemed to be a residential area, narrow streets lined with quiet apartment buildings with laundry hanging from balconies.

It was charming. Suspiciously charming.

I rang the buzzer. Once. Twice.
Nothing.

Maybe they were running late?

I decided to wait, pacing up and down the street. There was no sign of anyone coming or going, and the longer I lingered, the more unsettled I felt. The street was unusually quiet, like it was holding its breath.

After about fifteen minutes, my phone rang. It was the owner.

"Hola?"

There was a pause, then a low, measured voice spoke.

"The street doesn't want you. Forget about the apartment. Go now, and nothing will happen."

I froze.

My brain scrambled to process what had just happened.

"What?" I stammered, my voice shaking.

The line went dead.

I stood motionless, the phone still pressed to my ear. My heart jackhammered against my ribs, and suddenly the quiet street felt... too quiet. Like it was watching me.

Was it a prank? A mistake? But the voice had been calm, deliberate, like they meant every word.

Panic took over, and I bolted down the street, barely registering my surroundings. My heart pounded in my chest, and I kept glancing over my shoulder, half-expecting someone to follow me.

When I reached the main road, I exhaled in relief. The familiar noise of traffic and people brought me back to reality.

My chest heaved as I caught my breath, my hands shaking.

What. The. Hell. Just. Happened.

That evening, I met up with Joshua for drinks, still rattled.

As soon as I saw him, the words spilled out. "You are not going to believe what happened."

I told him everything. The silent street, the phone call, the voice that sounded like it belonged to a mafia boss casually warning me off his turf.

He listened intently, his expression shifting from concern to disbelief. "Wait, wait," he said, holding up a hand. "They actually said the street doesn't want you?"

I nodded, still shaken. "Yes. It was so... creepy. Like something out of a movie."

Joshua stared at me over his wine glass. Then pulled out his phone.

"You're not gonna believe this," he said, holding up the screen for me to see.

I leaned in, squinting at the map. "What am I looking at?"

He tapped the screen. "That street? It's **the** street. The infamous one. The, uh... hooker street."

I stared at him, trying to process what he was saying. "Wait... what?"

Joshua cackled, shaking his head. "Yup. Apparently, it's been that way for years. Women line up at night, regular clientele, the whole setup."

Suddenly, everything made sense. The unusual stillness, the strange looks, the cryptic phone call.

"Oh my god," I groaned. "So you're telling me... they thought I was competition?"

Joshua burst into laughter so intense he nearly choked on his wine. "Well, you were pacing the sidewalk like you were working a shift! I'm guessing someone didn't like that."

"Oh my god." I buried my face in my hands, laughing despite the lingering unease. "That explains why they said the street doesn't want me."

Joshua wiped a tear from his eye. "I hate to break it to you, babe, but you're not cut out for the world's oldest profession."

I threw a napkin at his face.

Diego's reaction, however, wasn't as lighthearted. When I told him later that night, his expression darkened.

"You were on *that* street?" His jaw clenched, his voice sharper than I'd ever heart it. "Alone?"

"I didn't know!" I protested, throwing my hands up. "It was a listing! I thought I was being responsible!"

"Responsible?" He barked out a humorless laugh. "Nadia, you keep stumbling into danger like it's a hobby. First the traffic, then the stalker, and now this? How many warnings do you need before you start paying attention?"

The words hit harder than I expected, sharp and unyielding. My stomach twisted. "I'm not trying to be reckless. I just... I didn't know what that street was."

"That's the point!" His voice rose. "You don't know. You don't look around. You don't think. You walk through this city like nothing bad could ever happen to you, and one day—" He broke off, running a hand through his hair, frustration rolling off him in waves. "One day, it's not going to end with a warning phone call or a scare. And then what?"

I crossed my arms, anger sparking through my shame. "Do you think I don't know that? Do you think I don't replay every mistake in my head, wishing I could just be... normal? The kind of person who doesn't make everyone around her worry all the time?"

Diego's expression softened for a fraction of a second, but the tension lingered. "I just—" He exhaled hard. "I don't want to lose you because you couldn't see what was right in front of you."

The room went quiet. My throat ached. His words weren't

cruel; they were scared. But all I could hear was the echo of my own failures, the truth I already carried around like a stone in my chest.

"I'm trying," I whispered, my voice cracking. "I really am."

For a moment, neither of us moved. He stood there, arms crossed tight like he was holding himself together, while I sat with my own hands balled into fists, hating myself for being the problem yet again.

Finally, Diego sighed and sat beside me, the anger ebbing into exhaustion. He didn't reach for me right away, and I didn't lean into him either. We just sat in that uncomfortable space, two people who loved each other but couldn't quite figure out how to close the gap between fear and trust.

The next few days weren't icy, but they weren't effortless either. Our rhythm was off. Less teasing, fewer lazy kisses in the kitchen. More sighs than laughter.

Finally, one night, I pushed. "Say it. Whatever's sitting on your chest, just say it."

Diego leaned back in his chair, jaw tight. "You walk into danger like you don't even see it. The traffic, now this street. I can't keep watching you gamble with your safety like it's nothing."

I bristled, but forced myself to meet his eyes. "You think I don't scare myself? You think I don't go over it a thousand times later, hating that I didn't see it coming?"

We stared at each other across the table, two stubborn people refusing to blink first.

Finally, he exhaled, shoulders dropping. "I just need you to be more careful. Because if something happened... If I lost you, I wouldn't survive it."

"And I need you to trust that I'm trying," I said softly. "Even if I mess it up."

It wasn't a magical fix. But it cracked the tension enough that, by the weekend, the banter was creeping back in. He'd roll his eyes, I'd shove his arm, and for a moment, it felt like us again—worn around the edges, but still steady enough to hold.

A few weeks after The Street That Rejected Me incident, Joshua, Enrique, and I decided we needed a reward.

Joshua declared it first. "We're celebrating. Nadia survived the sex-worker mafia."

Enrique nodded. "Also, I've made it to a third date. Which is basically a gay engagement."

"And I haven't murdered a man for texting 'lol' in three days," Joshua added. "We're thriving."

When I mentioned our brunch plans to Diego, I expected a

polite "have fun" and maybe a "please don't get arrested", not an eager "Can I come?"

Joshua nearly fainted. "Diego wants to join us for brunch?"

I shrugged. "Apparently."

Enrique grinned. "Oh, this is going to be fun."

And so, Diego was initiated into the sacred ritual of bottomless brunch.

It was a scorching Sunday afternoon when we arrived at one of the trendiest brunch spots in Eixample. The place was peak Barcelona aesthetics with high ceilings, hanging plants, and a waitstaff that appeared to have been handpicked from a Calvin Klein ad.

Diego took it all in as we sat down, his brow slightly furrowed. "So... is the shirtless thing just... normal here?"

Joshua, sipping his first mimosa, nodded sagely. "You'll get used to it."

Diego glanced down at his own fully-buttoned linen shirt and looked vaguely overdressed.

Enrique leaned in. "Take it off."

Diego choked on his water. "Excuse me?"

"You heard me."

Diego laughed nervously. "I'm keeping my shirt on."

Joshua sighed dramatically. "Fine. Be repressed."

The mimosas flowed freely as Enrique interrogated Diego with all the enthusiasm of a gay mom meeting her daughter's first boyfriend.

"So," Enrique said, topping off Diego's glass. "What's it like dating our girl here?"

Diego smirked at me, his fingers lazily playing with the stem of his glass. "It's an adventure."

I rolled my eyes. "That's code for 'she's mildly unhinged.'"

"You love it," he said, nudging my knee under the table.

My stomach did that annoying swoopy thing again.

Joshua, already two mimosas deep, leaned in. "So, do you have any hot scientist friends for me? Preferably with an accent and a trust fund?"

Diego chuckled. "I can't promise the trust fund, but I do know a guy in marine biology who's—"

"Marine biology?" Joshua clutched his chest. "You mean I could date a man who talks about whales for a living?"

Enrique nodded solemnly. "We support this journey for you."

And that's when it happened.

A stunning man—tall, tanned, devastatingly handsome—walked up to our table and rested a casual hand on Diego's shoulder.

"*Hola* handsome," the man purred, smiling at Diego with undeniable interest.

Diego, mid-sip of his mimosa, froze.

Joshua and I stared, fascinated.

Enrique grinned like a demon.

"Uh…" Diego cleared his throat, shifting uncomfortably. "Hi?"

The man's smile widened. "I saw you from across the room, and I just had to say… you have incredible arms."

I nearly choked on my drink.

Joshua grabbed my arm under the table. "Oh my God, this is the best day of my life."

Diego, utterly bewildered, turned to me like I could somehow rescue him.

I did not.

I sipped my mimosa, thoroughly entertained.

"Uh... thanks?" Diego said, clearly not sure of the etiquette in this situation.

The man's eyes sparkled mischievously. "Are you new to the scene? I don't think I've seen you around before."

"Oh, he's new, alright," Enrique said smoothly, barely containing his glee.

Diego shot him a murderous look.

Joshua clutched his face in delight. "I can't breathe. I'm so happy."

The man slid into the empty seat beside Diego, completely ignoring the rest of us. "So... Diego, was it?"

Diego stiffened. "Yeah."

"Diego," the man repeated, rolling the name off his tongue like a glass of fine wine. "Let me guess. You're into something adventurous. Rock climbing? Surfing?"

"I, uh..." Diego ran a hand through his hair, visibly struggling. "I'm a biologist."

The man's eyebrow quirked in delight. "Ah. A smart one."

I was living for this.

Diego, visibly panicked, turned to me. "Nadia?"

I blinked innocently. "Yes?"

He narrowed his eyes. "Help me."

Joshua, clearly having the time of his life, fanned himself dramatically. "Nadia, why are you interrupting Diego's moment?"

Diego let out a long-suffering sigh. "I'm, uh, flattered, but I'm actually—"

"Taken," I cut in sweetly, sliding my hand onto his arm.

The man's smile faltered slightly, but he gave me an appraising look. "Lucky girl."

I grinned. "Oh, I know."

With a playful wink, the man stood. "Well, if you ever decide to switch teams... look me up."

And with that, he walked off, leaving Diego looking like he'd just survived a natural disaster.

Joshua immediately burst into applause.

Enrique wiped a fake tear from his eye. "I'm so proud."

Diego, visibly exhausted, turned to me. "You enjoyed that, didn't you?"

"Deeply," I admitted.

Diego groaned, downing the rest of his mimosa in one go.

Joshua leaned over. "So… how does it feel to be a gay icon?"

Diego shoved his glass at him. "More mimosas. Now."

Enrique laughed. "Ah, acceptance. A beautiful thing."

As we walked out of the brunch spot, Diego slung an arm around my shoulders and muttered, "You're never letting this go, are you?"

I grinned up at him. "Oh, absolutely not."

And just like that, Diego had been officially baptized into the chaotic world of my friends.

CHAPTER 22 – The Hustle Never Looked This Fabulous

Job hunting in Barcelona was a full-time job in rejection.

And not the cute, ambiguous kind. I mean soul-crushing, ego-bruising, "thanks but no thanks" rejection served with a side of please-don't-apply-again.

It felt like playing the lottery where every ticket said: "You're underqualified, underpaid, and unfortunately, too foreign to function. Try again!"

Between the endless scrolling, the carefully curated cover letters, and the eerie silence of unanswered applications, my confidence was officially on life support. And don't even get me started on the language barrier, which loomed over me like a stubborn rain cloud.

Every listing required Spanish fluency, and yes, my Spanish had improved. It really had! I could confidently order coffee, argue with taxi drivers, and gossip about my neighbor's dog in full sentences.

But working in Spanish? That was a whole different battle-field.

And then there were the qualifications.

In Singapore, my Associate's Degree was a big deal. A well-earned badge of academic survival which seemed to fall short in Spain. It might as well have been a certificate in napkin folding.

Here in Spain, a bachelor's degree was considered the bare minimum. Everywhere I looked, employers were asking for bachelor's, master's degrees, or specialized certifications. At this point, my best bet was either selling snacks at the beach or becoming a human statue on La Rambla.

I groaned, flopping onto the couch dramatically.

"I'll figure something out," I muttered to myself. But even I didn't believe me.

Eventually, desperation and vermouth conspired to push me into a new phase: The Gig Era.

I became a jack-of-all-trades and master of none. Some gigs were fun. Some were weird. Some were *"did that actually happen?"*-level bizarre. But every job added a new thread to the patchwork chaos quilt that was my Barcelona life.

One of those threads? A radio DJ gig for a local English-speaking station.

The ad described it as an "exciting opportunity to develop broadcasting skills." Which was code for "unpaid but you'll have a good story for brunch."

I almost didn't apply. I mean, yes, I had radio experience in Singapore. Three years, to be exact. But I'd been in the promotions and production team. I wrote trailers, organized events, and planned marketing campaigns. That was it.

Still, something about the ad made me feel... itchy. In a good way.

So I applied.

I showed up at the station, a small, tucked-away studio on the outskirts of the city. The manager, James, was a wiry British man with round glasses and a nervous energy that somehow felt reassuring.

"Alright," he said, after we exchanged pleasantries. "Let's hear what you've got. Can you do a demo?"

"A demo?" I repeated, suddenly unsure if this had been a good idea.

"Yeah, just pretend you're on air. Talk about a topic for a minute or two. Whatever comes to mind."

My palms instantly became clammy, and I was about one breath away from fainting, but I stepped up to the mic and started talking about my favorite churro café in Barcelona. Why their chocolate dip should win awards. Why calories don't count when joy is involved.

By the time I finished, James was nodding.

"Not bad," he said with a small smile. "You're a bit stiff, but that's normal. You've got potential."

To my surprise, he offered me the job on the spot. It was unpaid, something he stressed immediately, but I didn't care. I was going to have my *own radio show*.

Every weekend for the next year, I nervously stumbled my way through playlists, weather jokes, and shoutouts to imaginary listeners. Slowly, I grew into it—learned how to breathe on the mic, how to improvise, how to sound less like a socially anxious Roomba.

And then came the day I announced our biggest giveaway: tickets to a burlesque show.

I could feel the buzz through the airwaves. Callers flooded the line, each hoping to snag a pair of tickets. It was one of those rare promotions that felt electric, even over the phone. Burlesque wasn't just a performance; it was a statement.

As part of the deal, I got my own pair of tickets and I didn't hesitate. I invited Diego to join me. He raised an eyebrow when I told him. "Burlesque?" he asked, grinning. "This is new."

"Trust me," I said, handing him the glossy flyer with a photo of a glamorous performer mid-dance. "You'll love it."

The night of the show, the theater was packed. Dim, red-tinged lights bathed the room, and the air carried a faint scent of perfume and excitement. Diego and I settled into our seats, surrounded by couples, bachelorette parties, and exactly one very excited elderly woman in a hot pink boa.

When the music started and the first performer appeared, I was captivated. It wasn't just the costumes, though those were dazzling, or the sensual choreography. It was the confidence, the artistry, and the sheer electricity of the performers. They danced with a kind of joy and abandon that was intoxicating, weaving between sultry and playful with a wink and a shimmy.

Halfway through a particularly steamy routine, I glanced at Diego. His eyes were locked on the stage, his expression somewhere between awe and disbelief.

I leaned over, whispering, "Are you enjoying yourself?"

His breath was warm against my ear as he murmured, "This is blowing my mind."

I grinned, squeezing his hand under the table. So was I.

Then, a performer stepped into the crowd, scanning for a volunteer.

And before I could even nudge Diego, he was already raising his hand like a straight-A student volunteering for extra credit.

I blinked.

I barely had time to process what was happening before the dancer took his hand and led him to the stage.

"Oh my god," I whispered. "This is the greatest thing that's ever happened."

Most men who get pulled onstage at a burlesque show look like deer in headlights.

Diego?

He smirked at the crowd like he'd been waiting for this moment his entire life.

The music swelled. The dancer twirled around him, draping a feather boa around his shoulders.

He caught it effortlessly, adjusting it as if he was born to wear one.

Then, AND I SWEAR TO GOD, he did a full, slow-motion exaggerated hair flip. Despite having *no long hair*.

The crowd erupted into laughter and applause.

I was equal parts in love and terrified.

The dancer, clearly enjoying his enthusiasm, guided him through a ridiculously dramatic routine—a teasing strut, a hip pop that made the audience lose it, and finally, a flirty wink and finger gun at the crowd.

By the time the act ended, the entire room was cheering.

Diego gave a deep, theatrical bow before strutting back toward our table. Strutting.

I was never going to hear the end of this.

Diego collapsed into his chair, laughing, still wearing the boa.

I stared at him, speechless.

Diego turned to me, grinning smugly. "Well?"

I exhaled, shaking my head. "I cannot believe you just did that."

He grinned wider. "You loved it."

I folded my arms, trying to suppress my laughter. "I definitely think you should consider leaving your day job."

By the end of the night, I was obsessed. Burlesque was everything I hadn't known I needed—sexy, empowering, and unapologetically bold.

Months later, the burlesque world came calling again, but this time, it wasn't Diego stealing the spotlight.

I met Lucia at a friend's dinner party. She was opening a restaurant and wanted something bold for the grand opening. When she said "burlesque theme," I basically levitated.

"Do you need help?" I asked, practically jumping at the chance.

Lucia's face lit up. "I wouldn't say no. Are you interested?"

Interested was an understatement. I volunteered my time, diving headfirst into the project. I worked with a team of talented people—dancers, costume designers, and choreographers—each of them bringing a slice of magic to the event.

Then, one day during rehearsal, one of the performers turned to me. "You should join us," she said, hands on her hips.

I froze mid-tea sip. "You mean... on stage? With my face?"

"Yeah. You've been watching us rehearse for weeks. You

know the moves. You've got the energy."

The energy? Was that code for chaos?

Still... the idea stuck.

That night, I stood in front of my mirror and tried a few steps. At first, I looked like I was fighting an invisible bee. But then the music kicked in, and I began to feel something shift. A confidence I hadn't known I possessed.

I moved. I laughed. I started to believe I could actually do this.
So I did.

By the time opening night rolled around, I was ready. I slipped into my costume, a daring, glittering outfit I never imagined I'd wear in public, and joined the performers backstage. The nerves hit me like a freight train, but then I spotted Diego in the crowd, sitting with a group of our friends. His smile was wide and supportive, and when he caught my gaze, he mouthed, *You've got this.*

When it was my turn to perform, the adrenaline took over. The lights, the music, the crowd—it all blurred together as I moved across the stage, each step bolder than the last. By the time I finished, the applause was thunderous, and I felt exhilarated in a way I hadn't in years.

But as I stepped offstage and scanned the crowd, my stomach dropped. Standing near the back, holding a flyer, was a face

I hadn't seen in years.

"Is that—" I started, but Diego followed my gaze and answered before I could finish.

"An ex?" he asked, his tone light but his expression suddenly sharp.

It was Adrian, an Argentinian man I'd dated briefly in Singapore. He'd been sweet, but we'd grown apart, and our goodbye had been mutual but distant.

Before I could decide whether to approach him, Adrian made his way over, a friendly smile on his face. "Nadia," he said warmly. "I was traveling and I saw the flyer. Thought it'd be a nice surprise. You were incredible."

"Thanks," I said, managing a polite smile, though my heart raced. "I didn't know you were in Barcelona."

Diego stepped forward and extended a hand. "Diego," he said, his tone polite but firm. "Nadia's boyfriend."

Adrian shook his hand, the unspoken tension between them thick enough to cut with a knife. Diego stayed close for the rest of the evening, like a lighthouse reminding passing ships that I already had a home.

The night carried on, but the air between us had shifted. Diego was quiet, his arm draped around me, but I could feel the tension thrumming beneath his calm exterior.

Later, as we walked home, the city buzzing faintly around us, Diego finally broke the silence.

"So… Adrian," he said. The name landed heavier than it should have.

I sighed. "Yeah. From Singapore. We dated for a bit."

Diego stopped walking, turning to face me. "You never mentioned him."

Heat rushed to my cheeks. "Because it wasn't serious."

His brows lifted. "Nadia, you've grilled me about every woman who's ever served us coffee. And now an ex shows up out of nowhere, and it's 'not serious'?"

"That's different!" I snapped, then instantly regretted it. "I just… Look, he was the last guy I dated before I left Singapore. And I didn't think it mattered."

Diego shook his head, frustration flickering in his eyes. "It matters when you keep things from me. Do you have any idea how it feels to constantly reassure you about colleagues, waitresses, anyone who so much as breathes in my direction while you leave out the fact that an ex just so happened to be visiting the city where you now live?"

His words landed like slaps, too fast to deflect. Guilt, hot and choking, surged up my throat. "I didn't ask him to come here. I didn't even know he would. I just…" I swallowed hard.

"Sometimes I'm scared I'll never measure up. That one day you'll realize someone else—someone who fits better, who speaks your language, who isn't a constant mess—would be easier."

The silence that followed was unbearable.

Then Diego exhaled, shoulders dropping. "Nadia, I don't want easy. I want you. But I can't fight for trust if you're hiding pieces of yourself from me."

I bit my lip, the shame and fear mixing into something messy and raw. "I'm sorry," I whispered. "I should've told you."

Diego exhaled slowly, then stepped closer, cupping my face in his hands. "No more secrets, okay? Not about exes, not about anything. I need us on the same team."

I nodded, tears stinging my eyes. "Same team."

And then he kissed me. Slow, grounding, forgiving. The kind of kiss that felt like both a truce and a promise.

By the time we reached home, my mascara was smudged, my feet ached, and my costume feathers were sticking out of my bag like guilty confetti.

But Diego pulled me close, his lips brushing my temple. "For what it's worth, you were amazing tonight."

I smiled through the lump in my throat. "You're not so bad

yourself."

And just like that, the fight didn't disappear, but it folded into something sturdier. A reminder that love isn't all glitter and applause. Sometimes it's calling each other out, saying the hard things, and choosing again and again to stay.

Especially when staying feels just a little terrifying.

CHAPTER 23 – Testing, Testing... Is This Life Thing On?

When I wasn't on-air pretending to know what I was doing, I was everywhere else in the station trying to actually figure it out.

I attended events. Shadowed producers. Fiddled with buttons I definitely wasn't supposed to touch. I wrote and rewrote scripts until they didn't sound like they were written by a sleep-deprived AI. I even practiced transitions in the mirror, whispering things like, "And now, your smooth Sunday sounds..." while holding a spoon like it was a mic.

I didn't earn a single cent. But I was head-over-heels, totally, embarrassingly in love with radio.

There was something magical about sitting behind that mic, knowing my voice was floating through kitchens, taxis, and earbuds across Barcelona. Maybe someone was laughing at my lame joke while chopping onions. Maybe someone was writing down that indie band I just played.

It felt intimate. Powerful. Unlike anything I'd done before.

It was at one of these station events, a music showcase for up-and-coming bands, that I met Javier. He was the station's go-to photographer, effortlessly charming, with a perpetual camera slung around his neck. Javier had a way of making everyone around him feel seen, both literally and figuratively. He called it "capturing underrated potential."

"You should try modeling," he said casually one evening as we packed up after an event, totally casual, like he was suggesting I try a new toothpaste.

I laughed, nearly choking on my drink. "Me? Modeling? That's hilarious."

Javier tilted his head, studying me like he was already framing a photo. "Why not? You've got an interesting look—unique but relatable. People love that right now."

I blinked at him. "Relatable like... I-cry-at-commercials relatable? Or relatable like... girl-next-door who might burn pasta but still deserves love?"

He shrugged. "There's an open audition coming up. You should go."

I waved him off, convinced he was just being polite or maybe slightly delusional. But when I mentioned it to Diego later, he latched onto the idea immediately.

"You should do it," he said, nudging me as we scrolled through the audition listing together.

I frowned, skeptically. "Why are *you* encouraging this? I don't even know how to pose for photos."

"You don't need to," he replied, his grin infectious. "They're looking for real people, not supermodels. You're beautiful. And you don't know it. Which, ironically, makes you even more beautiful."

Okay, rude. And flattering. And now I was blushing like I'd been personally serenaded by the sexiest singer in the music world.

Despite my reluctance, their enthusiasm wore me down. I found myself standing in a bright, airy studio a week later, surrounded by people who seemed to glow with confidence and beauty. My jeans and sneakers felt woefully out of place next to the tailored outfits and high-heeled boots.

I stood there awkwardly, clutching the portfolio of hastily taken photos Diego had snapped in our apartment the night before, with questionable lighting and a potted plant I used for "ambience."

I waited for my turn, trying not to bolt for the exit.

And somehow, don't ask me how, they signed me. "You've got a fresh, relatable energy," one of the agents had said, as if I was a new yogurt flavor.

Naturally, the first person I told was Joshua.

The second I mentioned the words "signed with an agency," he actually snorted into his gin tonic.

"Modeling? You?" He laughed so hard I considered pouring my drink over his head.

I crossed my arms. "Wow. Thanks for the support."

"I mean, listen," he said, wiping his eyes, "you're gorgeous. But come on, Nadia. You're treating this like it's your big career move. It's not. You're avoiding the hard stuff. Jobs that pay. Jobs that make you practice Spanish. Jobs that keep you here for real. Honestly? Even working at Starbucks would give you more stability than this."

My jaw dropped. "Wow. Did you rehearse that speech, or is this your natural gift for killing dreams?"

"I'm serious," he said, softer now. "I just don't want you to keep chasing distractions instead of doing the thing that'll actually help you build a life here."

I hated that he had a point. I also hated that he was right in a "big brother who annoys you but also weirdly knows your soul" kind of way.

I stared at him, my pride smarting. "Thanks, Dad."

"I'm not trying to kill your vibe," he said, softening a little. "I just don't want to see you burn out chasing stuff that was never meant to hold you up."

I wanted to argue, but the sting of his words stuck.

When I told Diego later, expecting full cheerleader energy, his response wasn't what I expected either.

"I have all along thought you were doing this just for fun," he said.

I frowned. "What do you mean, for fun?"

"I mean," he said carefully, "I love that you're trying it. You'll be great. But don't lean on it like it's a foundation. It's not a job; it's an adventure. Like a side quest in a video game. You need something steady to pay the rent. This isn't it."

I groaned, flopping onto the couch. "You sound like Joshua."

Diego chuckled, sitting beside me. "Smart man."

And just like that, the excitement dulled a little. Not gone, but less shiny. Because if both of them thought I was treating this like an escape hatch, maybe I was.

Still, I showed up at the castings. I learned to say "relaxed but sultry" in Spanish. I sat on glossy benches pretending not to sweat through my T-shirt.

But deep down, their words followed me into every waiting room. This isn't it.

At first, the novelty carried me. I strutted (okay, shuffled nervously) into castings like the underdog in some indie movie. The kind where everyone else has symmetrical faces and cheekbones sharp enough to slice cheese, and I'm just... me, trying not to sweat through my shirt.

But reality doesn't care about movie underdogs. Slowly, the shine wore off. The world of glossy portfolios, designer loafers, and girls who somehow knew how to pose without looking constipated? Yeah. Not mine.

The worst moments were when the intimidation was so overwhelming that I couldn't even bring myself to go through with the casting. I'd walk into the room, see everyone looking effortlessly put together, and feel my heart sink. There were times I turned right back around and left without even checking in.

The breaking point came when I finally booked something. A beverage campaign. I called Joshua and screamed into the phone. I called Diego and nearly cried from excitement. I even started practicing "candid" sipping poses in the mirror.

And then? Two days before the shoot—canceled. No explanation. No apology. Just a casual, "it happens."

Something inside me snapped.

Every crowded hallway I sat in. Every polite-but-condescending smile. Every pep talk I gave myself in a bathroom mirror before daring to walk into another room of cheekbone royalty. All of it collapsed under the weight of one shrugged-off email.

I dragged myself to a couple more castings, but my heart had already packed its bags and left.

Joshua had been right. Diego too. Modeling wasn't a career ladder; it was glitter. Sparkly, distracting, but one gust of wind and it's gone.

And the wild part? Quitting didn't crush me.

It felt... good. Like I'd been stuffed into a dress two sizes too small, and someone finally unzipped it.

I went back to the station, where my voice—not my jawline—was the currency. The booth felt like home. It reminded me that I was a voice, a presence, a woman with a very specific playlist for crying in the shower.

But as much as I loved it, even I had to admit the truth: passion doesn't pay rent.

I needed something steady. Something real. Something that wasn't going to vanish with one careless email.

And just when I was beginning to lose hope, it happened.

An email pinged into my inbox. Interview invitation – Content Creator Role For a company that sold tickets to international sporting events.

Not modeling. Not radio. But writing. Creativity. Sports! (Okay, I googled the teams. Still.)

I stared at the screen, hope fluttering like a timid bird.

This one felt different.

CHAPTER 24 – From Unpaid DJ to Red-Lace Queen

The interview room looked like someone had decorated it during a caffeine high and never looked back.

There was a bright orange beanbag chair that sat proudly in the corner like it had just won a personality contest, a poster that screamed "WE SELL EXPERIENCES, NOT JUST TICKETS" in big, motivational startup font, and, because apparently the universe was in a good mood that day, a tiny dish of gummy bears next to my writing test.

I was obsessed.

Not with motorsports, because let's be honest, I once thought Formula 1 was a skincare brand.

But this company? This energy? I wanted in.

The recruiter handed me two writing assignments and said, "No pressure, just show us what makes you... you." Then she smiled in that way that made it feel like maybe, just maybe, this wasn't going to be one of those interviews where my soul melted into the office carpet.

I was still nervous, but also hopeful. These were clearly my people.

Even though I knew absolutely nothing about motorsports, I did know how to write about enthusiasm. And pretending I totally knew what a pit crew did.

I had exactly one hour to prove that I could be the kind of person who made motorsports sound sexy.

The first task seemed simple enough: write a short promotional newsletter to sell tickets to a Formula 1 event.

I took a deep breath as I picked up my pen and tried to summon the energy of an overenthusiastic sports commentator. This is it, Nadia, sell the thrill, even if your entire knowledge of racing involves cartoon cars with eyeballs.

"Feel the roar of the engines, the rush of adrenaline, the heart-stopping battle for first place. Formula 1 isn't just a race; it's an experience. Don't just watch it, live it. Get your tickets now!"

I sat back, reread it, and nodded. Decent. Not Pulitzer-worthy, but solid.

Then came the second task, which threw me completely off balance. I was to create engaging social media captions for the same event.

I frowned, tapping my pen against the desk. I had zero professional experience in social media, but then I remembered that I once spent 45 minutes crafting the perfect Instagram caption for a photo of me eating gelato. Surely that counted for something?

"Join the roar of the crowd and make a date with the legends of Formula 1! 🏎️=3 #FeelTheRush"
"For the love of speed, for the thrill of the moment—don't miss it. 🏆 Grab your tickets now!"

Boom. Hashtag glory.

The hour flew by, and when the recruiter came to collect my work, I felt a quiet sense of pride. I didn't know if I'd nailed it, but at the very least, I hadn't embarrassed myself.

One week later, I was back to scrolling job boards and contemplating whether "professional dog walker" was a viable career path when my phone buzzed.

"Hello?" I answered, already bracing myself for another polite rejection.

"Nadia?" The voice on the other end was cheerful, almost suspiciously so. "This is Claudia from the ticketing company. We just wanted to say that we loved your writing and we'd like to offer you the job!"

For a moment, my brain stopped functioning.

"I... I... Really?!" I spluttered. "Oh my God, thank you!"

Claudia laughed. "We were especially impressed by your social media work. You've got a real knack for engaging content."

Me? Social media? Engaging content? Diego was going to have a field day with this.

After pretending to know how salary negotiations worked ("Yes, that number sounds... very salary-ish"), I officially handed in my notice at the academy.

Daniela took it surprisingly well, though I may have seen a flicker of pain in her eyes as she marked yet another English teacher departure in her mental tally.

And just like that, I became a full-time content creator for a company that sold motorsports event tickets.

The office was chic and aggressively modern with sleek desks, glass-walled meeting rooms, a ping pong table, and a coffee machine so fancy it could probably predict the stock market.

My colleagues were a mix of locals and expats, a friendly and vibrant group who made me feel welcome right away. During my first team meeting, we brainstormed ideas for a campaign promoting Formula 1 tickets. Everyone tossed out ideas effortlessly, mixing enthusiasm with casual banter.

I, on the other hand, was terrified someone would realize I had no idea what I was doing.

But somehow, I managed to hold my own, pitching ideas and writing promo blurbs while trying not to internally scream every time someone said "engagement metrics".

One of my captions even got approved for an actual upcoming campaign. I nearly cried as I sat there giddy with an odd sense of accomplishment. Then I celebrated with overpriced churros.

Maybe I could actually do this.

For the first time, I had a job that didn't involve unpaid overtime, student cancellations, or the emotional damage of being asked "Why is English so weird?" four times a day.

One of the best parts? Regular hours. No more late-night lesson planning or unpredictable student cancellations.

I could clock out at 6 PM, meet Diego for dinner or join Joshua and Laura for drinks without feeling like a corpse in lipstick.

By December, I had fully settled into the job just in time for the office Christmas celebration.

The party was a lively, chaotic affair, held in a cozy downtown venue that looked like Santa's Pinterest board exploded.

Tables were decked out in tinsel and fairy lights, cava flowed freely, and tiny Santa hats that made everyone look like underpaid elves were passed around.

Diego, upon seeing the photos, declared, "Deeply unflattering, but delightfully festive."

As the night went on, I found myself in a circle of coworkers discussing cultural holiday traditions.

"In Spain, Christmas Eve is the big family gathering," Marta explained. "But New Year's Eve? That's when the real partying happens."

"Speaking of," another coworker interjected with a grin. "Do you know about the grape tradition yet?"

I blinked. "Grape tradition?"

Marta leaned in conspiratorially. "At midnight on New Year's Eve, you have to eat twelve grapes—one for each chime of the clock. It brings good luck for the year ahead."

"That doesn't sound so bad," I said.

"Yes, but you have to eat them in time with the chimes," she added. "If you mess up the timing, it's bad luck."

I squinted at her. "So you're telling me that on New Year's Eve, instead of counting down and screaming 'Happy New Year,' everyone is just shoving grapes into their mouths like their lives depend on it while a clock rings ominously?"

"Exactly!" Marta said, beaming.

Spain was a chaotic fairy tale and I loved it.

The rest of the night was a blur of dancing, holiday snacks, and dramatic re-tellings of office printer meltdowns. Marta asked about holiday traditions in Singapore, and I explained how Christmas wasn't as much of a family-focused celebration there.

"For us, it's more commercial with gifts, lights, and big shopping mall displays," I said. "It's different, but still fun."

"That's so interesting!" Marta said. "And what about New Year's? Do you have any funny traditions like our grapes?"

I opened my mouth to answer, but before I could speak, someone leaned in with a mischievous grin.

"Wait, you don't know about *the* tradition yet, do you?"

"The what now?" I asked, confused.

A ripple of laughter spread through the group as Marta gave me an almost conspiratorial look. "Oh, you'll see. Just wait until New Year's Eve."

I didn't trust her sparkle-eyed tone one bit.

I tried to press them for details, but they wouldn't budge, their teasing smiles making me both nervous and curious.

What on earth had I gotten myself into this time?

When New Year's Eve finally arrived, I was equal parts excited and apprehensive about whatever "tradition" my colleagues had hinted at. Diego and I were invited to Marta's house party for the evening, a warm and inviting space filled with the scent of roasted meats, laughter, and the clinking of glasses.

The evening started traditionally enough. The dining table groaned under the dishes—*jamón ibérico*, roasted lamb, seafood platters, and endless bottles of *cava*. All so pretty that they deserved their own Instagram accounts.

Diego's hand lingered on my back as we were introduced to Marta's friends and family, all of whom welcomed us with the warmth I'd come to associate with Spanish hospitality.

As the hours ticked closer to midnight, the energy in the room shifted. Everyone began gathering in front of the television, where a live broadcast showed the clock in Madrid's Puerta del Sol. Bowls of grapes were handed out, 12 in each bowl, perfectly counted.

I turned to Diego, whispering, "Okay. I'm ready for my grape speed-eating debut. But what's this other mystery tradition everyone's been teasing me about?"

He smiled, his dimpled cheek betraying a hint of mischief. "Patience. You'll find out soon enough."

The countdown began. The chimes of the clock rang out, and I frantically stuffed one grape after another into my mouth, trying to chew and swallow while keeping up with the crowd's laughter and cheers.

"Uno!"
"Dos!"

By the twelfth chime, I was victorious. Slightly choking, but victorious.

The cheers went up. People hugged and kissed, shouted *"Feliz Año Nuevo,"* and toasted with *cava*. I thought that was it.

But as I turned to Diego, I noticed Marta and a few others disappearing into another room, whispering and giggling.

"Diego," I said suspiciously, narrowing my eyes. "What's going on?"

He grinned, pulling me into a quick kiss. "Just follow me."

I followed him into the hallway, where Marta stood holding a box and the world's most mischievous grin.

I blinked. "What fresh chaos—"

She opened the box and held up… a pair of red lace underwear.

"Okay, Nadia," Marta said, barely containing her laughter. "Here's the real Spanish New Year's tradition: you have to wear red underwear to bring good luck for the year ahead!"

I blinked, caught completely off guard. "Wait, what? Are you serious?"

"Absolutely," Marta said, her grin widening. "But it has to be new and it's best if it's gifted to you."

"Which is why we got you this," Diego said, taking out the underwear.

I took it, laughing so hard I nearly dropped that delicate red lace set. "You planned this?"

"Of course," Marta said. "You're practically Spanish now. You have to do it!"

The room filled with laughter as they insisted I go along with the tradition. Diego leaned in, his eyes sparkling. "Trust me, it's fun. And who couldn't use a little extra luck?"

Despite my initial embarrassment, I couldn't help but laugh as I dashed off to change, the sound of their teasing and cheers echoing in the background.

When I rejoined the party, red lace firmly in place, I felt

ridiculous and strangely… empowered.

Diego's eyes sparkled with mischief. He pulled me aside, pressing a kiss to my cheek. "You look good in red."

I smiled, wrapping my arms around his neck. "I bet you say that to all the girls."

"No," he murmured, brushing his lips against mine. "Just you."

The rest of the night passed in a blissed-out blur. Music. Dancing. Me, in a ridiculous Santa hat and red lace. Diego's hands on my waist, the warmth of his touch grounding me in the moment.

We clinked glasses sometime after 2 a.m.

"To new traditions," he said.

"To red underwear," I added.

I couldn't stop smiling, thinking about how much my life had changed since I'd arrived in Barcelona. Sometimes, you don't just adapt to a new culture—you let it pull you in, red lace and all.

CHAPTER 25 - One Ticket, Please
(For Fish and Patience)

Adjusting to life in Spain wasn't just about learning the language. It was an entirely different rhythm of life, full of quirks, traditions, and cultural surprises that kept me on my toes.

Some things I loved immediately, while others were... let's just say, more of an acquired taste.

One of the hardest things for me to get used to was how slow everything felt. I was terrible at it.

Back in Singapore, everything moved at lightning speed. Malls and supermarkets thrived on weekend shoppers, bustling late into the night. Sundays were perfect for errands; if something wasn't available at 10 p.m., it simply didn't exist. There was always something to do, somewhere to be, and everything was available at the click of a button.

Spain? Spain was built for naps. And wine. And naps after wine.

One of the first things I had to learn the hard way was that nothing happens on Sundays. Not groceries. Not errands. Not even impulse purchases.

Sundays, the day of rest, were almost sacred. Shops, supermarkets, and even some restaurants closed entirely, leaving me in a lurch more than once.

I can't count how many times I would open my fridge on a Sunday afternoon, realize I was missing a key ingredient, and then smack my forehead in frustration.

One Sunday afternoon, I was struck by a deep, all-consuming desire to bake banana bread. I had the bananas. I had the cinnamon. I even had the pan greased. But when I opened the fridge, the eggs were gone. Vanished like my productivity.

"No problem," I thought, like the naïve, pre-Spain version of myself. "I'll just pop out and grab some."

I grabbed my bag and headed to the nearest supermarket, only to find the doors firmly shut.

Second store? Also closed.

Third store? May as well have had tumbleweeds blowing

past the doors.

Was there a national holiday? A city-wide egg strike? Was I being personally punished by the banana bread gods?

I called Diego, balancing my phone between my shoulder and ear as I peered into yet another closed shop window.

"Hey," I said. "Are the stores closed today?"

"It's Sunday," he said, like that explained everything.

"Yes, I know that. But why is everything closed?"

"Because it's Sunday," he repeated with a laugh.

I groaned. "What kind of logic is that? People still need to buy things on Sundays!"

"Next time, plan ahead," Diego teased, and I could hear the smile in his voice.

Frustrated but amused, I hung up and trudged back home, muttering under my breath about how backward it all seemed.

Later that evening, when Diego stopped by, I was still sulking on the couch.

"No banana bread?" he teased as he set down a bag of groceries he'd brought over.

I gave him a mock glare. "No eggs."

Diego grinned, pulling out a carton and waving it in front of me. "Problem solved."

"You're lucky you're cute," I muttered, snatching the eggs from his hand.

"And you're lucky I brought snacks," he replied, leaning down to kiss my cheek before collapsing next to me.

And I'll admit it, I swooned. Just a little.

It wasn't just Sundays that threw me off, though. Even during the week, I'd sometimes walk to a store in the middle of the afternoon, only to find a sign on the door that read *Cerrado por siesta* (Closed for siesta).

"*Siesta?*" I muttered, staring at the sign. "People still do that?"

Apparently, they did.

I thought siestas were a cute myth, like unicorns or job postings that didn't require five years of experience for an entry-level role.

But no. They were real. Whole neighborhoods would go suspiciously silent, like the city had collectively decided to take a nap and not tell me.

At first, it drove me crazy. I was used to convenience, to

efficiency. I couldn't understand how anyone got anything done when businesses kept closing in the middle of the day.

"I swear Barcelona has a vendetta against productivity," I ranted to Diego one day as we walked past a shuttered bakery at 3 p.m.

"Nadia," he said, pulling me into a side hug. "Life here isn't about rushing. It's about enjoying."

"I enjoy getting things done," I grumbled.

He kissed the top of my head. "Soon, you'll learn to love it."

And, ugh, he was right. Slowly, I did.

One afternoon, I met Joshua in Gràcia for coffee. We sat at a sunny outdoor table, watching people wander past like life wasn't something to race through but something to linger in.

"It's weird," I said, sipping my sangria. "Everything's so… slow."

Joshua nodded, sipping his drink. "I know what you mean. But honestly? I kind of love it."

I raised an eyebrow. "You love it?"

He shrugged. "Back home, I felt like I was always running on a treadmill. Like I couldn't stop moving or I'd drown. Here? People actually live and take time to enjoy things. I breathe more."

That stuck with me. That breathe more thing.

Maybe Joshua was right. Maybe I needed to stop fighting the slow pace and start embracing it.

So I started trying.

Over time, I learned to embrace the Spanish approach. Sundays stopped being panic days and started becoming rituals. Diego and I would sleep in, then take long walks along the beach or get lost in little neighborhoods we hadn't explored yet. We'd stop for tapas at tiny bars, share *croquetas* and glasses of vermouth, and end up sprawled on the couch in a happy, food-induced haze.

One Sunday afternoon, we were sprawled on the couch after a lazy brunch. Diego traced lazy circles on my arm, his voice soft.

"You know what I love about Sundays?"

"Hmm?" I murmured, feeling content and sleepy.

"I get to have you all to myself."

Cue my heart melting like butter on toast.

But the cultural adjustments didn't stop at naps and week-ends. Mealtimes in Spain were basically a form of time travel.

Lunch wasn't at a time that I was used to… It usually happened at 2 or 3 p.m.
Dinner? 9 p.m. if you were early. Midnight if you were fancy. I once had dinner at 11 p.m. and felt like I was living a double life.

At my first Spanish dinner party, I showed up at 7:45 p.m., tummy growling and cheeks politely flushed. By 8:30 p.m., we were still on olives. I was this close to chewing on the tablecloth.

When Diego saw me glancing nervously at my watch, he leaned over and whispered, "Relax. Appetizers haven't even come out yet. It's going to be a while."

"But I'm starving," I whispered back, pouting slightly.

He kissed my cheek. "Patience. The best things are worth waiting for."

Eventually, I learned that mealtimes aren't just about eating, but they're also about connection.

The Spanish have what they call *sobremesa*, lingering at the table after a meal, and it is a Spanish art form. Long after the last plate is cleared, people chat over wine or coffee, laughing and sharing stories. It's a far cry from the rushed meals I was used to back home.

It became one of my favorite things.

"One of my favorite things, though we're in a very complicated, on-again, off-again relationship, is the supermarket."

Grocery shopping in Spain was like wandering through a foreign film, and exploring supermarkets quickly became one of my favorite pastimes. There were new characters (pig cheeks!), dramatic plot twists (why does the cereal aisle have more wine than cereal?), and charming side characters like the fresh orange juice machine.

You heard me.

In Singapore, fresh orange juice was a luxury you paid for at fancy brunch spots. Here? Every supermarket had a machine where you could make your own.

Almost every supermarket had an orange juice maker. A hulking machine that takes whole oranges and juices them right in front of you. You pick your bottle size, press the lever, and it becomes this beautifully noisy, citrusy performance. The machine would come to life with a series of satisfying whirs and clunks, grabbing oranges, slicing them in half, and pressing them until golden, fragrant juice poured into the bottle.

I stood there mesmerized, watching it work as if I'd never seen orange juice before. I didn't even need orange juice that day, but I bought some anyway, just for the fun of it. It felt like magic.

Also magical? The bread section, which felt like walking into a bakery.

Rows of freshly baked baguettes, sourdoughs, and multigrain loaves filled the air with the warm, comforting scent of bread. What really amazed me, though, was the automatic bread slicer.

You'd place a whole loaf into the slot, close the lid, and press a button. Boom. Perfect even slices, ready to be bagged. It was ingenious, and I found myself looking for excuses to buy bread just so I could use it.

But nothing prepared me for the fish counter.

One day, I decided to be brave and make *merluza*, the delicate hake, a popular fish in Spain. Fancy, flaky, slightly intimidating.

I headed to the supermarket, proud of myself for stepping out of my culinary comfort zone. I marched to the fish counter, excited and ready. Until I wasn't.

The fish section smelled exactly as you'd expect, with rows of ice-covered counters displaying everything from prawns to squid to whole fish with their eyes still staring at you. I stood there, waiting my turn, while the fishmongers worked at lightning speed, cleaning, gutting, and wrapping fish for the customers ahead of me.

Ten minutes passed. Then fifteen.

People kept walking up and being served right away. Meanwhile, I was invisible.

I watched, confused, as they handed tiny slips of paper to the fishmonger.

What's going on? I wondered, starting to feel impatient.

After 40 minutes—yes, 40—I was the only one left. Finally, one of the fishmongers looked at me and asked, "*¿Número?*"

"Uh... *¿qué?*" I blinked, confused as to why he was asking me for a number.

He raised an eyebrow, clearly unimpressed, and gestured toward a small ticket dispenser on the wall nearby. I stared at it in disbelief. Of course, you needed a queue number to buy fish. Why hadn't I noticed it earlier?

Embarrassed, I grabbed a ticket and slunk back to my spot like a toddler who just realized their lollipop was actually a button.

Nothing quite says 'I've got my life together' like standing there, red-faced, while the fishmonger laughed and cut my hake like it was a comedy routine.

By the time I got home, I was still fuming at my own obliviousness. Diego was lounging on the couch, scrolling through his phone, his legs stretched out and looking perfectly at ease.

"What took you so long?" he asked, sitting up as I walked in.

"Don't ask," I groaned, setting the bag of fish on the counter with a dramatic thud. "Let's just say I learned a valuable lesson about Spanish supermarket etiquette."

Diego's eyes lit up with curiosity. "Oh, this sounds good."

I glared at him, though my lips twitched into a reluctant smile. "The fish counter. Apparently, you need a ticket to get served."

His grin widened as he leaned back against the couch. "Let me guess… You didn't take a number?"

"Nope. I stood there like an idiot for almost 40 minutes, wondering why everyone kept going ahead of me."

Diego burst out laughing, the sound filling the room and instantly easing my frustration. "I cannot picture you just… standing there," he gasped between chuckles.

"40 minutes, Diego. 40. Minutes."

He stood up, still grinning, and pulled me into a hug. "You're too cute," he said, his laughter still lingering in his voice.

"Not cute. Humiliated," I mumbled, my face pressed against his chest.

Diego pulled back slightly, tilting my chin up with his finger so I had to look at him. His eyes sparkled with amusement. "Well, next time, you'll be the first one to grab a ticket, right?"

I narrowed my eyes playfully. "If there is a next time, you're coming with me."

He smirked, leaning down to kiss my forehead. "Deal. But only if you promise not to leave me waiting for 40 minutes while you figure it out."

I laughed, swatting his chest. "You're impossible."

Later that night, we prepped the fish together in our tiny kitchen, with Diego still chuckling every few minutes as I gave him the side eye.

"What?" I finally asked, throwing a piece of parsley at him.

He caught it mid-air, still grinning. "I'm just picturing you standing there at the fish counter, looking so determined and so confused."

I shook my head, laughing despite myself. "Yeah, yeah. Laugh it up."

The next day, I was determined to redeem myself. I marched into the supermarket, grabbed a number at the fish counter like a boss, and waited.

When they called me up, I was ready. Until I realized I didn't know how to ask them to clean the fish.

"Um… *limpio*? Clean?" I said, miming scrubbing motions and praying my dignity survived.

The fishmonger gave me the kind of smile you give a toddler who just put their shoes on the wrong feet. Patient. Kind. A little amused. Then he nodded and got to work.

And just like that, I left with my cleaned fish and my pride mostly intact.

Tiny victories. I was collecting them like wine corks.

For a second, I imagined calling my mom to tell her about it. How I'd navigated a Spanish supermarket, how I'd managed without anyone holding my hand. Back home, that would've been nothing. Here, it felt like scaling Everest.

And if I did pick up the phone? Mom would immediately ask if I'd eaten, Roselyn would want proof I wasn't living in squalor, and Kyra would ask if I was finally being practical for once.

Sometimes it was the tiniest wins, like buying fish, that cracked something open inside me. Because part of me wanted to call and brag about it, to prove I could stand on my own, and to hear that mix of love and exasperation, which was their way of saying they cared, even when it came wrapped in criticism.

But another part whispered that maybe, just maybe, no one would answer.

So I tucked the thought away, let the ache settle where it always did, and kept walking with my little plastic bag of victory.

Living in Spain was like signing up for a beginner's course in "How to Function Like a Grown-Up... Somewhere Totally Different."

Everything looked simple until it wasn't. Life became one long series of cultural speed bumps I kept hitting face-first, usually while holding a baguette and wondering why the pharmacy was closed at 2 p.m.

But somewhere between my fourth supermarket meltdown and learning to pronounce *merluza* without sounding like I was sneezing, it started to feel like home. Slowly, imperfectly, hilariously. Home.

And even though I still missed 24-hour convenience and the ability to buy eggs on a Sunday, I'd trade that in a heartbeat for slow mornings, juice machines, accidental siestas, and lazy Sunday strolls with a boy who made the weirdness feel magical.

I wasn't just adapting. I was becoming.

And I looked really good doing it with a glass of fresh orange juice in hand.

CHAPTER 26 – The Best-Kept Bathroom Secret (And I Used It for Shoes)

❧

You'd think by now, after months of living in Spain, navigating everything from siestas to supermarket ticket dispensers, I'd have gotten the hang of basic domestic appliances.

You'd be wrong.

Because there, in the bathroom of my apartment, sat a mysterious little porcelain fixture. Not the toilet. Not the sink. The other thing. It looked like a sink for garden gnomes. Or maybe a tiny trough? Some kind of old-school foot spa?

Whatever it was, it sat smugly next to the toilet like it had earned its place in the world and didn't feel the need to explain itself.

I stared at it for the first few months, tilting my head as if a different angle might unlock the mystery. But when no brilliant realization came, I shrugged it off and ignored it. For months.

I wasn't about to ask Diego what it was, because that would've meant admitting I didn't know, and I was already the foreign girlfriend who didn't understand public holidays or why lunch was at 3 p.m. I had to keep some dignity intact.

So the bidet and I coexisted. Quietly. Respectfully. Like awkward roommates who nod in the hallway but don't make eye contact.

I didn't touch it, didn't think about it, and certainly didn't use it.

That is, until a rainy Tuesday upended everything.

I'd just come home from running errands, soaked to the bone and tracking muddy footprints through the apartment. My sneakers squelched with every step. I peeled them off like two soggy marshmallows and stared at them in horror.

They needed to be cleaned. Immediately. But the bathroom sink was too small, the bathtub too dramatic, and the kitchen was already teetering on the edge of salmonella.

Then my eyes landed on it.

The bidet. A porcelain basin. With running water. And a

faucet.

Perfect.

I plopped my shoes into it, turned on the tap, and watched as dirt swirled dramatically down the tiny drain. "Look at you," I cooed to the bidet. "Who knew you'd finally find your calling?"

I left them there, completely forgetting about them, until later that evening when I heard Diego calling from the bathroom.

"Nadia?" His voice echoed through the hallway, a mix of confusion and amusement.

There was a pause. A very long pause. The kind of pause that usually precedes discovering your partner has done something either adorable or deeply concerning.

I wandered over, half expecting him to be holding up one of my rogue socks.

Instead, he was standing in the bathroom, one eyebrow raised, staring at my sneakers like they'd personally offended him.

"Why," he asked slowly, "are your shoes in the bidet?"

I blinked, caught off guard by the question. "Wait, that's a bidet?"

Diego burst out laughing, shaking his head. "*Sí*. What did

you think it was?"

I crossed my arms, suddenly feeling defensive. "I don't know! A foot washer? Or maybe a pet sink!"

"Pet sink?" he gasped, tears forming in his eyes.

I crossed my arms. "Well, it cleans, doesn't it?"

He couldn't even speak. He just leaned against the doorframe, laughing until he slid down to the floor, clutching his stomach.

"You've been living here for how long, and you've never used it?"

"Nope," I said, reaching over to grab my shoes from the bidet. "Clearly, I've been using it wrong."

Diego took a breath, trying to calm his laughter. "Okay, lesson time. A bidet is for washing yourself."

I frowned. "Washing what, exactly?"

He wiggled his eyebrows. "The south pole."

I let out a horrified gasp. "So you're telling me I just gave my sneakers a butt bath?!"

That sent him into another laughing fit.

"Exactly," he said, grinning. "It's more hygienic than just using toilet paper. It's pretty common in Europe."

I stared at the bidet, my expression shifting from confusion to mild horror. "People really use this? Like... regularly?"

Diego nodded. "Every day. It's normal here."

I shook my head, still processing. "And I've been using it to soak my shoes."

Diego burst out laughing again, wrapping an arm around my waist and pulling me into a hug. "Yes. And this is why I love you."

"This is why I need a user manual for Europe," I muttered, my face burning.

I groaned, burying my face against his chest. "This is mortifying."

"It's adorable," he murmured, pressing a kiss to my hair.

Later that night, as we curled up on the couch, I tried to regain some dignity.

"So," I said, raising an eyebrow, "do you use it?"

Diego shrugged casually. "Of course. It's what it's there for."

I shuddered dramatically, leaning back against the cushions.

"I don't think I'll ever be able to look at it the same way again."

Over the next few days, I avoided the bidet like it had betrayed me. I walked past it suspiciously. I eyed it while brushing my teeth. I even briefly considered taping a sign to it that said not for shoes or butts, just vibes.

But eventually, curiosity got the best of me.

One morning, I stood in front of it, hands on my hips, wondering if I should give it a try.

"This feels ridiculous," I muttered to myself.

Diego walked past the bathroom, peeking in with a smirk. "Need another lesson?"

I shot him a glare. "Nope. I Googled. I'm a woman of the internet now."

But the embarrassment didn't end there.

A few days later, I found myself at Joshua's apartment for our usual Friday night hangout—complete with popcorn, a reality TV show we pretended not to care about, and enough rosé to qualify us for honorary membership in a bachelorette party.

We were mid-episode of The Real Housewives of Beverly Hills when I casually mentioned the Bidet Incident. I thought I was telling a mildly embarrassing story.

CHAPTER 26 - *The Best-Kept Bathroom Secret (And I Used It...)*

I forgot who I was talking to.

Joshua spat out his drink.

"Okay, that's it," he said, hopping up. "Time for a visual aid."

"No, Joshua—"

But he was already headed to the bathroom. I stayed planted on the couch, arms crossed and deeply suspicious.

"Okay," his voice called out. "Come in. Bidet 101 is now in session."

I peeked in cautiously. Joshua was standing beside his bidet, looking far too proud, like he'd invented it himself.

"So," he began, gesturing like a TED Talk presenter, "this unassuming porcelain friend is not, in fact, a foot jacuzzi. It's for your—" he paused, made a dramatic swirl with his hand "nether sparkle."

"I'm leaving," I said, turning on my heel.

"Oh no you don't," he laughed. "You traumatized an entire plumbing fixture. You're staying."

He reached down to turn the water on. "Observe the gentle stream. It's dignified. Respectful. Not ideal for Nikes."

I rolled my eyes. "Thank you, Captain Hygiene."

But then, and I swear to this day he did it on purpose, he dropped his pants.

"Joshua!" I shrieked, spinning around so fast I nearly took out a potted plant.

"What? I'm demonstrating!"

"I don't need a demo of your shiny white butt! Oh my god, I just saw the moon and it's not even night yet!"

He howled with laughter while I stood there, frozen like an uptight Victorian aunt who'd just walked in on a scandal.

"I need bleach," I whispered. "For my eyes. For your apartment. For everything."

He finally pulled his pants back up, wiping away tears. "You are *so* repressed. It's adorable."

I pointed a finger at him. "You, sir, are never allowed near porcelain and me in the same sentence again."

"You're welcome," he said with a wink. "Now you'll never misuse a bidet again."

I stomped back to the couch, plopped down, and shoved a handful of popcorn into my mouth like it owed me something.

Joshua sat beside me, still grinning. "So… you want to try

mine later?"

I threw a cushion at his face.

"Absolutely not."

Despite the humiliation (and the aggressive teasing from both my boyfriend and my best friend), I eventually came around.

One quiet Sunday, that bidet and I had a moment. A bonding experience. A truce. It was no longer the weird porcelain stranger in the corner; it was an official part of my hygiene routine. A deeply European rite of passage.

Was I fully converted? Not entirely. But I'd stopped using it as a shoe spa, and that felt like progress.

Just one more delightful little quirk to add to my growing collection of "things I never thought I'd do in Europe but now weirdly love."

CHAPTER 27 – Forget Santa, We've Got a Pooping Log

Like everything else in Spain, it took time to adjust to new customs, to let go of my expectations and embrace the local way of doing things. Even traditions I thought I knew, like Christmas, came with their own unique twists.

Goodbye, turkey dinners and mall carolers. Hello, seafood feasts and... well, logs that poop presents. But we'll get to that.

Diego's family had invited me to his hometown, León, for the holidays, and I was both thrilled and wildly nervous. Spending Christmas with his entire family? That felt big. Like, does-this-mean-we're-married-in-Spanish-family-terms kind of big.

"You're going to love it," Diego promised as we packed. He

slid an arm around my waist and kissed my cheek, probably to distract me from the fact that I was currently folding pajamas into little Marie Kondo–inspired stress balls.

"And they're going to love feeding you," he added.

"Are you sure?" I asked, biting my lip. "What if I mess up some cultural thing and offend your mom? Like, I don't know, use the wrong fork or insult someone's octopus?"

He chuckled, tucking a strand of hair behind my ear. "Just be yourself. That's all you need to do. And also, there's no wrong way to eat an octopus."

"Okay, but… will there be turkey?" I teased, trying to lighten the mood.

He laughed, shaking his head. "Not exactly. Trust me, you'll be surprised."

And surprised I was.

Christmas dinner was a full-blown feast. No turkey in sight, but an ocean's worth of seafood spread across the table like Poseidon had catered the event. Prawns, crab, clams, octopus… and not a single marshmallow-covered yam in sight.

"This is Christmas?" I whispered to Diego, my eyes wide with delight and mild terror.

"Welcome to seafood heaven. It's traditional for Christmas," he said, cracking a crab leg like it was second nature. I, on the other hand, needed a YouTube tutorial and an emotional support fork.

The second course was a parade of roasted meats that included lamb so tender it practically whispered "you're welcome," and a suckling pig that looked like it could have won a beauty pageant.

Diego's mom served it all with such pride, I didn't dare ask if the suckling pig was looking at me.

"You're spoiling me," I told her in clunky but earnest Spanish.

She placed a warm hand on my shoulder and smiled. *"Eres parte de la familia ahora."*

Cue emotional heart explosion. I was now part of the family. Me. The girl who once used a bidet to rinse sneakers.

Diego squeezed my hand under the table, his touch grounding me in that moment.

Then came dessert, which threw me for another loop.

Back in Singapore, Christmas desserts were over-the-top— Yule logs, chocolate truffles, fancy cakes. Here? It was all about *turrón*, Spain's crunchy answer to, "No, you will not have room for cake."

Diego's mom placed a tray of it on the table—thick slabs of nougat made with almonds, honey, and chocolate.

I picked up a piece, curious. "Is this it?"

Diego grinned. "Try it."

I bit into the *turrón*, and immediately grabbed three more. It was sweet but not overly sugary, with a satisfying crunch from the almonds.

Diego just winked. "Told you."

It struck me that my relationship with Spanish food was basically my relationship with Spain. At first, strange and intimidating—too much shell to crack, too many words I didn't know. But then, little by little, I learned to lean in. To taste, to try, to belong.

And yet, as I crunched through another piece of almond *turrón*, my brain betrayed me.

Suddenly, I was back in Singapore, stealing my mom's pineapple tarts before Eid dinner, or sitting in a fluorescent-lit coffeeshop at 1 a.m. with my sisters, greasy prata between us and laughter spilling across the table like it was free refills.

I hadn't sat at one of those tables in over a year, and sometimes the missing hit me out of nowhere. Not in a dramatic, constant way, but like a pinch of salt sneaking into something sweet—sharp, unexpected, impossible to ignore.

Guilt, grief, and longing all tangled up inside me as I sat at Diego's family table, surrounded by people who treated me like I'd always been there.

For the first time, I let myself hold both truths at once: I could ache for my family and still find pieces of home here too.

That night, stuffed with seafood and sugar, I realized belonging doesn't always come with fireworks. Sometimes it slips in quietly, as gentle as Christmas Day itself.

But Spain wasn't done dazzling me with its Christmas chaos.

On January 5th, the city turned into a glittery fever dream for *Reyes Magos*—Three Kings Day.

The streets were decorated in dazzling lights and the promise of a grand parade. Diego insisted we watch it, and I was completely unprepared for the spectacle.

Floats rolled through the streets, each more elaborate than the last. There were performers dressed as the Three Kings— Melchor, Gaspar, and Baltasar—waving regally to the crowd. There were camels. There were more sequins than a Taylor Swift concert.

But the real stars of the parade were the candies.

There were candies raining down from every float like Willy Wonka had been elected parade manager.

Children ran through the streets with baskets, buckets, and even upturned umbrellas to collect as much as they could, while parents joined in, catching candies for themselves or sneaking a piece here and there.

"Did you ever do this as a kid?" I asked Diego as I ducked to avoid a stray caramel.

"Of course," he said, grinning. "It's a rite of passage. Here, catch!"

He tossed me an umbrella, and before I knew it, I was laughing along with the children, collecting candies like I was six years old again.

So there I was, cackling like a maniac while running towards the areas with the best candies. At one point, I may have body-checked a six-year-old for a lollipop, but in my defense, he was really fast.

The next morning, the celebrations continued with the traditional *Roscón de Reyes*, a sweet, ring-shaped bread decorated with candied fruit and sometimes filled with cream. Diego placed it proudly in the center of the table, explaining the tradition.

"There's a surprise baked inside," he said. "If you find the king figure, you'll have good luck for the year. But if you get the bean, you have to buy next year's *roscón*."

I took my slice cautiously, trying to avoid the dreaded bean.

But as luck would have it, I bit into something hard. Pulling it out, I found the tiny king figure, to the cheers of everyone at the table.

"I'm the queen!" I announced, shoving the paper crown on my head like the sugar-gobbling monarch I was born to be.

Diego leaned in, kissing my cheek. "Always. Enjoy it while it lasts. Next year, you might get the bean."

But the strangest yet most delightful Christmas tradition? That honor went to *Caga Tió*.

When Diego first told me about it, I thought he was joking.

"You have a what?" I asked, wide-eyed.

"A pooping log," he repeated, laughing at my expression. "It's called *Caga Tió*."

I stared at him, waiting for him to explain.

"It's a log with a face painted on it," he said. "Kids take care of it in the weeks leading up to Christmas, and then, on Christmas Eve, they hit it with sticks and sing a song to make it poop out presents."

I blinked. "You're making this up."

"I'm not! It's a real tradition."

The kids gathered around the log, which had a painted-on face and a tiny red hat, and sang the traditional Catalan song.

"*Caga, Tió! Caga!*" they chanted for the log to poop presents and candies, as they hit it.

I tried not to cry from laughing as they lifted the blanket and found goodies tucked underneath.

"Okay," I told Diego that night. "This beats Santa. Hands down."

But perhaps the funniest moment came courtesy of Diego's cousin, Luis.

Now, Luis was charming in a way that made you instantly suspicious. He was tall, stylish, always smelled faintly of bergamot and bad decisions, and had a twinkle in his eye that said trouble, but like, the flirty kind.

On our second night in León, as we were all lounging in the living room in various states of seafood coma, Luis plopped down beside me and nudged my arm.

"So," he said casually, "do you have any hot, funny friends who like men who own a ring light?"

I nearly choked on my *turrón*. "That's... specific."

He grinned. "I'm just saying. The universe brought us together for a reason."

I narrowed my eyes. "You're hitting on me or asking for matchmaking services?"

"Both?" he offered with a wink.

I laughed and shook my head. "You're out of luck on the first one. But… now that you mention it…"

My mind immediately went to Daniela, my formidable, perfectly blow-dried boss who terrified most people into submission but secretly loved tequila and used the skull emoji unironically. She was terrifying and magnetic, and honestly?

Luis might be the only man alive brave enough to handle her.

That night, after a few glasses of wine and questionable judgment, Luis and I recorded a short video for her. In it, he introduced himself with a dramatic hair flip and said, "Hola Daniela. I hear you like power and sarcasm. I own several button-down shirts and once cried during an episode of The Crown. Call me."

I sent it, giggling into my scarf like a teenager.

The next morning, Daniela replied with her own video. She was sipping coffee, sunglasses on, giving full international spy energy.

"Well hello, Javier," she purred, arching a perfectly sculpted brow. "Let's chat after the holidays. I'll bring the sarcasm, you bring the ring light."

I screamed. Out loud. In front of Diego's entire family.

Luis leaned over, looked at her message, and whispered, "I think I'm in love."

"Good luck," I muttered. "She once made a man cry with just her LinkedIn summary."

He beamed. "Perfect."

So the year ended with seafood, pooping logs, parade candy, and accidentally launching a flirtationship that could either end in a wedding or international scandal. Honestly, I was rooting for both.

Christmas in Spain was nothing like I imagined and somehow, it was everything I didn't know I needed. It wasn't just about the quirky traditions; it was about the warmth, the laughter, and the way Diego made me feel like I belonged.

And honestly? I wouldn't have it any other way.

CHAPTER 28 - It's Always Fiesta O'Clock in Barcelona

Just when I thought the holiday whirlwind was slowing down, Barcelona tapped me on the shoulder, handed me a drink, and shouted, "Surprise! We party all year!"

Seriously, I used to think New Year's Eve was the climax of the festive calendar. Barcelona looked at that and said, "Cute. Now buckle up."

Carnival showed up first, like a glitter-drenched guest who never RSVP'd, complete with costumes, music, and dancing in the streets. But it was Sant Jordi that truly made my heart flutter.

Every April, the city transformed into a real-life rom-com. Stalls popped up with books and roses, couples strolled hand-in-hand, and I'm pretty sure I saw at least three spontaneous declarations of love in Plaça Catalunya.

"This is amazing," I whispered, taking it all in.

"Sant Jordi," Diego explained as we strolled through the crowd, "is about books for boys and roses for girls. It's our version of Valentine's Day."

Sant Jordi, or Saint George's Day, is one of Catalonia's most beloved holidays. Legend has it that Saint George saved a princess from a dragon, and from the dragon's blood grew a rose bush. On this day, it's tradition for men to give roses to women and for women to give books to men.

I was halfway through scanning a vendor's table when Diego pulled a rose from behind his back like a magician with a romantic streak.

"For you," he said, and I basically melted into the pavement.

I tried to act cool though I could feel my cheeks flushing. *"Gracias.* Which book do you want or should I surprise you?"

"I'm waiting to see what you pick," he said, dimples on full display.

We spent hours wandering from stall to stall, browsing through books and soaking in the festive atmosphere.

Eventually, I found the perfect one—a travel guide to hidden spots in Catalonia.

"You always say we should explore more," I told him, handing it over. "Now we have no excuses."

He grinned. "I love it. And I love you for finding it."

My knees went soft. Right there, sandwiched between a poetry stall and a churro stand.

I blinked, surprised by his words, but the warmth in his gaze made my heart skip a beat. "I love you too," I whispered.

We stood there in the middle of the crowd, surrounded by laughter and music, and for a moment, it felt like the world had melted away, leaving just the two of us.

The festivals didn't stop with Sant Jordi.

There was Sant Joan in June, a wild celebration of the summer solstice, where the city came alive with fireworks, bonfires, and late-night beach parties.

"People stay up all night," Diego said, as if that were a selling point and not a direct threat to my eight-hour sleep cycle.

The beach was packed with revelers, the sky lit up with colorful explosions, and music blared from every direction.

Joshua was there too, dancing barefoot in the sand with a sparkler like he was the unofficial King of Summer.

"This is insane!" I shouted over the noise.

Joshua raised his arms to the sky. "Welcome to Spain, baby!"

Diego leaned down, kissed my shoulder, and said, "This is just the beginning."

We spent the night dancing, laughing, and watching the fireworks. By the time we stumbled home at sunrise, I had sand in places sand should never be and a newfound respect for Spain's stamina.

"Barcelona never sleeps," I said as we walked back home.

Diego chuckled. "And neither do you, apparently."

Since then, I'd come to expect street celebrations, parades, and fireworks at the drop of a hat. But nothing prepared me for La Mercè.

"Trust me, you're going to love it," Diego said as we walked through the narrow streets of El Born. "It's the biggest festival in Barcelona."

La Mercè was a week-long celebration honoring the city's patron saint, packed with concerts, art installations, and street performances. There were even people dressed as devils, because obviously. It was like a street party and a medieval exorcism had a baby.

But the highlight? The *correfoc*—the fire run.

I'd heard about it from my students, who always delivered

with the same breathless awe usually reserved for roller coasters or celebrity sightings. Words like "crazy" and "dangerous" got thrown around with the kind of wide-eyed enthusiasm that made me question whether I needed a helmet... or a waiver.

As we approached Plaça de Sant Jaume and spotted the gathering crowd, I glanced nervously at Diego. "Okay, seriously, what exactly is a fire run?"

He just grinned. That annoyingly sexy, I-know-something-you-don't grin. "You'll see."

Not helpful.

We wriggled our way to the front like two eager tourists who clearly didn't read the safety disclaimers, and just as I was about to ask if I could chicken out, I felt Diego's arm wrap around my waist.

"Stay close," he murmured in my ear. Which sounded both protective and mildly ominous.

Then all hell broke loose.

The drums started pounding, and suddenly, people dressed as actual devils—horns, capes, the whole nine yards—came strutting out of the shadows holding giant sticks. With fireworks attached.

"Nope," I said instinctively. "Nope, nope, no. OHMYGOD."

Before I could fully process what was happening, everything exploded into sparks. Literal, actual, flying sparks.

"Is this safe?" I screamed over the noise, already preparing my internal monologue for the ER nurse.

Diego just laughed—laughed!—and spun me around like we were ballroom dancing in a furnace. "Not really!"

And then the devils started running. Yes. Running.
With flaming sticks.
Through a crowd of cheering, clapping, cheerfully combusting people.

Sparks rained from the sky like we'd offended a very dramatic fireworks god, and everyone around us acted like it was totally normal.

It was chaos. Beautiful, exhilarating chaos.

I watched in awe as people threw themselves into the dance, completely unafraid of the fire.

"Come on!" Diego shouted, grabbing my hand.

"I'm not dressed for this!" I protested, wildly gesturing to my very flammable-looking outfit.

Too late.

He yanked me into the madness, and suddenly we were

twirling and dodging sparks while laughing like kids. The air smelled like gunpowder and singed hair extensions, and I was both terrified and… kind of loving it?

At one point, a devil zipped past me with a crackling staff of doom, and I dolphin-level squealed and jumped out of the way. Diego pulled me into a spin, laughing like a maniac, and we kept dancing through the sparks like we were extras in a musical set in hell.

When the last firework fizzled out, we stumbled out of the square, breathless, sweaty, and probably mildly toasted.

"That was insane," I gasped, pushing my hair off my face and wondering if I still had eyebrows.

Diego looked at me with stars in his eyes and soot on his forehead. "Welcome to *La Mercè*."

There was definitely no shortage of traditions in Barcelona that made me question people's sanity, because after all that, I discovered the *Castellers*.

We were on our usual Sunday stroll through the neighborhood when we stumbled upon a small square filled with people. A team of *Castellers*, dressed in white pants and colorful sashes, was preparing to build one of their iconic human towers.

"What's going on?" I asked Diego.

"It's a *castell*," he said, his eyes lighting up. "A human tower. You've never seen one?"

"Only in photos."

"Well, you're in for a treat."

The process was fascinating.

It started with a large base, called the *pinya*, made up of dozens of people locking arms and holding each other steady. Then, one by one, more people climbed on top, forming layers of the tower.

The higher it got, the more nervous I became.

"This doesn't seem… safe," I whispered to Diego.

He laughed. "It's been a tradition for centuries. They know what they're doing."

At the very top, a child no older than six or seven climbed to the top like it was just a regular Sunday and not a feat of athletic madness.

I stood there blinking like someone had handed me a live baby goat.

My heart stopped. "They send kids up there?"

"They're the *enxaneta*," Diego explained. "They're the lightest, so they climb to the top and raise their hand when the tower is complete."

I watched in awe-slash-mild panic as a tiny girl in a helmet scaled a literal mountain of humans like she did this every Sunday. When she reached the top and threw one hand in the air like a tiny, triumphant gladiator, the crowd erupted in cheers.

Meanwhile, I was still trying to process how a child with a bedtime just defied gravity while I needed a snack break after climbing three stairs.

"That's incredible," I said, genuinely impressed and maybe just a little emotionally unstable.

"It's all about trust and teamwork," Diego said, his eyes soft. "It's a symbol of Catalan culture."

Which, apparently, included small children casually risking their lives for applause and tradition. No biggie.

A few weeks later, Enrique, Barcelona's unofficial Minister of Bad Ideas, dragged me to a castell practice session. That's how I ended up locking arms with total strangers and praying I didn't become a human pancake with a side of embarrassment.

"They're always looking for new members," he said cheerfully, like we were joining a knitting club and not a vertical human Jenga tower.

"Fun," I raised an eyebrow. "You want me to climb a human tower?"

"Not climb," he corrected. "You'll just be part of the base. Very safe. Very grounded. You won't have to go higher than the first level."

"So I'm the foundation? Like cement?" I squinted. "Unpaid, nervous cement?"

Still, I agreed, mostly because I was terrible at saying no to enthusiastic friends and partly because I wanted to prove I could handle more than Google Translate and sangria happy hours.

The session was held in a gym that smelled like adrenaline and determination. One of the team leaders greeted us with the kind of energy you'd expect from someone about to build a literal person pyramid.

"*¡Hola!* Ready to build a castle?"

"Sure," I said with the enthusiasm of someone who had not yet grasped the gravity, pun intended, of the situation.

We got a crash course in arm-locking, shoulder-bracing, and "do-not-let-your-knees-buckle" posture. Which is how I ended up shoulder-to-shoulder with strangers, pretending I wasn't three seconds from toppling like a fainting goat.

"Steady!" the leader called out as the first level was built.

Easier said than done when you're in a denim skirt and regretting your life choices. I braced myself, feeling the pressure of the people above me.

Enrique beamed beside me. "This is awesome!"

"I'm glad you think so," I muttered, eyes wide as someone stepped onto the base and the whole structure shifted. "This is the most intimate I've ever been with anyone who wasn't contractually obligated to love me."

The tower climbed higher, and I held my breath as a helmeted kid once again monkeyed their way up to the top. When they raised their hand in victory, the entire room exploded in applause.

Somewhere between the wobble, the sweat, and the minor existential crisis, I actually smiled.

"You did great!" the leader said, patting me on the back.

And weirdly? I felt proud. Like, proud-proud. Like I survived something that might make my mom clutch her pearls and book me a flight home.

Because it wasn't just about the tower. It was about saying yes to something wild, pressing close to strangers who suddenly felt like teammates, and realizing that maybe Barcelona wasn't just a place I was living in.

Maybe it was starting to live in me.

With every festival, every shared meal, and every unexpected adventure, I found myself slipping deeper into the city's rhythm. Slowly. Boldly. Often while sweaty and confused, but slipping in nonetheless.

And let's be honest, there were still so many parties left to survive.

In Singapore, I thought I knew what a late night out was. But Spain? Spain rewrote the rules entirely.

The first time Diego invited me to a club, I made the rookie mistake of suggesting we leave at 10 p.m.

"Leave? At 10?" Diego laughed, his eyes crinkling with amusement. "That's when people are starting dinner."

I groaned. "Are you serious? I'll be asleep by midnight!"

Diego grinned like the mischievous night owl he absolutely was, and bent down to press a quick kiss to my lips. "Not tonight, you won't."

We didn't leave the house until midnight. As in, Cinderella had already lost her shoe and I should've lost consciousness, but no. In Spain, that's just when things get started.

By the time we strolled into the club, the place was just beginning to fill up. The music was thumping loud enough to realign my spine, the lights were flashing like a rave inside a lava lamp, and the bartenders? They moved like cocktail-slinging wizards in tight T-shirts.

Diego grabbed my hand and tugged me toward the dance floor. "Come on, Singapore. Time to show me what you've got."

I laughed, letting him lead me into the crowd. "Don't judge! I'm more of a karaoke girl."

He just laughed and spun me under his arm like I was born in a Beyoncé video. "Then pretend it's karaoke night in your living room and shake it like your dignity's already gone."

It was both horrifying and... weirdly freeing?

His hands found my waist and we fell into step, moving to the rhythm like we had absolutely no business being that adorable in public. The music pulsed around us, the crowd swayed like one giant glittery organism, and I let myself get swept up in it—Diego's steady hands anchoring me, his cheek brushing mine as he whispered corny lines in my ear just to make me laugh.

The hours melted into a blissed-out haze of dancing, laughing, and enough flirty eye contact to short-circuit a small robot. We kissed in shadowy corners like teenagers with poor impulse control. By the time the music started to fade, I was sweaty, slightly tipsy, and fully ready to go home and sleep for approximately three business days.

Then Diego, my beautiful, evil boyfriend, turned to me with

a grin that should've come with a warning label.

"There's an after-party," he said casually, as if he hadn't just turned me into a disco raisin.

I looked around for hidden cameras. "An after-party? It's literally morning. Like, tomorrow morning.

He shrugged, his dimpled smile weaponizing itself against my last ounce of resistance. "You said you wanted to experience Spain. This is it."

I groaned like someone who had just realized there was a second part to leg day. "Fine. Lead the way, *Señor* After-Party. But if I fall asleep mid-sentence, I'm blaming you and Spanish culture."

We ended up in a dimly lit alleyway that looked like the setting for a spy movie or a very chic kidnapping. Diego knocked twice on a nondescript door like he was part of a secret cult. A woman opened it, gave him a knowing smile, and let us in without a word.

Inside, it was... a vibe.

The room was full of beautiful zombies—people who looked like they hadn't slept in forty-eight hours but still somehow had glowy skin and impeccable outfits. The music was more subdued, a dreamy beat that pulsed through my bones, saying "you don't need sleep, you need this mojito."

"Do people ever sleep here?" I asked Diego, half-joking as we leaned against the bar.

Diego leaned in, brushing a strand of hair behind my ear with a touch that made my entire frontal lobe reboot. "Eventually."

I sipped my drink, something citrusy and probably illegal in three countries, and surveyed the room. It felt like a secret society, with everyone murmuring in cozy corners, laughing at inside jokes, hugging friends like it had been years, not hours.

There was something weirdly magical about it, like we'd stepped into an alternate timeline where time didn't matter and nobody judged your under-eye bags.

Diego's thumb traced lazy circles on the back of my hand, grounding me. "You okay?" he asked softly.

I nodded, leaning into him. "Tired. But weirdly... good."

"We can leave whenever you want."

I glanced up at him, his face illuminated by the soft glow of the bar lights. "You're too good to me, you know that?"

He chuckled, pressing a kiss to my temple in that devastatingly soft way that made my ribcage feel like it needed reinforcement. "I'm just trying to make sure you survive your first after-party."

We stayed a bit longer, met some people with names like Gorka and Luna who swore they were professional "party planners" (which I think just meant they didn't have day jobs), and soaked in the smoky, glitter-dusted air.

And then it happened.

A tall, glossy-haired woman, the kind of person who looked like she always got what she wanted, slid up to Diego with a smile that could power half of Barcelona. She leaned in close to say something over the music, her hand brushing his arm like they were old friends… or something more.

My stomach clenched so hard it felt like it was trying to climb into my throat. Maybe it was the alcohol. Maybe it was the exhaustion. Maybe it was me, all of my insecurities packed into one fragile body. Before I could stop myself, the words tumbled out: "Well, isn't she friendly."

Diego blinked, startled. "Nadia, she was just asking if we wanted another drink."

"Sure," I snapped, "and I only wear mascara because it's hydrating."

His brows shot up. "Are you seriously jealous right now?"

The tension that had been simmering in my chest boiled over. "I just don't get why women feel the need to hang off you. Like, do I have 'insecure foreign girlfriend' stamped on my forehead?"

Diego's jaw tightened. "You're making something out of nothing. I didn't even notice—"

"Exactly! You didn't notice! Because you're too busy being charming and smiley and..." I waved my hand helplessly, "...you!"

His voice rose, low but firm. "What do you want me to do, Nadia? Stop talking to people? Walk around with blinders on? Because that's not me."

The words hit like shards of glass. He was right, and that made it worse. My hands curled into fists at my sides, nails digging into my palms. My heartbeat hammered in my ears.

Then he blurted, raw and unguarded, "Do you know how exhausting it is? Every time you doubt me, it feels like you're waiting for me to fail. Like no matter what I do, it'll never be enough."

I froze. The music, the chatter, the lights... All of it receded into a blur. His words slashed through me sharper than the bass pounding beneath our feet.

He shook his head. "Sometimes I feel like you don't even see how much I want this. Us. I bring you into my world, introduce you to my friends, my city... and you still think I could want someone else?"

A hot rush of shame, fear, and longing coiled tight in my chest. Part of me wanted to yell back, fling my messy baggage, my broken-engagement ghosts, all at him like shards of a shattered mirror. Another part of me wanted to collapse into his arms, vanish into the quiet of his warmth, and pretend the fight had never ignited.

So instead, I crossed my arms. Classic defense mechanism. "Well, maybe if you didn't smile at every woman like you were auditioning for a reality TV show—"

"Nadia." His voice was low, steady, a warning and a plea in one.

I glared at the floor, my stubbornness clinging on for dear life. My pulse was still racing, my pride screaming at me not to fold. Because if I folded too fast, didn't that just make me the girl who always caved?

The silence stretched, heavy with everything I wanted to say but couldn't. Finally, I let out a long breath, the fight draining out of me slower than I wanted to admit.

"I hate how insecure I get," I whispered, almost to myself.

Diego's shoulders softened. He exhaled too, then stepped closer, slipping his hand back into mine like a truce flag. "Don't do that. Don't tear yourself down like that." His voice was gentler now. "You're the only one I see, okay?"

And just like that, the heat in my chest turned into something else—still sharp, still uncomfortable, but laced with the ache of knowing he meant it.

I didn't melt instantly. I was still mad at myself. Still bristling. But I let him hold my hand anyway.

Because even if my brain was a battlefield, some small, stubborn part of me wanted to believe him.

I hated myself for picking a fight. Again. For letting insecurity crash a perfectly good night.

We stayed a bit longer, but eventually, my eyelids started staging a rebellion.

By the time we left, the sky was pinking up with sunrise, and Barcelona was yawning back to life. Bakeries opened their shutters. Someone walked by with a bag of fresh bread that smelled like heaven and childhood.

Diego slipped his fingers through mine again, but the silence between us wasn't the soft, content kind. It was heavier. The kind you feel in your chest. My head leaned on his shoulder out of habit more than ease, the leftover fight still humming in my ribcage.

"You survived your first after-party," he said finally, voice lighter than the mood deserved. He was trying.

"Barely," I muttered. My words came out more clipped than I wanted. I shut my eyes for a beat, then forced a softer one. "I feel like I've aged six years. But... worth it."

His lips twitched into a grin, but it didn't quite reach his eyes.

Not yet. And I hated myself a little more for putting that shadow there.

As we walked, the city kept tugging at me wiith the smell of bread, the hum of voices, the sky opening up like a watercolor wash. Barcelona refused to let me sulk, even when I wanted to.

And through it all, there was Diego, still holding my hand, still here, even after my spirals. The boy who could frustrate me, infuriate me, make me jealous out of my own skin… and then still look at me like I was worth the trouble.

Something shifted in me. Not a full surrender, not yet. But a tiny step toward believing him when he said I was the only one he saw.

I thought about how different my life had been before—neat, predictable, built on color-coded calendars and backup plans. And here I was, stumbling home at sunrise, mascara smudged, bread-scented air in my lungs, learning to unclench one shaky step at a time.

Turns out, life doesn't always need a five-year plan. Sometimes it just needs a good pair of walking shoes, a cute boy with strong forearms, and a willingness to follow the music even if you don't know the steps.

Diego squeezed my hand as we reached my building. "Ready to collapse?"

I fake-sobbed. "Collapse is my new favorite activity."

He laughed and kissed me gently, like a reward for making it through the night.

But sometimes, Barcelona's celebrations weren't all joy and tradition. Sometimes, they were pure chaos.

CHAPTER 29 – When the Streets Turned Into a Party

"Barça! Barça! Barça!"

The chants rolled through the city like a tsunami of chaos, joy, and possibly beer fumes. Joshua and I exchanged a look that said, Are we about to walk into a flash mob or a riot?

"Did I miss a memo?" I asked, trying not to trip over a rogue cava bottle on the sidewalk. "Why does it sound like the entire city is on the verge of either proposing or combusting?"

Joshua tilted his head toward the horizon, where fireworks were painting the sky with questionable enthusiasm. "It's either a celebration or a very festive apocalypse."

We had just wrapped up a chill day wandering the Gothic

Quarter, eating our body weight in *croquetas*, and judging overpriced artisan soap. But as we got closer to Rambla de Catalunya, the buzz turned into a full-on roar.

"What's going on?" I asked, squinting at a sea of flags.

Joshua shrugged. "No idea. Maybe a protest?"

A logical guess, given Barcelona's love affair with spontaneous activism. But this crowd wasn't angry; they were ecstatic. Face paint, flags, shirtless men singing at decibels that should require a permit. Something big had happened.

We wormed our way to the police barricade and were immediately hit with a wall of sound, color, and euphoric chaos. Drunken joy radiated from every pore of the crowd, fireworks crackled in the distance, and the air smelled like beer and smoke.

Joshua squinted at a banner someone was holding. "Something about Barça winning…"

I blinked. "Winning what?"

A man nearby overheard and shouted, *"La Champions!"*

Joshua blinked. "Wait, Barça won the Champions League?"

"That's football, right?" I asked, because I'm nothing if not consistent in my sports ignorance.

He nodded, slowly. "A big deal."

"A huge deal," said another stranger, handing us mini Barça flags like we'd just joined a cult.

"We need to cross this street," I muttered, eyeing the carnage.

Joshua gave me a skeptical side-eye and then eyed the crowd warily. "Do we really? Maybe we should wait it out."

But I was determined. "I live on the other side, remember? Come on. It can't be that bad."

It was worse.

We lasted about 30 seconds before realizing this was a mistake. The crowd was dense. People danced in the streets with the kind of unhinged energy that usually required an exorcism. Someone poured beer down his shirt like it was holy water. Others waved red-and-blue flares, turning the night into a smoky rave.

Suddenly, a loud cheer erupted from the far end of the street, and we saw a man perched precariously on a light pole, waving a flag and chugging from a bottle of wine.

The police tried to coax him down, but he ignored them, singing at the top of his lungs.

"This is madness," I said, laughing despite myself.

"They're climbing everything," Joshua muttered, pointing out more fans scaling trees, traffic lights, and even storefronts.

"Is this a celebration or a jungle gym?" I asked, watching as one man scaled a traffic light like it was Mount Everest.

We weren't the only ones worried. The police were out in full force, trying to keep the crowd under control. Officers shouted warnings, telling people to get down, but no one listened.

"*Viva Barça!*" someone yelled, popping open a bottle of *cava* and spraying it into the crowd.

Joshua dodged the spray, laughing. "This is insane."

And then came the tree.

As we edged closer to my street, we saw a group of fans gathered around a tree. They were pouring beer on each other and cheering as one man climbed higher, balancing precariously on a branch.

Then it happened.

One spark hit a dry leaf, and whoosh. Fire. Like, actual flames.

"Holy shit," Joshua gasped.

People screamed. The man on the branch kept singing,

totally unfazed by the fact that he might be the first human marshmallow in Barcelona history.

The police rushed in, shouting and waving their batons, but the fans were too far gone in their celebration. They chanted louder, drowning out the warnings.

"We need to go. Now." I grabbed Joshua's arm and fled down a side street, dodging *cava* spray and flying *churros* like a seasoned local.

By the time we made it to my building, we were sweaty, breathless, and potentially slightly buzzed from secondhand celebration.

As we climbed the stairs, we could still hear the distant chants of *"Barça! Barça! Barça!"* echoing through the city.

Once inside, I locked the door and leaned against it, letting out a long breath.

"I just survived a sports-induced street riot."

Joshua flopped on the couch, shaking his head in disbelief. "You think they even noticed the tree fire?"

"Nope."

I grabbed two chocolate bars from the kitchen and handed one to him. "Here. We deserve this."

We sat there in silence for a moment, both processing what we'd just witnessed. Then Joshua burst out laughing.

"I mean, it's just football, right?" he said.

I laughed too, unwrapping my chocolate. "Apparently not in Spain."

We turned on the TV and found live coverage of the celebrations. The news anchor was practically yelling over the noise of the crowd, describing the scenes we'd just walked through.

The footage showed people climbing statues, lighting flares, and jumping into fountains. The commentator excitedly recapped the match, but all I could focus on were the images of the fans turning the city upside down.

"They've officially lost their minds," Joshua said, taking a bite of his chocolate.

"And we almost got caught in the middle of it."

The news cut to footage of a burning tree. Our tree. On fire. On TV.

Joshua pointed at the screen. "Hey, that's our tree!"

I cackled. "Great, we're now part of Catalan sports history. As witnesses to tree arson."

"Admit it. You loved it."

I took a bite of my chocolate bar. "Okay, maybe a little."

Just as I was recovering, my phone buzzed.

Diego: *"Game at the park tomorrow with Luis. You coming? Ask Daniela if she wants to come too. Wear something you don't mind grass stains on."*

Oh no. More football madness.

Clearly, I needed to start Googling "Football for Dummies" if I was going to survive in this country. Or at least fake enough knowledge to not embarrass myself during small talk.

The next day, I decided to contribute what I could... Which turned out to be a pep talk for Diego.

Was it motivational? Questionable. Did it involve snacks, a shoulder massage, and me yelling "Kick it like it owes you money"? Absolutely.

"It's nothing serious," he said, lacing up his cleats like this wasn't the fourth time he'd mentioned "nothing serious" while adjusting his socks to a military standard. "Just friends, a park, a ball, and maybe bragging rights for the next decade."

Daniela came with me, partly because she wanted to cheer Luis on, and partly because she thought it would be hilarious to watch me try to understand football in real time.

We found seats, or rather, a patch of grass, and sat down with sangria and enough sunscreen to bathe in.

"Okay, explain the rules again," I whispered, squinting at the field. "Who's winning?"

"No one's winning yet. They just started," Daniela said, without looking at me. Her eyes were locked on Luis, who had just done something vaguely impressive involving a spin, a kick, and a mild shirt lift. She didn't blink once.

"Right, right. And we're cheering for…?"

"Diego and Luis's team. The ones in black."

"Got it. Black jerseys. Enemies of the neon orange ones."

I nodded like a woman who had learned something new about the world.

The match was actually fun to watch. Diego looked hot in a sweaty, rugged, semi-feral kind of way, and Luis kept shouting things in Catalan that I assumed were compliments to his teammates but may have also included light curses. Either way, the vibes were strong.

That is, until I decided to help.

A player in a neon jersey made a slick move—fancy footwork, total sprint, kicked the ball straight into the net—and I shot up like a jack-in-the-box on espresso.

"YES! WOOHOO! NICE SHOT!" I cheered at full volume, throwing my hands up like I'd just won the lottery.

The field went silent.

Daniela dropped her drink in horror.

Luis stared at me in disbelief.

Diego looked like someone had just slapped him with a *churro*.

"Nadia," Daniela whispered, dragging me back down by the arm, "that was their own goal."

I blinked. "Wait, what?"

"They accidentally scored on themselves. That's bad."

"But it was such a good kick."

"It was. For the wrong team."

I sank into the grass like I could disappear into the soil. "Oh no. Do you think Diego noticed?"

Daniela looked at me. Then at Diego. Then back at me. "He was mid-sprint and literally stopped running. So yes."

Luis jogged past us and called out, "Thanks for the support, Nadia!"

I wanted the Earth to open up and swallow me whole, possibly while wearing a 'Go Team' shirt ironically.

When the game finally ended, and I had made zero additional commentary, Diego came over, sweat-drenched and grinning.

"Well," he said, pressing a kiss to my cheek, "you definitely made an impression."

"Do I get points for enthusiasm?"

"Oh, absolutely," he said, pulling me close. "Negative points, but still points."

Daniela and Luis were already deep in some flirty banter that involved him offering her his water bottle and her accepting it like it was a diamond necklace.

Despite my football faux pas, I couldn't help but smile.

Even if I didn't understand the rules, I was starting to understand what mattered—these people, this city, and the way I was slowly, awkwardly, lovingly becoming part of it.

CHAPTER 30 - Barcelona, You're a Little Bipolar And I Love It

After surviving the football-induced street riot that was Barça's big win (still can't believe I dodged a flaming tree and lived to tell the tale), I was officially due for a quiet weekend and a therapist. Or at least a calming cup of tea.

Barcelona, it turns out, is not just a city of late-night parties, flag-waving grandmas, and shirtless men swinging from lampposts. It has a softer, more introverted side too. A side that doesn't smell like *cava* and crowd sweat.

On Sundays, Diego and I turned into our gentler alter egos. Gone were the Friday-night wild children. In their place? A couple who explored the city's hidden corners and held hands in Ciutadella Park while debating the superiority of almond versus oat milk.

"This," I said one morning, sipping my tea, "is the version of Barcelona I want to marry."

Diego smiled, brushing a crumb from my cheek. "So I'm off the hook?"

My heart skipped. It should've been a throwaway line, but something about the way he said it made my brain go full neon-sign mode: marriage.

I tilted my head, trying to sound casual. "Would you even want to? Get married, I mean."

He leaned back, thoughtful, not rattled in the least. "Honestly? I don't really care either way. It's not something I think about much. If it happens, cool. If it doesn't, also fine."

I blinked at him, tea halfway to my lips. "That's it? Just... fine?"

He shrugged, all effortless nonchalance, like we were discussing sandwich fillings. "I don't need papers or rings to know how I feel."

Meanwhile, I sat there rethinking my entire genetic code. Because I was still Asian after all, and marriage wasn't just some optional side quest. It was the endgame. The family, the future, the badge of stability my mom could brag about over pineapple tarts.

I tried to cover the crack in my voice with a laugh. "Wow.

Guess I'll cancel the order for our his-and-hers wedding thrones."

Diego smiled and squeezed my hand. But his eyes lingered on me, like he could tell I was spiraling under the table. He didn't press, though. He never did.

And maybe that was the problem. While he could live happily in the present, I was still counting steps to a finish line he didn't seem to care about.

We let the conversation drift away, back into safer waters about oat milk and weekend plans, but the question hung between us like steam off my tea.

Later, at Ciutadella Park, kids were chasing pigeons with all the determination of FBI agents. Elderly couples walked by, their intertwined hands so steady it made my chest ache. For a second, I wanted to stop them and ask, *how did you get here? Did you both want the same things?*

Instead, I smiled too brightly at Diego when he pointed out a dog wearing sunglasses.

And then there were the neighborhood markets.

Yes, La Boqueria was bright and loud and wonderful, but it was also full of selfie sticks and couples aggressively arguing over whether passionfruit was too weird for a smoothie. I used to be a La Boqueria girl until I got elbowed by a tourist trying to take a selfie with a pineapple.

I now preferred the smaller neighborhood markets where the fruit seller knew my name and once gave me a peach so perfect it deserved its own fan club.

"Sweet as honey," he said with a wink, handing it to me. "You'll love this one."

I bit into it, and it dripped down my chin in true peach-advertisement fashion. A small child clapped. A woman gasped. Diego laughed so hard he dropped his baguette.

I laughed too, but even as juice slid down my wrist and Diego teased me about my peach-eating technique, a quiet thought tugged at me. He could laugh like this forever without needing a ring. Could I?

The market buzzed around us, alive with chatter and color. It should've been nothing but joy.

And yet, tucked beneath the sweetness of the peach was the tang of uncertainty, a question I wasn't ready to swallow.

It was magical. Messy, complicated, unplanned, and magical.

But of course, this is Barcelona. And this city doesn't let you get too comfortable for too long.

One Friday night, Joshua and I decided to explore the nightlife of El Born. It had been a while since we'd had a proper night out, just the two of us, and he insisted we start with a drink he'd heard about from one of his colleagues.

"It's time," he declared, eyes wide with mischief. "We're going to try *leche de pantera.*"

"Panther's milk?" I repeated, skeptical. "Is that a drink or a Harry Potter potion?"

Joshua laughed. "It's a real drink. Apparently, it's a mix of condensed milk, gin, and a bunch of other secret stuff. Sounds weird, but everyone swears by it."

He dragged me to a bar in El Born that looked like it had been decorated by someone who really missed the '70s and had unresolved feelings about lava lamps. A frosted glass bottle arrived like a mysterious elixir, and the bartender poured out the creamy, pale drink.

One sip later? I was a believer.

"This is dangerous," I said, pouring another round. "It tastes like melted ice cream but punches like gin. It's actually really good."

"Right?" Joshua agreed, already reaching to refill our glasses.

We worked our way through the entire bottle, chatting and laughing until the world blurred pleasantly around the edges. By the time we left the bar, we were hungry and giggly, the night air buzzing with our drunken enthusiasm.

"What should we eat?" Joshua asked, clutching my arm to steady himself as we wandered down a cobblestone street.

"Something greasy," I said, scanning the late-night options. We eventually stumbled into a tiny hole-in-the-wall serving hot *bocadillos*, simple Spanish sandwiches stuffed with everything from fried calamari to *chorizo*.

I went for the *jamón serrano* with manchego combo, because nothing says "classy drunk girl" like fancy ham and cheese. Joshua ordered some grilled mushroom situation with melted brie, which felt extremely on brand for him.

And then, because moderation has never been our strong suit, we added a *tortilla de patatas* to share.

"These are ridiculous," Joshua mumbled, eyes wide, crumbs snowing onto the table like baguette confetti.

"I'm sorry," I said, holding my sandwich with both hands, "but I think I love you."

Joshua paused mid-bite. "Me?"

"No, the sandwich." I stared down at it, utterly smitten. "This *jamón* is tender. This *manchego* is bold. I feel seen."

He snorted, nearly choking on his brie. "Are you proposing to your sandwich right now?"

"Obviously," I said, already cradling it like a newborn. "If it says yes, you're invited to the wedding."

"We are never forgetting this place," I added solemnly, eyes still locked on my future spouse.

Spoiler: We absolutely forgot that place. Couldn't tell you the name, the street, or if it even legally exists. But in that moment? It was the most beautiful love story Barcelona had ever seen.

The next morning, I was a *leche de pantera* cautionary tale, nursing a glass of water at the kitchen table while questioning my life choices.

Diego walked in, sleepy-eyed and rumpled, looking like a sexy indie film character and making me regret my puffy-eyed, messy-bun state.

"Rough night?" he teased, placing tea in front of me like the thoughtful menace he was.

"Joshua and I discovered *leche de pantera*," I admitted, rubbing my temples.

Diego's laugh filled the kitchen. "Ah, the drink of legends. Did you finish the bottle?"

"Of course," I said with mock pride. "And then we found this amazing sandwich place."

He shook his head, amused. "Sounds like a proper night out."

I sipped the tea gratefully, the warmth soothing my frazzled nerves. Diego sat across from me, his gaze lingering a little longer than usual, and for a moment, the conversation lulled. His foot brushed against mine under the table, a small, grounding touch.

And maybe it was the hangover. Maybe it was the fact that my defenses had all been melted down with gin and condensed milk. But before I could stop myself, the words slipped out.

"Would you ever want to marry me?"

Diego blinked. Not shocked exactly, but still caught off guard, like I'd tossed a grenade into our quiet kitchen.

I immediately groaned, hiding my face in my mug. "Forget I said that. It's just… hangover brain. Ignore me."

But he didn't. He reached over, tugging the mug gently from my hands, forcing me to look at him. His expression was serious, but soft. "Nadia. Don't hide."

My throat went dry. "I just… I don't know if you even think about marriage. And I'm… Well, I'm me. I grew up with the idea that it's the goal. The endgame. And sometimes I wonder if we're…" I trailed off, too embarrassed to finish.

Diego pulled his chair closer, cupping my face in his warm, rough palms. "Listen to me. If marriage is what you want, if we get there, then yes. I'll marry you." His lips curved into the smallest, sweetest smile. "Not because I need papers or rings to know I'm yours. But because if it matters to you, then it matters to me."

Cue my heart, melting into an unidentifiable puddle right there on the kitchen table.

"You'd really—"

"Of course." He brushed his thumb along my cheekbone. "I don't think about it much, that's true. But I think about you. And if you want that, then I want it too. Because I'm not in this halfway."

Tears pricked embarrassingly fast, and I blamed the hangover. "You're annoyingly good at this, you know that?"

He grinned, pressing a kiss to my forehead. "Good. Then stop worrying. We'll figure out our future together, step by step. No rush."

And just like that, the knot in my chest loosened.

When he let me go, I was still puffy-eyed, still hungover, but now dangerously close to swooning in my mismatched pajamas.

Diego sat back, smirk firmly in place. "Now finish your tea before you cry into it and make it salty."

I laughed through my tears, knowing I'd remember this moment long after the hangover faded.

Diego sat back after his forehead kiss, watching me cradle my tea like it was a life raft. "Better?" he asked.

"Marginally," I muttered. "My brain is still made of gin and condensed milk, though."

His grin was wicked and way too handsome for a Sunday morning. "Perfect. Nothing fixes a hangover like garlic and butter."

I groaned, laughing despite myself. "Is this your way of telling me we're trying something new?"

"Exactly," he said, tugging me gently to my feet. "Come on. Let me take care of you."

And maybe it was the hangover or maybe it was the fact that he had casually promised he'd marry me someday if that's what I wanted, but when he said it, my chest squeezed. Not in a scary, future-is-uncertain way. In a this-man-makes-me-feel-safe-even-when-I'm-a-mess way.

I groaned playfully, still recovering from the night before, but I let him guide me out the door.

He stopped in front of a small tapas bar I hadn't noticed before, probably because it was hidden between a shop that sold mismatched socks and a cat café that always smelled faintly of judgment.

When I first moved to Spain, I thought I was a culinary daredevil. A spice-loving, menu-pointing, "surprise me" kind of girl.

But the truth? The second I saw a dish I couldn't pronounce or something that looked vaguely tentacled, I panicked and clung to my comfort foods like a tourist clutching their emergency peanut butter.

My holy trinity? *Tortilla de patatas, croquetas,* and *jamón ibérico* if I was feeling brave and slightly bougie.

And listen, those dishes are delicious. Like, I'd-write-a-sonnet-about-them delicious. But they're also the training wheels of Spanish cuisine. I thought I was living boldly, when really, I was just ordering off the safest part of the menu.

Then along came Diego with his smolder, his smirks, and his complete refusal to let me be boring.

Inside, the bar was warm and bustling, filled with the clinking of glasses and the hum of casual conversation. Diego slid onto a stool and waved me to sit beside him.

"Alright," he said with a grin. "We're starting with *gambas al ajillo.*"

"What's that?" I asked, scanning the menu as if it might offer me a clue.

"You'll see," he replied with a wink.

A few minutes later, a steaming clay dish arrived, filled with shrimp sizzling in golden garlic-infused olive oil, flecked with red chili. The aroma was intoxicating, and Diego handed me a piece of bread.

"Dip it in the sauce," he instructed.

I hesitated for only a second before doing as he said.

I dipped.
I bit.
I ascended.

The flavor was incredible—rich, garlicky, and just the right amount of spice. The shrimp were perfectly tender, and I found myself reaching for more.

"This is what angels eat," I whispered.

"I know," Diego replied, smirking. "You've been missing out."

His gaze lingered on me, softer now, like he was memorizing the way I lit up with each new bite. I felt my cheeks flush, not just from the heat of the food but from the way he looked at me like I was the only thing in the room.

Then came *carrilleras*—slow-cooked beef cheeks braised in a rich red wine sauce. The meat was melt-in-your-mouth tender, each bite infused with deep, savory flavors that spoke of hours of careful cooking.

I moaned a little too loudly, and Diego shot me a look that said, *Careful, or we're not making it to dessert.*

"How have I never had this before?" I asked, savoring the flavors.

Diego's smirk. "Because you were too busy playing it safe with *tortilla* and *croquetas*." He leaned in closer, his voice teasing but affectionate. "But don't worry, I'm fixing that."

I rolled my eyes, but I couldn't stop the smile that spread across my face. "Okay, you win. This is incredible."

But my favorite part of the day? The market detour that turned into absolute comedy gold.

I spotted a tray of pastries and made a beeline for what I thought was an innocent cream puff. I took a giant bite before Diego could stop me... and instantly burst into tears.

"T-That's not cream," I choked.

"Nope," he said, clearly trying not to laugh. "That's *sobrasada*. Spicy pork paste."

I had just emotionally bonded with a meat cupcake.

"I'm suing this market," I mumbled, wiping my eyes. "False advertising."

He kissed the top of my head, still chuckling. "Barcelona's just keeping you on your toes."

As the sun dipped low and the world turned golden, I realized he was right.

Barcelona was all kinds of unpredictable. Loud and soft. Sweet and spicy. Beautifully bipolar. And I was falling in love with every ridiculous, delicious, chaotic part of it.

CHAPTER 31 – When Food Becomes a Love Language

Tapas were supposed to be small. Dainty. Bite-sized. What they didn't mention in the travel brochures was that they also came with existential crises, full-blown flavor meltdowns, and a dangerously inflated sense of culinary confidence.

Basically, they ruined me in the best way.

Every dinner with Diego was like dating a food tour guide who was also a mind reader. From the crispy edges of *pan con tomate* (bread rubbed with fresh tomato and olive oil) to the delight of *berenjenas con miel* (crispy eggplant drizzled with honey), he knew exactly what my taste buds wanted before I did.

"You've officially graduated from *tortilla*-only dinners," Diego teased one night as I soaked up garlic oil with bread like I had just discovered religion.

I threw him a dramatic look. "You say that like *tortilla* isn't the Beyoncé of Spanish food."

He grinned. "Beyoncé's great. But Spain's got a whole girl group."

He wasn't wrong. And apparently, I was now the group's biggest fan.

Diego didn't just stop at tapas. Over time, he introduced me to regional specialties from all over Spain, turning every meal into an adventure and every bite into a memory.

We road-tripped through Spain one forkful at a time.

In Valencia, I met *paella* in its "authentic" form, which Diego claimed involved rabbit, chicken, and stern disapproval of anything resembling seafood.

"Trust me," he said, leaning in with that playful smirk of his as he spooned some onto my plate. "This is the real deal."

"And what if I like the tourist version better?" I teased, raising an eyebrow.

"Then," he said, brushing a strand of hair from my face, "I'll mourn quietly while questioning all your life choices."

"Noted."

The Basque Country came with *pintxos*—tiny, artistic snacks skewered with toothpicks and served with the quiet judgment of locals who definitely knew we were tourists. Diego would guide me through the bar like we were in a museum.

"This one's crab. That one might be anchovy. That one's probably cheese, but take a bite and roll the dice."

I still remember the creamy *txangurro*—a dish of spider crab cooked with onions, peppers, and breadcrumbs that was both delicate and decadent.

And then there was Andalusia, where we split *flamenquín*: deep-fried pork rolls stuffed with ham and cheese, which tasted like heaven and clogged your arteries with a kiss.

"You've got something," Diego murmured, reaching over to wipe a crumb from the corner of my mouth.

My heart promptly forgot how to beat properly.

I caught his hand, holding it for a moment longer than necessary. "Thanks," I said softly, my heart fluttering in my chest.

In Galicia, I fell in love with *lacón con grelos*, a hearty dish of boiled ham, turnip greens, and potatoes. It sounds rustic, but somehow made me feel like a peasant in the best possible way.

Diego wrapped his arm around me as we strolled through

the cobbled streets after dinner, the cold air biting at our cheeks, and I wanted to marry both him and the meal.

"Still warm enough?" he asked, pulling me closer.

"Perfect," I whispered, leaning into him.

In Asturias, we drank *sidra* (cider), poured theatrically from high above the glass to aerate the drink.

"It's about the tradition," Diego insisted, spilling half the bottle.

"Is the tradition wasting half of it on your shoes?" I asked sweetly.

But the most... dramatic culinary moment came in León, his hometown.

The region was famous for its hearty cuisine, and Diego's friends were eager to show me the best of it.

"You have to try the *morcilla*," one of them, Pablo, insisted as we sat around a cozy table in a small, rustic restaurant.

"What is it?" I asked, slightly wary. Rookie mistake.

"It's a local specialty," Pablo said, grinning like he was about to gift me with a life-changing secret or an accidental allergic reaction. "Trust me, you'll love it."

Diego shot him a look. Not a full-blown warning, but definitely a *this better not end in tears or a breakup* kind of glance. I caught it, raised an eyebrow, but before I could interrogate either of them, the waiter appeared with a sizzling plate of sausage that looked suspiciously… shiny.

"Voila," Pablo said, serving me a piece like a magician presenting his final trick. "Prepare to have your mind, and possibly your taste buds, blown."

I leaned in, gave it a cautious sniff, and then a very brave bite.

And oh. Oh yes. It was delicious. Like earthy, savory, slightly sweet magic dusted in paprika and mystery. The kind of flavor that made you question why you'd wasted years eating boxed mac and cheese.

"This is… actually amazing," I said, nodding, while mentally preparing a Yelp review and a backup plan in case this turned out to be snail guts or something equally traumatic.

Pablo beamed. "See? I told you."

But as I reached for a second piece, I made the mistake of asking again, "So, what's in it?"

"Oh, just rice, onions… and blood." Pablo said, grinning like someone about to commit a prank on live TV.

"Wait. Blood?" I froze, my fork hovering mid-air.

"*Morcilla* is blood sausage," Diego said gently, placing a comforting hand on my knee under the table like that would somehow soften the blow.

I stared at the remaining pieces on my plate as if they might come alive and confess their sins.

My stomach did a tiny somersault, the kind that says *abort mission, we're eating blood*.

"Wait... like, actual blood?" I asked, voice squeaking up an octave.

"Yeah," Pablo said, clearly enjoying my slow descent into horror. "But you liked it, right?"

I very calmly, and by calmly I mean dramatically, set my fork down like it had betrayed me. "I think I liked it better when I thought it was, I don't know... boring spicy rice."

I pasted on my best *mmm, delicious* smile for the rest of the meal while avoiding the sausage like I owed it money. I was all for culinary adventures, but I'd just found the line, and apparently, it was made of coagulated pig plasma.

Later that night, as we strolled back to the hotel, Diego nudged me with his elbow, grinning like the smug, sexy tour guide he was.

"You know," he said, "you actually handled that better than I thought you would."

I shot him a look. "Yeah, well, that was before I knew I was a vampire."

He chuckled, wrapping an arm around my shoulders. "Fair enough. But hey, you tried it. That counts for bravery points in my book."

"Sure," I said, giving him a look. "It's a story I'll tell someday… preferably when I'm trying to win a dare or make someone throw up a little in their mouth."

Diego stopped walking and turned to face me, that annoyingly perfect streetlight casting a glow on him like he was in a cologne ad. I probably had *morcilla* breath and he still looked like that.

Rude.

"Nadia," he said, brushing his thumb along my cheek in that soft, movie-scene way that made me forget how blood sausage had just emotionally traumatized me. "I love that you're willing to try these things. Even when they're, you know… mildly horrifying. It means a lot to me."

My heart did a weird cartwheel and then flopped dramatically like it needed a fainting couch.

"Well," I murmured, smiling up at him, "it's easy when you're next to me looking all swoony and distracting. Even blood sausage doesn't stand a chance."

From that moment on, *morcilla* became the running gag among Diego's friends. They'd dramatically present it at dinners like I was on some twisted reality show. I'd laugh. Smile sweetly. And then shove the plate as far away from me as legally possible.

The truth? I wasn't smiling just to be polite. I was smiling because every bite, even the ones that made my taste buds stage a protest, felt like my ticket into belonging. Like my way of saying: *I'm here. I'm willing. I want to belong.*

Back home, food was about family duty—showing up at the table, eating what was served, being part of the collective. Here, it was the same, but different. Trying Spain's food became my way of proving that I wasn't just visiting; I was investing.

And sometimes, yes, I thought about pretending I adored blood sausage when my taste buds were quietly filing a lawsuit. Because I didn't want to disappoint Diego's friends, or worse, look like I was rejecting a piece of them.

But somewhere between *paella* and *morcilla*, I realized something: belonging shouldn't come at the cost of lying to myself. If I swallowed everything with a forced smile, I wasn't being brave. I was being a bad improv actor with terrible taste in sausage.

So the next time morcilla made its dramatic entrance, I was brave enough to shake my head, laugh, and say, "Nope, still not a vampire."

Diego caught my eye. He didn't look disappointed. He didn't tease. He just gave my hand a quick squeeze under the table and murmured, "That's my brave girl."

And somehow, that meant more than pretending ever could.

Because exploring food with Diego wasn't just about saying yes blindly. It was about trying, being open, and also trusting myself enough to say no when I needed to. That balance between courage and honesty felt like its own small victory.

Now, I no longer cling to *tortilla de patata* like a security blanket. I scan menus like a thrill-seeker. Sometimes I say yes to the mystery dish. Sometimes I politely pass. And either way, I don't feel like I'm failing anyone.

Sure, I still draw the line at blood sausage, but I've come a long way.

And I'd like to think the girl who once ordered "bread, but like… safe" has become someone who says, "Bring the mystery shrimp thing… and if it tastes like regret, I'll still survive."

Still, nothing, and I mean nothing, could've prepared me for what happened the next night with Joshua and Enrique.

We were in this tiny, bougie tapas place that looked like a Pinterest board exploded. Joshua wanted dessert. Enrique wanted drama. So they ordered something that was literally on fire.

"It's called *crema catalana flambée*," Enrique announced, as if he was about to win a Michelin star.

The waiter set it ablaze tableside, the flames licking the edges of the sugar crust.

Joshua clapped. "This is the most exciting thing I've seen since that time you choked on a wasabi peanut and blamed colonialism."

"That was valid," Enrique said, completely deadpan.

But then Joshua leaned too close. Like... too close.

"Do not singe your lashes," I warned. "You just grew them back from that questionable serum."

He waved me off. "Relax. I'm a professional."

Two seconds later, his napkin caught on fire.

Cue chaos. Shrieking. Me launching a glass of water at the table. The flame sputtered. Enrique fanned smoke with a menu like he was auditioning for Moulin Rouge. The waiter looked like he was rethinking all his life choices.

Joshua blinked. "Did we... still get dessert?"

"You almost became dessert," I hissed.

And that night, we added a new food rule to the list: No

flammable desserts unless all parties are sober and/or wearing fire-retardant scarves.

CHAPTER 32 – In a World of Chocolate Cake, I Chose Flan

"Do you ever get tired of eating *flan*?" I asked Diego one evening, lazily twirling my spoon through the caramel pool that was halfway between dessert and syrupy miracle. We were camped out in his parents' kitchen again, pretending like we weren't about to eat an entire dish of flan meant for four people.

He blinked at me like I'd asked if air was optional.

"Tired of *flan*?" he gasped. "You don't ask the sun if it's tired of shining, Nadia."

I snorted and took another bite. Creamy. Velvety. Offensively smooth. The caramel had that perfect, almost-burnt edge. I was starting to understand the hype.

Diego nudged the plate toward me. "You're starting to like it."

"Maybe," I said, dipping my spoon back in. "But it's still not chocolate cake."

He leaned back, eyes twinkling. "Chocolate cake is overrated. *Flan* is honest. It knows what it is. No layers. No frosting to hide behind. Just fuss, no excess."

I narrowed my eyes. "You say that about everything in Spain."

"Because it's true. Simplicity is the soul of Spanish living." His gaze softened, lingering on me for a moment before he added quietly, "Besides, sometimes simple things are the best."

I rolled my eyes, but a smile tugged at my lips. Because even though I'd never admit it out loud, not just yet, he was kind of right.

When I first got to Spain, I was underwhelmed by the dessert scene. The options seemed simple, understated, and nowhere near as sweet. I wasn't sure they'd ever win me over.

Back home in Singapore, we didn't hold back. Chocolate lava cake, rainbow *kueh lapis* (a steamed, colorful layered cake), pandan chiffon cakes so fluffy they doubled as pillows; our desserts were indulgent. Loud. Centerpieces. Here, desserts whispered instead of screamed.

Then Diego's mom handed me a slice of her homemade *bizcocho*.

It looked... unassuming. Just a golden sponge cake dusted with powdered sugar. But then I took a bite.

Lemon. Vanilla. A hug in cake form. It was perfectly moist, with a subtle citrus tang that lingered on my tongue.

"How does something this plain taste so good?" I mumbled through a mouthful.

"Olive oil," his mom said, holding up a little bottle like it was magic potion. "Butter is for birthdays. Olive oil is for everything else."

"Butterless cake?" I gasped.

She winked. "Lighter. Healthier. More Spanish."

And just like that, I became a *bizcocho* believer.

"Between your mom's cake and this *flan*, I feel betrayed by my own dessert history," I said, licking powdered sugar off my fingers.

Diego watched me with a soft smile as I took another bite. "She'll be thrilled to hear you've switched teams."

But Spain didn't just change how I looked at desserts. It changed how I ate everything.

358

Somehow, despite eating like every meal was my last—hello, tapas—I wasn't gaining weight. My jeans were actually getting loose. Which made no sense.

"Am I crazy," I asked one night, standing in front of the mirror, "or am I losing weight?"

Diego glanced up from his book, one brow arched so high it practically hit his hairline. "Crazy? Absolutely. Losing weight? Also yes. Why?"

I pointed dramatically toward the kitchen, where the aftermath of our dinner, a gloriously garlicky pile of *gambas al ajillo* and fall-apart-soft *carrilleras*, still sat like delicious little crime scenes. "Because I'm eating. All. The. Time. How is this possible? Explain your witchcraft."

He laughed, shut his book, and tugged me onto the couch like he'd been waiting for this moment all day. "It's the Mediterranean diet, baby. You've been converted."

"Converted how?" I asked, curling my legs under me like a human croissant.

He broke it down for me like a food-loving professor.

He held up a finger. "One: We use olive oil instead of butter. Less saturated fat, more delicious sass."

Another finger. "Two: Our portions are smaller. You eat everything, just... not like you're prepping for hibernation."

I squinted at him. "So you're saying I've been unknowingly portion-controlled?"

"I'm saying tapas have happily tricked you."

I paused, thinking it through. He wasn't wrong. Spain's food philosophy was basically: Live your life, but maybe don't drown it in butter and frosting.

Even bread here came with restraint. Like, "Hi, I'm a polite little slice of baguette, not an entire loaf screaming for cheese."

"And the desserts?" I asked, narrowing my eyes because this was where things got suspicious.

He leaned in, all smug and adorable. "They're not loaded with sugar. They let the ingredients do the talking."

Okay. That checked out. *Bizcocho*, *flan*, even *turrón*—they all whispered sweet nothings instead of screaming DIABETES like some of my old favorites back home.

"And," Diego added, smirking now, "you walk everywhere. No car, remember? All those steps add up."

I groaned. "Ugh, fine. Spain wins."

Over the next few weeks, I found myself falling hard for this whole Spanish way of eating. Everything was simple, unfussy, and annoyingly good for you. Like a lifestyle magazine that didn't make you feel bad about loving carbs.

Diego's mom kept sneaking me her magical homemade treats, and I, being the overachiever that I am, decided to try making *bizcocho* myself. I followed her recipe to the letter. Poured my heart into it. Even wore an apron like someone on a baking show.

When it was done, I marched it over to Diego with the pride of a woman who had just conquered Mount Spongecake.

He took a bite. Chewed. Smiled. And then... the look.

"What?" I asked, hands on hips.

"It's really good," he said slowly, "but maybe... a smidge more olive oil next time?"

I groaned. "Betrayed. In my own kitchen. I'm never going to be able to make anything that resembles your mom's."

He kissed my forehead, laughing. "She's got a 40-year head start on you. But you're catching up."

Living in Spain had rewired my brain. And my taste buds. Chocolate cake still called my name sometimes, sure, but more and more, I found myself reaching for *flan*. Or a slice of airy *bizcocho*. Or, you know, the entire tray.

Because somewhere between the garlic prawns, the sidewalk strolls, and Diego's smug little grin, I realized... simple could be swoon-worthy too.

"Alright," I said one evening, licking the last bit of *flan* off my spoon like a woman with zero shame. "What's next on the Spanish dessert tour? Enlighten me."

Diego's eyes sparkled. Which was usually a warning. "Have you ever tried *polvorones*?"

"Polvo-what-now?" I tilted my head like a confused puppy.

"Polvorones," he repeated, grinning like he'd just told me the secret to eternal happiness. "They're these crumbly little cookies we eat around Christmas. But honestly, they should be eaten every day, all year, forever."

A few minutes later, we were at a bakery that smelled like roasted almonds and dreams.

Diego pointed out flavors like he was giving me a VIP tour—almond, lemon, chocolate. He handed me one, wrapped in pastel paper that made it look like a present from the dessert gods.

I peeled it open like it was a delicate artifact. Powdered sugar dusted my fingers. I took a bite… and immediately saw heaven.

The cookie crumbled instantly, melting into a buttery, nutty sweetness that felt like eating a cloud. It was as if someone had baked nostalgia and wrapped it in carbs.

362

"Oh. My. God." I froze mid-bite. "Where has this been my whole life?"

Diego just laughed. "Told you. You're welcome. Side effects may include addiction."

Addicted? Please. I was already planning our wedding.

The next day, I went back. This time for vanilla and cinnamon. The day after that, hazelnut and coconut. Each time, I found myself marveling at the variety, the delicate wrapping, and how each flavor was somehow better than the last. At one point, I swore I blacked out in front of the display case and came to holding six varieties and no regrets.

Eventually, the bakery owner, a jolly, older man with a thick Catalan accent and permanent powdered-sugar fingerprints, started greeting me like we were old friends.

"Another batch today, *guapa?*" he said one afternoon as I stepped up to the counter.

I blushed like a girl caught texting her crush. "Yes, please. Do you have pistachio?"

Diego, who had tagged along this time, leaned against the counter with the kind of smirk that should've been illegal. "She's your best customer now, isn't she?"

The shop owner chuckled. "Every day this week."

"Diego!" I elbowed him so hard he nearly dropped his wallet. "You traitor."

"What?" he said innocently, hands up. "You're famous now. The *reina de los polvorones*. The *polvorones* queen."

The title stuck. So did the teasing. Every time we went back, he'd wink at the owner and say something like, "Careful, she might start a riot if you run out."

He wasn't wrong.

Polvorones became my emotional support snack. I'd stash a few in my bag for afternoon snacks. Hid a backup in my coat pocket. I even started gifting them to friends, insisting they try them too.

One night, as I reached for my third cookie during a movie, Diego raised a brow.

"You think you'll ever get sick of them?"

I looked him dead in the eye, my mouth full of almondy goodness. "Absolutely not. But you know what would make them even better?"

He paused. "If they came with a side of hot chocolate?"

"Nope. If we learned how to make them ourselves."

Diego raised an eyebrow. "You want to make them yourself?

Aren't you already buying half the shop's stock?"

"I'm serious! Think of the money I'd save. And the power I'd hold."

He laughed, already pulling out his phone. "Alright, *polvorones queen*. Let's find you a recipe."

But no matter how many sweets I tasted or recipes I tried, some flavors lived in a place Spain couldn't touch.

One afternoon, while folding up the bakery bag with a fresh batch of almond cookies, I was hit with a pang so sharp it knocked the air out of me.

I missed my sisters.

Roselyn, bossy in the kitchen but somehow still lovable. Kyra, dramatic and flour-covered within minutes. Our annual Eid tradition of baking pineapple tarts in our family's tiny, flour-dusted kitchen with Mom standing over us like the Dessert Police, arms crossed, lips pursed.

"Too much jam," she'd scold. "Press the edges tighter, Kyra."

"I'm literally pressing with all my ancestors' strength," Kyra would grumble, shoving the tray toward the oven.

"Guys," I'd say, trying to play mediator while sneakily licking jam off my thumb. "Let's just get through this so we can eat the rejects."

Even the rejects were divine.

Now, thousands of miles away, I could almost taste the buttery pastry melting on my tongue, smell the cloves and sweetness wafting through the kitchen. My phone buzzed. I reached for it, heart fluttering. Maybe today they'd reply.

Nothing. Still.

It was the kind of homesickness that sat quietly with you. It didn't scream. It just… lingered. Like the ghost of cinnamon in an empty cookie tin.

I hugged the bakery bag to my chest and whispered, "You guys would love these."

Diego came over, pressing a kiss to my temple. *"Polvorones* again?"

I nodded, blinking fast.

"They're healing," I said. "Like edible therapy."

He pulled me into a hug, no questions asked.

In a world of chocolate cake, I chose *flan*. And a dozen *polvorones*.
And a little piece of home that lived in flour, jam, and three sisters squabbling over pineapple tarts.

CHAPTER 33 - Flan-tasy Denied: My Sweet Comeback Story

We never got around to making the *polvorones*. Life, as it often does, had other plans—plans involving errands, overtime, and the occasional "let's just order in" night. But my love for sweets? Alive. Thriving. Flourishing like basil in a Mediterranean window box.

Flan? Yes.
Turrón? Obviously.
Polvorones? Please.

I was basically on a dessert tour of Spain, minus the souvenir magnets.

And then came the headaches. The bloating. The "why do my jeans hate me" fatigue. At first, I blamed stress. Or Diego's mom's *bizcocho*. Or the moon. But when things didn't improve, I dragged myself to the doctor.

"You have candidiasis," she said, very casually for someone who just ruined my week.

I blinked. "Candi-who?"

"Candidiasis," she repeated, probably used to this exact reaction. "It's an overgrowth of yeast in your body. Usually caused by diet. Too much sugar, too many refined carbs… they feed the yeast."

I froze. In my mind, a slideshow of recent crimes flashed before my eyes. *Flan* on Tuesday. *Polvorones* on Wednesday. That entire bar of *turrón* on Friday that I swore I'd only "taste."

"So you're saying I have to… stop eating sugar?"

She nodded. "Low-sugar, low-refined carb. Brown rice, sweet potatoes, leafy greens. Nothing that feeds yeast."

I stared at her like she'd just suggested I give up oxygen. "But… sugar is my love language."

"You might need to get creative," she said, handing me a pamphlet like it was a peace offering.

Walking out of the clinic felt like my world had tilted on its axis. No dessert? No white bread? Instead of a lost boyfriend, I was mourning desserts. My love for sweets was practically a personality trait.

The first week was brutal. Eating out felt like walking through a minefield. Bread baskets landed on the table like tiny edible betrayals, smirking at me like *"Remember us? We used to be happy."*

"Hidden sugar" was apparently everywhere, from sauces to salad dressings. My brain screamed for *flan* while my gut begged for mercy.

I researched obsessively, diving into blogs, forums, and even a few scientific articles. Lists of "safe foods" scrolled through my screen, filled with brown rice, quinoa, sweet potatoes, garlic, and probiotic yogurt. Things I'd previously filed under "boring side dishes" were suddenly my salvation.

And still, I cheated. A bite of *churro* here. A sliver of cake at a birthday party there. Every slip left me doubled over in guilt and stomach cramps.

But little by little, I started learning to pause. To make choices. To breathe through the craving instead of letting it steamroll me. It was my crash course in distress tolerance, the kind I'd never had to practice before.

Slowly, self-care became less of a buzzword and more of a lifeline. Long walks when I wanted to binge. Herbal teas when I wanted a soda drowned in sugar. Saying no to tapas nights that would wreck me, and yes to cooking at home, where I controlled the ingredients.

And yet... somewhere between reading way too many sugar-detox blogs and crying into a bowl of plain yogurt, I discovered something fascinating. Apparently, some Asian bodies process sugar differently. More sensitivity to insulin. More prone to yeast overgrowth.

It wasn't just that I liked sweets; it was that my body had apparently made a lifelong frenemy pact with them.

So when I finally turned to baking again, it wasn't from a place of denial but from curiosity. Could I make something both safe and satisfying?

The answer was a very burnt, very crumbly no.

Was I qualified? No. Was I desperate enough to Google "can I bake cake with chickpeas?" Absolutely.

My venture into my sugar-free baking journey could've been sponsored by the word "nope."

First attempt? Disaster. My almond flour cookies disintegrated like they were allergic to structure, and the coconut-sweetened cakes? Imagine chewing on a memory foam pillow.

Diego, bless his taste buds, took one bite of my banana bread and immediately reached for water like he'd just eaten a mouthful of cinnamon.

"It's... interesting," he managed, which in Diego-speak translated roughly to "I love you, but please don't make me eat that again."

But I refused to give up.

I rolled up my sleeves, stocked up on bananas, coconut flour, and whatever else Pinterest said would change my life, and got to work. My kitchen became a food lab. I adjusted ratios, whispered prayers to my mixing bowls, and Googled more alternative baking techniques than anyone should.

And then, cue the angelic choir, I had my first win.

Filthy Rich.

A chocolate bar so decadent, so fudgey, so melt-in-your-mouth dreamy, it practically winked at you from the plate. Made with almond flour, dark chocolate, and just enough coconut oil to make it scandalous.

I handed Diego a square with the kind of hope usually reserved for lottery tickets.

He took a bite and paused. "You made this?" he asked, chewing like he couldn't believe his own taste buds.

"Yes," I said, trying to play it cool even though I was vibrating with pride.

He reached for another piece, already nodding. "This is incredible. You should sell these."

From there, things snowballed, but not without effort. Every new recipe was a lesson in patience. Every "cheat" meal was followed by recommitment. And every success in the kitchen reinforced that maybe I wasn't just surviving this diagnosis; I was reshaping myself.

And just like that, my sugar-free dessert empire was born— from banana bread tragedy to chocolate triumph, one monk fruit miracle at a time.

The praise lit a fire under me. I created Monkey Business (peanut butter banana muffins) and Sexy Tarts (zesty lemon tarts with coconut crusts that looked like they belonged in a centerfold). I gave them all scandalous names because, well, if you can't have sugar, you can at least have drama.

Somewhere in the middle of all this whisk-slinging joy, I had a thought that stopped me cold.

This never would've happened in Singapore. Not because of ingredients or ovens, but because of expectation.

If I'd told my family back home I wanted to quit sugar and start a dessert business, I could practically hear their collective gasp. *Don't be ridiculous*, my eldest sister Roselyn would've said. *Stick to something stable.* Kyra would've nodded quietly, but I'd see the concern in her eyes.

And my mom? She'd supervise my life the same way she supervised our Eid cookie baking—hovering, correcting, making sure everything looked proper.

There wasn't exactly a blueprint in my family for whimsical dessert pivots. In Singapore, I was supposed to work hard, climb the ladder, and not take wild chances involving almond flour and Instagram logos.

But here in Spain? With Diego cheering me on and friends like Joshua and Enrique literally taste-testing my success, I'd found space. Support. Room to dream.

Joshua and Enrique were there from the start, showing up like my own glittery taste-test task force.

"These muffins?" Joshua declared, mouth full. "They're like emotional support snacks."

"I want to marry this tart," Enrique moaned, dramatically wiping away a fake tear.

Joshua pointed at me. "You should do this for real. Like real real. Start a business. Open a bakery. Call it 'No Sugar, Still Sexy.'"

"That name is horrifying," I said, passing him another Sexy Tart.

"I know," he beamed. "I'm a visionary."

Fueled by their encouragement (and the sight of Joshua dramatically fanning himself after a bite of cinnamon monkey muffin), I made a menu, created an Instagram account, and gave my desserts names that would make my mother gasp.

Orders started trickling in, first from friends, then strangers, then one terrifying corporate email asking for fifty Sexy Tarts for an event.

I turned my kitchen into a war zone of mixing bowls and muffin trays. The air smelled like toasted coconut and ambition. I slept maybe four hours in two days, but delivered those tarts like a sugar-free superhero in leggings.

After the event, I called Joshua.

"They loved them," I whispered, almost in disbelief. "One guy said they were life-changing."

Joshua screamed so loud I had to hold the phone away from my ear.

"You're a genius!" he yelled. "A sexy, almond-flour-wielding genius!"

That night, Diego and I sat on the couch sharing leftovers, our feet tangled under a blanket.

"This is your thing," he said softly. "You turned a food breakup into a full-blown love story."

I leaned on his shoulder, eyes fluttering closed. "I guess I did."

And maybe, just maybe, I was starting to believe I could rewrite the rules. Even if every glossy photo was trial, error, and a girl teaching herself resilience one sugar-free cookie at a time.

Because this wasn't just a baking pivot. It was self-care with an apron on.

It was learning that sometimes discipline looks like brown rice, sweet potatoes, and restraint at a café table. Sometimes it looks like crying over almond flour and trying again anyway.

And maybe those cracks where sugar used to live were now filled with something sturdier, like the stubborn ability to keep myself standing even when it was hard.

CHAPTER 34 – The Silent Battle for My Wallet

The first time I stepped into a Chinese store in Barcelona, I thought I'd be in and out in five minutes. Ten, tops. I just needed batteries.

Instead, I emerged 45 minutes later with a feather boa, three packs of neon pens, a rice cooker, and a pair of novelty slippers shaped like unicorns.

Why? No reason. Did I need them? Absolutely not. Did I feel alive? One hundred percent. Batteries? Absolutely forgot about them.

It was my ex-boss-turned-friend Daniela who first clued me in. "You haven't lived until you've been to a Chinese store," she'd said with the kind of reverence most people reserve for religious experiences or Taylor Swift concerts. "They have everything. And I mean everything. And they're cheap. Like dangerously cheap."

She wasn't lying.

It was the Disney World of random shopping. Organized chaos. Aisles that multiplied when you blinked. And price tags that made you question how capitalism even worked.

Toaster? Check. Hair dryer? Check. A tiara, extension cords, a rubber chicken, and thirty types of glitter pens? Check, check, and triple check.

It was like someone had taken every item from a dollar store, a party store, a beauty salon, and a mildly unhinged online catalog, and squeezed them all into one magical fluorescent-lit box.

"How does one store have this much stuff?" I muttered, wandering from one aisle to the next, eyes wide and wallet trembling.

It quickly became my version of retail therapy. I'd pop in for something specific, like a mop, and leave with an egg slicer, three mugs, a candle shaped like a cactus, and a sudden belief that I could probably organize a flash mob if needed.

Joshua, of course, was no help.

"We're here for balloons," I told him before a party.

30 minutes later, he was cradling a plastic pineapple lamp and a tiara.

"Stick to the list," I hissed.

"Ma'am, I am the list," he replied, placing the tiara on my head with great ceremony.

It became a thing. Our chaotic Chinese store tradition. We'd go in with purpose and come out with emotional support stationery and questionably translated notebooks that said things like Dream Big Potato.

But then... came the betrayal.

A Sunday morning emergency—no eggs, no bread, and a craving for French toast so intense I nearly started sobbing into my empty fridge. Everything in Barcelona shuts down on Sundays.

Everything except the Pakistani-run convenience stores, known here as "paki stores."

At first, the term made me flinch. Back in Singapore, "paki" was an actual slur. But here, it was casual, used like "corner shop" or "lifesaver on Sundays when everything else is closed." Cultural dissonance? Yes. But also, accurate.

The paki stores, however, were open on Sundays. That was a big deal.

Need milk? Bread? Eggs? Cigarettes? The paki store was your savior.

So off I went, armed with a canvas tote and irrational confidence.

Only to discover that eggs, on a Sunday, cost roughly the same as my dignity. Five euros. For eggs. The same ones I bought for three euros at Mercadona, the local supermarket. Were these eggs laid by golden hens?

I hesitated, sighed, and paid anyway. Toast cravings wait for no woman.

"Highway robbery," I muttered on the way out, to which the owner responded with a knowing shrug. He knew. They always know.

"That's the Sunday tax," Diego explained later. "They charge extra 'cause they can."

But I wasn't mad. They were my always-there friend, always open. Always smiling. And somehow, the owners knew everyone's names. Diego was basically family.

Still, I noticed the quiet turf war on our street. This unspoken rivalry between the Chinese stores and the paki stores. They were often just a few doors apart, each fighting for the same turf.

Sometimes, you'd see the owners standing outside, glaring

at each other from their respective doorways, like characters in a Western standoff.

"Gang war," Diego joked one day as we passed two stores on the same street.

I laughed so hard I snorted in public. "Honestly, it feels like it."

One week, I tried to organize my chaotic life with a planner I found at the Chinese store. I made a budget spreadsheet, printed out weekly menus, and even color-coded my spending.

"I'm turning over a new leaf," I told Joshua.

Two hours later, I spent 20 euros on glitter pens, a mug that said Live Laugh Lemon, and a phone ring light I definitely did not need.

My wallet wept quietly in the corner.

"You need an intervention," Joshua said, sipping iced tea from a new straw cup I bought for him. (Also from the Chinese store. Obviously.)

"But look how cute this measuring spoon set is," I argued.

"Girl, you don't even measure. You just pour and hope."

Fair.

So, as you can imagine, I was riding high on my store-hopping adventures. That is, until my card was declined on a random Tuesday.

Declined. Twice.
Cue full-body sweat.

Turns out, I had, without realizing it, completely overspent my weekly budget on spontaneous store trips, bakery detours, and a last-minute online order of a jumpsuit I was certain I needed for "future vibes."

I went home, sat on my bed, and stared at my glitter planner like it had betrayed me.

"This is why we can't have nice things," I told it.

The worst part? I had to cancel lunch with Joshua and Enrique.

"I'm grounded," I texted. "Financially."

Joshua responded with a GIF of a raccoon stealing chips.

I snorted, but the laugh didn't stick. When the screen went dark and I set my phone down, the silence in the apartment came rushing in like an uninvited guest.

I sat at my little kitchen table with a mug of tea that had gone cold and tasted vaguely like regret. And suddenly, homesickness wasn't some cute little longing; it was a full-body ache. Like someone had stuffed a brick in my chest and forgotten to take it out.

Back home, if I were broke, I'd have wandered into the kitchen and eaten leftovers until my mom noticed and yelled at me for not eating properly. My sisters would've roasted me for spending all my money on "nonsense," then slipped me cash on the sly because that's what family does.

There was always a net. Always a backup. Always someone who knew when to shove a plate in front of me and say, "Eat first, panic later."

Here? There was no net. Just me, an empty fridge, and a city that kept spinning whether I could keep up or not.

And God, it stung. Not just the broke part. The lonely part. The "if I trip, there's no one to catch me" part.

I curled up on the couch with a throw pillow that smelled faintly of laundry detergent and desperation. "I miss home," I whispered to no one, and immediately hated how wobbly my voice sounded.

There it was—the truth. I missed being known, being cared for, being someone's responsibility in the best way. Instead, I was the girl crying into a pillow because she couldn't afford brunch.

For five solid minutes, I let myself wallow. Full pity party. No snacks provided because, well, broke. Then I sat up, blew my nose on a questionable napkin, and gave myself the world's shortest pep talk:

Fine. You're homesick. You're lonely. But glitter pens aren't going to fix it, and unicorn mugs don't pay rent.

I couldn't control the loneliness. But I could control the budget.

I needed the mini crash. I needed the reminder that glitter pens weren't going to save me from homesickness, and unicorn mugs weren't going to pay my rent. Budgeting wasn't about restriction; it was about power. About being the version of me who could afford eggs and emotional breakdowns on the same day.

CHAPTER 35 - Wait, Protests Are Legal Here?

※

I'd learned the hard way that budgeting wasn't glamorous. No fun shiny things. Just the quiet satisfaction of not overdrafting.

Apparently, two weeks of avoiding the Chinese stores and cooking my own meals made a significant difference in my bank account. I hadn't even noticed how much savings I had until one morning I opened my wallet and realized… wait.

I had money. Like, actual money. Enough that when Daniela suggested hanging out, I didn't have to fake a tragic cough and claim I was "saving for rent."

Which is how I found myself on a sunny Saturday afternoon wandering the cobblestone streets of Barcelona's Gothic Quarter, on my way to meet Daniela for a drink and pretending I hadn't tried on five outfits to look effortlessly casual.

We had met at the metro station and as we walked to the bar, I was halfway through saying, "I need to look less like I just Googled 'Barcelona expat starter pack' and more like I belong here," when Daniela practically dragged me by the arm into Zara.

She had become more than just my ex-boss by this point; she was my European fairy godmother, armed with a credit card and a ruthless sense of style.

"You need basics that scream effortless, not touristy," she said, handing me a black blazer that somehow looked expensive and intimidating at the same time. "And no more leggings as pants. This is not a yoga retreat."

An hour later, I was buried under a pile of jeans, cropped jackets, and flowy blouses.

"This one," Daniela declared, holding up a satin midi skirt. "It says, 'I brunch in three languages.'"

By the time we reached Primark, I was emotionally spent but fashionably reborn. She had picked out boots that made my calves look toned and a tote bag that screamed "Barcelona local" louder than I ever could.

"How do you feel?" she asked as I paid for my final haul.

"Like I just passed a European citizenship test without studying," I said, clutching my new wardrobe like it was armor.

We emerged from the store triumphant, bags in hand, ready to parade my Euro-chic transformation down Passeig de Gràcia.

And that's when I saw it.

At first, I thought it was a street performance. There was a crowd gathered, people chanting in unison, some clapping, others waving flags and holding signs. But as we got closer, I realized; this wasn't flamenco.

It was a protest.

My whole body tensed. In Singapore, the only time I'd ever seen a crowd shouting in the streets was during a mall's mega sale. Protesting was illegal. Even holding up a sign with a smiley face could earn you a court summons. The idea of joining a demonstration on purpose? In broad daylight? In a place with traffic police just watching? My inner Singaporean was internally filing a police report.

I instinctively reached for Daniela's arm.

"Oh my god, am I going to get arrested?" I muttered to myself, clutching my shopping bags and dragging Daniela across the street to distance ourselves.

"Should we... should we leave?" I whispered, heart racing.

Daniela blinked at me. "Why would we leave?"

"There's a protest. What if we get arrested? Do we just... stand here? What if someone sees us? Are there cameras?"

She laughed, completely unbothered. "Nadia, this is Spain. Protests happen every weekend. Sometimes twice a day."

My eyes darted between the crowd and the police standing calmly at the edge of the square, chatting and sipping from tiny plastic cups.

"Nobody's being tear-gassed," she added. "You're fine. You can even join if you want."

"Join??" I gasped like she'd just invited me to commit treason in broad daylight. "My mother would faint. My sisters would scold me over FaceTime."

I stood frozen on the sidewalk, staring at the demonstration, unsure whether to run or applaud.

Even from the other side, I couldn't resist watching. The crowd's energy was electric with people chanting, clapping, and waving banners. I could feel the passion in the air, though I had no idea what the protest was about.

When I got home, I practically burst through the door like I'd just survived a near-death experience.

"DIEGO!" I yelled. "I saw a protest!"

He looked up from the couch, chewing toast. "What were they protesting?"

"I don't know! I didn't stop to read the signs! I thought if I got caught near it, I'd be thrown into jail!"

Diego's expression shifted from concern to disbelief. "Thrown into jail? For what?"

"For being near a protest!" I said, as if it were the most obvious thing in the world.

He stared at me for a moment before laughing. "Nadia, this is Spain. Protests are legal here."

"You could have even joined in," he continued, laughing.

I flopped onto the couch beside him, dazed. "Wild. Absolutely unhinged. My mom would faint."

He snorted. "Let her. You're in Europe now."

I wasn't convinced.

Still, a few months later, I did something I never thought I'd do. I decided to attend a protest on purpose.

It was about Catalan independence, which, if I'm being honest, I only half understood. Like, I knew there were flags, and history, and a whole lot of feelings, but ask me to explain it in detail and I'd sound like a kid giving a book report on a novel she only skimmed.

"I don't even fully understand the issue," I admitted to Diego as we walked toward the meeting point. "I just want to see what it's like."

Diego raised an eyebrow. "You're dragging me into this for the experience?"

"Exactly," I said with a grin.

"You don't even know what side you're on," he pointed out, amused.

"Details," I said. "I'm here for the sociology. The vibes. The snacks, if there are any."

Plaça de Catalunya was packed. Spanish flags waved in the air like it was a football match, and the chants were loud, passionate, and surprisingly rhythmic. Children perched on their parents' shoulders waving smaller flags, teenagers snapped photos, and older women yelled slogans with the confidence of people who'd done this every week since the '70s.

And here's the thing, I'd lived in Barcelona for years by then, but in moments like this? I still felt like the girl on the outside, peering through the glass at someone else's family dinner. Everyone around me was rooted in something—

history, culture, identity. And me? I was just… visiting.
Observing.

Until a group of masked protesters started throwing fire-
crackers near the police barricade. The sound made me
jump so high I smacked a stranger with my bag.

The crowd surged, chanting louder, and suddenly I had a tiny
existential crisis right there on the pavement. If I picked up
a flag, which one should it be? What did it mean if I didn't?
Was I allowed to stand here without an opinion? Was that,
like, illegal?

A man next to us shouted something I didn't understand, but
the way Diego stiffened told me it wasn't *let's all hold hands
and bake a cake.*

"I think I've seen enough," I whispered, suddenly overwhelmed.

He nodded, grabbing my hand. "Let's go get you a *bocadillo*
before you start a revolution by accident."

We found a café tucked away on a quieter street, where I
inhaled a sandwich the size of my head and two glasses of
vermouth while Diego patiently explained the historical and
political context. I nodded like I understood more than 30%
of it.

But even with my dramatic exit, something about it stuck.
People weren't afraid to show up, wave flags, and yell at the

top of their lungs. And no one was dragging them away in handcuffs for it.

Back in Singapore, if I'd even thought about standing in the street with a sign, my mom would've staged an intervention involving incense, prayer, and a lecture about "why can't you just focus on your job." Classic Mom.

And yet here I was, in a city that let its people be loud, messy, passionate. I wasn't part of it, not really, but watching from the edges made me wonder what it would mean if I ever was.

Would I always be the outsider peeking in for entertainment, or could Barcelona ever feel like more than borrowed chaos?

By the time we walked home, hand in hand and slightly deaf from chanting, the whole city seemed to hum with tension. Slogans spray-painted on walls, headlines glowing from shop TVs, strangers whispering heatedly at café tables. It felt like Act One of a very complicated sequel.

And I couldn't help thinking about what would happen if this sequel actually took. If Catalonia really does break away, what does that mean for me?

Would my visa suddenly be void? Would I need to stand in line for another residency card, this time under a new flag? Would I have to relearn how to say "hi, I'm foreign, please don't kick me out" but in even more Catalan?

The idea of moving again made my stomach lurch. I'd barely

figured out which store sold the good peanut butter, and now I might have to start over somewhere else? Absolutely not.

It was both terrifying and, somehow, weirdly funny. Because only I could move halfway across the world, finally start to feel like I might belong, and then realize the entire country might change underneath me.

Barcelona: come for the *churros*, stay for the political identity crisis.

And yet, even in the middle of all that unrest, Spain still somehow had the bandwidth to run a high-speed train that could shoot you across the country at 300 kilometers per hour while smelling faintly of *churros*. Priorities.

I still remember the first time Diego casually suggested we take the AVE, the high-speed train, to Madrid for the weekend. Like it was no big deal. Like we were just hopping over to the next town and not hurtling across the country at 300 kilometers per hour in something that felt like a spaceship but smelled faintly of *churros*.

CHAPTER 36 - Spain on Tracks, Europe in Sight

"It's only two hours," Diego said, like he was not casually shattering my entire concept of distance.

"Two hours?" I blinked. "That's how long it takes to get from one end of Singapore to the other, twice."

He smirked. "And this time, no MRT train breakdowns."

As it turned out, Spain's AVE train was basically teleportation with snacks. The ride to Madrid was smooth, scenic, and, dare I say, romantic. We glided past golden fields and tiny fairytale villages, olive trees dotting the landscape like confetti from nature's party cannon.

Diego sat beside me, flipping through a guidebook, occasionally pointing out landmarks through the window.

"See that?" he said, gently tapping my arm and motioning toward a distant castle perched on a hilltop. His excitement was contagious. "That's from the medieval period. Imagine the stories those walls could tell."

Meanwhile, I was internally hyperventilating over the fact that anyone could live that close to castles. I had castles as my laptop's screensaver. Spaniards had castles outside their train windows.

When we stepped into Madrid, it hit me like a slap of sunlight and possibility. The city buzzed—electric, elegant, and slightly chaotic, like a fashionably late guest who still manages to be the life of the party.

We hit the weekend markets first, an explosion of colors, scents, and people trying to sell you vintage sunglasses or antique forks for "just five euros, *amiga*." One stall sold handmade notebooks. Another sold cured meats in cones. I bought both, obviously.

That night, Madrid's nightlife punched me in the face in the best way. Diego and I wandered into a bar where someone was singing flamenco live, and the passion in her voice cracked something open in me. We danced until 3 a.m. with strangers who felt like old friends, then devoured *churros* with hot chocolate in silence, our feet aching and souls buzzing.

"I could live here," I whispered, half-joking as we walked back to our Airbnb.

Diego glanced at me, grinning. "You're already halfway here."

He wasn't wrong.

From there, weekend train trips became our love language.

We hiked in San Sebastián, where the sea breeze flirted with my hair and the *pintxos* flirted with my taste buds. The beaches were postcard-perfect, bluer than my jealous little Singaporean heart could comprehend. I used to think Sentosa was a beach. Turns out, Sentosa was a suggestion.

Then came Cádiz, with its cobblestone alleys and seafood so fresh I half-expected it to leap off the plate and reintroduce itself. We rented bikes and cruised along the coastline, stopping for ice cream and unsolicited photos of sunsets.

One afternoon, Diego suggested a "hidden beach" he remembered from childhood.

"It's quiet," he said. "Crystal clear water. Not many tourists."

Sold.

We locked our bikes and hiked down a sandy path flanked by cliffs, the sound of waves growing louder. It really was stunning—turquoise water, golden sand, not a single overpriced umbrella rental in sight.

I kicked off my sandals and ran into the surf, squealing when the cold water hit my ankles. Diego hung back, setting up our towels while I splashed around like a toddler on a sugar high.

And that's when it happened.

Out of the corner of my eye, I saw an old man sauntering along the shoreline.

At first, I noticed nothing unusual. Broad shoulders. Slight sunburn. Confident walk.

Then my eyes drifted lower. And… OH. OH NO.

"OH MY GOD!" I shrieked, nearly tripping over a wave as I turned and sprinted out of the water like a woman possessed.

Diego looked up just as I launched myself into his arms like I'd just seen a sea monster.

"WHAT. WAS. THAT?" I panted, burying my face in his chest and pointing frantically behind me.

He blinked once, then followed my gaze.

A slow smile spread across his face. "Ah," he said, way too calmly. "Yes, this is a nudist beach."

"You KNEW?!"

"I forgot until just now," he said, absolutely not sorry.

"You let me go frolic! Among strangers! Who were just... Out there!"

He tried to keep a straight face, but the laughter was bubbling up like a shaken soda can.

"I didn't think he'd walk right past you like that," he said, grinning. "Although, technically, he wasn't walking past you. More like... swinging."

"STOP IT," I cried, clutching his shirt and refusing to ever look behind me again. "This is trauma. This is an origin story for a future phobia."

Diego just hugged me tighter, still chuckling. "Welcome to Cádiz."

Even León, Diego's hometown, made the list. When he first said it was eight hours away, I was hesitant. "Eight hours? That seems... a lot?"

"Trainhotel," he said, eyes twinkling, clearly amused by my hesitation. "It's a night train with sleeper cabins, like a moving hotel."

We boarded at night, cozied up in our little cabin, and watched the sunset streak the sky pink and gold.

Eight hours later, we woke up in León to the smell of mountain air and Diego's mom waiting with open arms and a pot of *cocido* so large it had its own gravitational pull.

Now listen. *Cocido* isn't just a dish. It's an event. A three-act play. A spiritual experience.

When Diego's mom placed the steaming pot in the center of the table, the scent hit me like a warm, meaty hug to the face. Simmering spices, rich broth, and what I could only assume was a small farm's worth of protein danced through the air.

Across the table, Diego was already watching me like a kid waiting to see if I liked his favorite movie.

"You've been hyping this up for months," I teased, arching a brow as I ladled some of the golden broth into my bowl. "If this doesn't blow my socks off, I'm holding it against you forever."

"Oh, it will," he said, smirking like a man who knew his mom's cooking was about to change my life. "Prepare to be converted."

The first course was the broth—light, golden, and served with delicate noodles that looked like they'd been placed with tweezers by a soup artist. Diego nudged my bowl toward me like it was a love letter in liquid form.

"Well?" he asked, eyes wide with anticipation.

I took a sip.

And promptly sighed. Loudly. Dramatically. Like I was in a commercial for cozy fall weather and oversized sweaters.

"It's like a hug in a bowl," I said, pressing a hand to my chest. "A hug from a grandmother I never met, but who somehow knew all my emotional needs."

Diego grinned, smug. "Told you."

Then came round two: the *garbanzos*. Plump little chickpeas that had clearly gone to culinary grad school, because they were soaking up the smoky, meaty drama like seasoned professionals. They arrived with a supporting cast of cabbage, potatoes, and carrots—vegetables so tender and flavorful I briefly considered writing them into my will.

And then, cue dramatic music, the grand finale. The meat platter.

Not just a meat platter. The meat platter. A glorious, glistening mountain of *chorizo*, pork belly, *morcilla* (which I looked at with suspicion, remembering that day with his friends), and thick, juicy hunks of beef. It was less a plate and more a Roman feast. All we were missing were togas and a servant fanning us with palm leaves.

This wasn't the kind of meal you ate. It was the kind you committed to. You paced yourself. You told family stories between bites. You pretended to hesitate before reaching for a fourth slice of bread, and everyone pretended not to notice.

Diego had spent months hyping up his mom's *cocido*, going on about how it was the best thing I'd ever taste, how no restaurant could compare, how I'd need to sit down after the first bite. I'd rolled my eyes every single time.

And now? I was eating those eye-rolls with a spoon.

Because sitting there with a full belly and a fuller heart, surrounded by clinking cutlery, cozy chatter, and the intoxicating scent of homemade comfort, I realized that this wasn't just food. It was family. It was warmth. It was a stew that said, you belong here.

Diego wasn't wrong. It was everything he promised, and then some.

I looked at him across the table. "You weren't exaggerating."

He beamed. "Told you. She's a *cocido* queen."

And she was. She even liked me—told me I had "sweet eyes" and served me an extra portion, which I took as a blessing and a threat.

After lunch, we went for a walk through León's quieter streets. It wasn't flashy like Madrid or beachy like Valencia, but it was calm. Solid. The kind of place that smelled like roasted chestnuts and felt like belonging.

I slipped my hand into Diego's.

"Your mom's amazing."

"She thinks you're amazing too," he said, squeezing my hand.

"I think you're stuck with us."

"Promise?" I whispered.

He looked at me then, really looked at me, like he was deciding something. "You know," he said slowly, "I don't talk about marriage much. But if we did get married, what would that even look like?"

My heart did the equivalent of an Olympic backflip. "Like... a wedding?" I squeaked, suddenly sweating despite the cool León air.

He smiled, but it wasn't teasing this time. It was soft, serious—the kind of smile that made you feel seen, and somehow exposed, all at once. "Would your family come? Would you even tell them?"

And just like that, the air thickened, pressing against my chest. My throat seized, a knot of shame, fear, and longing I couldn't unknot. Because I knew the answers, and I hated them.

"I don't know," I whispered, staring down at the cobblestones. "Probably not. My mom would light incense and pray for my soul instead of booking a flight. My sisters would say I'd lost my mind. And honestly?" My voice cracked. "I don't think they'd come. Not even for me."

The sadness hit me like a freight train. The kind of sadness that doesn't care you're in public, surrounded by quaint architecture and the faint smell of roasted chestnuts. The ugly cry kind.

And oh, did I ugly cry. Right there in León. Mascara streaking, nose running, hiccuping like a broken accordion.

Diego didn't hesitate. He pulled me into his arms, his coat swallowing me whole. His heartbeat pressed into mine, his warmth a shield against the ache.

"Hey, hey," he murmured against my hair, holding me so tight I thought my sadness might actually suffocate under his grip. "Don't cry about them. They don't get to decide your happiness."

I pressed my face into his chest, tasting the faint scent of garlic from dinner and the tang of his cologne. And then it hit me, this time my tears felt like they might belong somewhere, like someone else's strength could patch the holes left behind by everyone else.

"I just…" I sobbed into his chest, "I always thought I'd have a big wedding with my family there. And now the thought of standing in front of everyone without them—" My voice cracked again.

"It makes me feel like I'm not enough for either world. Not Singapore. Not here."

He tilted my chin up, thumb brushing away tears that immediately reappeared because my tear ducts are traitors.

"Listen to me," he said, steady and soft. "If it's just you and me in a town hall with terrible lighting and a witness who smells like cigarettes, I'd still marry you. If you want something bigger, we'll make it big. If you want it small, we'll keep it small. Whatever it looks like, you'll never be alone in it. Not as long as I'm here."

Cue more ugly sobbing, this time mixed with a laugh-snort because he'd just described my dream wedding as a fluorescent-lit government office with cigarette fumes. Romantic, really.

"Diego," I sniffled, "you can't just say stuff like that and expect me not to look like a raccoon in our wedding photos."

He chuckled, kissing my damp, blotchy face without hesitation. "Then we'll get married twice. One for us, one for the raccoon photos."

And somehow, in the middle of my public meltdown, I fell even more in love with him.

Because this man, who truly didn't care much about marriage, cared about it for me.

And even if my family never showed up, I knew he always would.

A few days later, we went to the Picos de Europa. I'd never seen mountains like that—towering, jagged, dusted with snow like someone had gotten carried away with a giant powdered-sugar shaker.

We hiked. We sweat. I questioned my life choices approximately every eight minutes.

And then we reached the summit, and I burst into tears. "It's too beautiful," I sobbed, blaming the altitude. "Why is no one warning people?"

Diego just laughed and handed me water.

Because here's the thing. I never thought I was a nature person. I used to say "outdoorsy" meant sipping iced chocolate on a patio.

Once, my sisters and I did the Henderson Waves trail and treated it like we had scaled Everest.

The Henderson Waves were this wavy, undulating pedestrian bridge surrounded by jungle and well-behaved joggers. We packed snacks. We took selfies. We took breaks. It was barely 1.5 kilometers, but at the time, it felt like a wilderness expedition. My mom even said, "You better not fall off, okay?" as if it were the Inca Trail.

Diego would've laughed himself breathless. That wasn't hiking. That was cardio with architectural flair.

But now? Now I had blisters from actual hikes. I had grass-stained jeans and a camera roll full of mountain views that made me want to cry. I wasn't just tolerating nature. I was falling in love with it.

And maybe that was the most unexpected part of all.

"I didn't grow up with this," I told him. "In Singapore, we have manmade beaches, not mountains."

He looked around at the vast silence, the sweeping view. "Think you're a nature girl now?"

I wiped my nose and nodded solemnly. "Yeah. But like, only with snacks."

Because maybe that was the truth of it. I didn't need a perfect backdrop or a perfect family cheering from the front row. I just needed the courage to show up, the snacks to keep me going, and Diego, always Diego, waiting at the top of the mountain.

Spain made room for me. Diego made room for me. And I, surprisingly, made room for nature, for spontaneity, and for things I never thought I'd love.

Like walking shoes. Or budgeting for train tickets instead of cute boots.

And just when I thought my heart couldn't stretch any further, it whispered, "Hey… what if there's even more?"

Because as much as I was head-over-heels for Spain—like, write-it-a-love-song level of obsessed—there was a little voice in my head (okay, more like a sparkly travel bug in heels) whispering, "Psst… Europe's right there. Go poke it."

One evening, somewhere between our second glass of wine and our third attempt at deciding whether our next weekend should involve mountains or beaches, I blurted out, "What about Europe? Like… the rest of it. Shouldn't we be flinging ourselves across borders like the free-spirited adventurers we pretend to be on Instagram?"

Diego raised his glass with the kind of look that could start a revolution, or at least a very impulsive Ryanair booking. "Where do you want to go first?"

Cue my internal confetti cannon.

"France. Italy. Germany. Greece. Literally anywhere that serves carbs and has questionable plumbing," I said, practically vibrating. "Everywhere, Diego. Everywhere."

He leaned back in his chair with a lazy, amused grin and that annoyingly calm energy he has when I'm being a complete travel goblin. "Then we better start planning."

And just like that, the rest of the continent didn't feel like a distant dream anymore.

It felt like a to-do list. With snacks.

CHAPTER 37 – When Europe Became My Playground

There's something downright magical about crossing borders in Europe. One moment, you're in Spain arguing over whether a *tortilla* should have onions, and the next, you're sipping coffee in a café where everyone's wearing berets unironically.

It's wild. It's wonderful. It's every travel-porn blog I ever read come to life.

Our first adventure? Perpignan.

"It's just over the border. A short drive, but it feels completely different from Spain," Diego said, like we were popping into a neighbor's backyard and not entering a whole new country.

And honestly, it kind of felt like that. One crisp Saturday

morning, we packed the car and headed north. The Catalan countryside rolled by in soft greens and golds, and then, bam!, we were in France. Like a magic trick, the signs flipped from Spanish to French, the hills flattened out, and suddenly there were baguettes everywhere.

When we got to Perpignan, I swear I walked straight into the pages of a fairytale. The scent of fresh bread wafted through the streets from boulangeries on every corner, and there were actual humans walking around in berets, carrying baguettes like it was their birthright. No joke, one man had two.

It was so cliché I half-expected a mime to pop out and serenade us with an accordion. And honestly? I was eating it up like a warm croissant. Zero shame. Ten out of ten. Would frolic again.

We wandered aimlessly through the narrow streets, past colorful buildings and charming cafés, which is the best way to do Europe, stopping for flaky croissants and hot chocolate at a corner café. I leaned back in my chair, soaking up the buttery air.

"This feels like we've stepped into a movie," I said.

Diego reached across the table and squeezed my hand. "And it's just the beginning. There's so much more to see."

As we continued exploring Perpignan, the sky gradually got darker. The rain held off for now, but the clouds gave the town an even more enchanting feel—like a city tucked away in a storybook.

We turned a corner and heard music, the kind of soft string melody that makes you feel like dancing in the rain.

"Do you hear that?" I asked.

Diego nodded, his brow lifting with curiosity. "Let's check it out."

The music floated toward us like some kind of musical breadcrumb trail, leading us through twisty little alleyways until we stumbled into a courtyard filled with ivy-draped balconies, centuries-old buildings leaning in like they had juicy gossip, and right in the center?

A whole band of musicians jamming out like they were born with instruments in their hands. Violins, guitars, an accordion—it was like someone accidentally dropped the soundtrack to my European fantasy onto real life.

I smiled, enchanted. "Okay, this is incredible."

Diego grinned. "Only in Europe."

The music was electric, the kind that gets into your bloodstream and makes your feet tap even if you have the rhythm of a stunned duck. The moment the band paused, one of the guitarists scanned the crowd and locked eyes with Diego.

"You play?" he asked in that very specific French-accented Spanish that somehow sounded both flirty and suspicious.

Diego laughed and lifted his hands in mock surrender. "A little."

Which was apparently the secret password, because the man didn't hesitate. He just handed over his guitar and pulled him into the circle.

"*¡Vamos!*" the crowd chanted, cheering him on.

I folded my arms, already laughing as I watched him charm the crowd. "Of course you're being cheered on by strangers. Of course."

Diego shot me the world's most sheepish—and smug—grin, then tested a few chords like he hadn't just hijacked the spotlight in the most swoony way possible.

He strummed a familiar Spanish song, all soulful and heart-felt, and the crowd immediately joined in, swaying and humming like we'd all rehearsed this in a previous life. But then, just when I thought he was done, he didn't stop. Instead, he caught my gaze and held it like a lifeline.

"This one's for you," he said softly, his voice carrying through the courtyard.

The first few chords were slow and tender, and I recognized the song immediately. It was *Besame Mucho*, a classic that always made my heart skip a beat.

"Diego…" I whispered, already turning into a puddle of emotions with very frizzy hair because, surprise, the rain had decided to make a dramatic entrance too.

He sang slow and low, voice warm and steady, each lyric curling around me like a hug I didn't know I needed.

Bésame... bésame mucho...
Como si fuera esta noche la última vez...

My heart swelled as I watched him, completely caught up in the moment. I might've melted into a nearby potted plant if he hadn't kept singing with those ridiculous eyes and that ridiculously sincere smile.

The courtyard glistened with rain, the crowd was dead silent, and for a full minute, it felt like we were the only two people on earth. Honestly? I didn't even care that my hair was puffing out like a mushroom cloud.

When the song ended, the crowd went wild. Clapping, cheering, and probably plotting to start a fan club. Diego returned the guitar and came straight to me, pulling me into his arms.

"Where did that come from?" I asked, still trying to recover from my public swoon.

He shrugged, his eyes sparkling. "You inspire me."

411

I laughed, shaking my head. "You're ridiculous."

"Ridiculously in love with you," he said, and yep, there went my last remaining brain cell.

We ducked under an awning as the musicians packed up and the drizzle turned into a polite downpour. I leaned into him, grinning like a lunatic.

"That was straight out of a movie," I said softly, resting my head on his shoulder.

Diego kissed the top of my head. "Perpignan's full of surprises."

I tilted my face up to his. "So are you."

And just like that, we walked back to the car, hands clasped, hearts way too full, and I knew this would be one of those stories we'd tell for years. The day it rained music and romance in baguette-scented air.

Perpignan had officially set the bar. And honestly? I couldn't wait to see what came next.

Later that year, my Singapore bestie, Kat, flew in.

"We're going somewhere," she announced the moment she landed. "I did not travel 17 hours to not cross a border.

She didn't have to twist my arm. One of the best things about living in Europe? The flights were ridiculously cheap.

"How is this possible?" she said, scrolling through flight options as we ate cereal from wine glasses (I hadn't done dishes).

We ended up booking Milan for 70 euros. Total. Round trip.

"70. That's like... a taxi ride during surge pricing," Kat said, both outraged and delighted.

The moment we landed, Milan hit us like a high-fashion slap to the face in the best way. The city practically oozed energy, like even the buildings were trying to strut. Everywhere we turned, there were ridiculously stylish people gliding past us like they were born in Gucci wombs, while we stumbled around gasping at the Duomo like freshly released forest goblins.

We spent that first afternoon gawking at the cathedral's façade, which looked like someone had carved it out of dreams and drama. We took approximately a thousand photos and maybe cried a little (just me, probably) because it was that beautiful.

"Can you believe we're here?" Kat said, eyes wide, grin wider, as we stood in the shadow of the Duomo.

"Not even a little," I said, still trying to convince my brain we weren't just in an elaborate airport duty-free hallucination.

That's when two men approached us with suspiciously cheerful grins and rainbow string bracelets in hand.

"*Bella, bella!*" one of them called out, grinning widely as he held out one of those bracelets. "For good luck!"

Before we could politely decline or do our awkward shuffle-away routine, they had already tied the bracelets around our wrists like we were being knighted by the Ministry of Tourist Traps.

"For free," one of them said, teeth gleaming like the villain in a soap opera.

We laughed. Silly, naive, optimistic us.

And then, "10 euros, just for luck!"

Kat and I exchanged a look that said, *we've been duped*. We dug around in our pockets, handed over some coins, and walked off like scammed-but-dignified queens.

"Well," Kat said, deadpan. "We've officially been swindled by street charmers in Italy. I think that makes us locals now."

"Totally," I nodded. "Next up: getting lost in a piazza and pretending it was intentional."

Despite our glittery bracelet betrayal, Milan more than made up for it. We carb-loaded like Olympians. Pasta? Yes. Gelato? Absolutely, even though it was cold enough to chill your soul.

Italian waiters? Flirty and bilingual. We were thriving.

One night, tucked away in a trattoria that smelled like garlic, basil, and sin, our absurdly attractive waiter slid a bottle of wine onto our table with a wink.

"This one's on the house," he said in a voice that could melt butter. "You ladies deserve it."

Kat raised an eyebrow at me the second he walked away. "Do you see now why I love this country?"

We clinked our glasses to friendship, to spontaneous trips, and to being shamelessly charmed by men who probably had five other tables of equally enchanted tourists.

On our last day, we made our way to the rooftop of the Duomo. The wind whipped our hair around like we were in a music video, and the city stretched out beneath us like a painting.

"I can't believe you're living this life," Kat said, quietly, her voice full of that kind of awe that makes you stop and feel it.

I exhaled slowly, my heart doing that fluttery thing it always did when I realized how far I'd come. "It still doesn't feel real. But I'm so, so glad it is."

And just like that, I flashed back to a family trip we once took to Phuket.

My mom, two sisters, and I squished into a tuk-tuk meant for three, bouncing through Thai traffic while my mom lectured us about stranger danger and Roselyn screamed because she thought she saw a lizard in her shoe.

We stayed at a resort that promised "ocean views," which turned out to be a glimpse of water if you stood on a chair and squinted. Still, we made the most of it—eating mango sticky rice, arguing over whose turn it was to reapply sunscreen, and singing off-key karaoke in our hotel room.

Back then, international travel felt like an event. Months of planning. Budgeting. Aunties chiming in with unsolicited opinions.

Now? I was booking flights like I ordered takeout.

That night, after Kat had fallen asleep (snoring softly like a human lullaby), I lay in the dark with the bracelet scam still tight around my wrist and the memory of Phuket clawing at me.

Being with Kat had been like cracking open a time capsule.

Suddenly, all the feelings I'd buried came rushing back. What it felt like to be known without explaining myself, to laugh without translating, to belong without effort. And it made me wonder if I'd made a catastrophic mistake.

Had I traded my family and everything that actually mattered for castles, *churros*, and budget airlines, only to end up orbiting a life I could never fully land in?

And suddenly, Barcelona felt like quicksand. A beautiful, glittering quicksand that I'd thrown myself into, smiling all the way down.

The more I thought about it, the heavier it got. My chest squeezed until I could barely breathe.

Pride told me to stay quiet, but my heart didn't get the memo. So I broke.

I cried so hard my body shook. The ugly kind—messy, snotty, desperate. The kind of crying that makes you feel hollow afterward, like you've leaked out everything you were holding inside. I buried my face in the pillow to muffle the sound, but the tears kept coming, wave after wave.

I missed my family so much it physically hurt. I missed my mom's nagging, my sisters' teasing, the noisy chaos of never being alone. I missed the safety of knowing that if I stumbled, there'd be people to catch me.

Here, all I had was the echo of my own choices, and it was deafening.

And the worst part? I knew if I called home, no one would swoop in with comfort. They'd just remind me I chose this. That I wanted this. And they'd be right.

By the time I finally drifted off, my throat was raw, my face was swollen, and my pillow was a crime scene of tears and questionable Airbnb detergent.

The next morning, Kat cheerfully shoved a croissant at me while I shuffled around in sunglasses indoors. When she asked why my eyes looked like I'd lost a boxing match, I shrugged.

"Milan's air quality," I croaked. "Absolutely brutal."

Before Kat left, we made a pact to do another trip. Maybe Greece next. Or Prague. Or, honestly, wherever had cheap wine and fewer bracelet scams.

As I watched her plane take off, I felt that familiar tug of mixed emotions.

I was doing this. I was building a life that twelve-year-old me, eating fishball noodles in Singapore and dreaming of cobblestones, would've been proud of. That quiet, timid girl who thought the world was too big, too bright, too intimidating... she'd have called this impossible.

And yet, here I was.

I still couldn't say if I belonged to one place or many. Singapore was home in my blood, but all the pieces of Barcelona felt like fragments of a version of myself I'd never dared to imagine.

But I knew that Europe wasn't just a playground.

It was a portal. And I had the golden ticket.

CHAPTER 38 – The Call I Avoided, the Journey I Needed

While I was busy collecting stamps in my passport and embarrassing myself in at least three different languages, there was one journey I kept ghosting like a bad Tinder date: the one back to my family.

Three years.

That's how long it had been since I last spoke to them. No calls. No texts. Not even a rogue meme in the group chat. Just radio silence.

At first, I told myself I needed space. (True.) Time. (Also true.) An emotional detox from years of expectations and unsolicited life advice. (Extremely true.)

But as the silence stretched, it stopped being about space

and started feeling like standing on the edge of a cliff where jumping meant vulnerability, and vulnerability meant... ew, feelings.

Then it happened.

A notification pinged on my phone. A photo from my eldest sister, Roselyn.

She was holding a baby, her third, apparently. Roselyn's hair was in a messy bun that screamed "I haven't slept in 47 years," and yet she was somehow glowing. The baby was wrapped in a soft blanket, with big, curious eyes and a tiny hand curled around Roselyn's thumb.

No message, no "hope you're well" or "we miss you." Just the photo.

Classic Asian family. We could discuss recipes, reality TV, and which brand of detergent actually got curry stains out of white shirts, but the second emotions tried to RSVP to the conversation? Left on read.

I stared at the photo for so long my screen went dark. And then I stared at the darkness some more, my heart twisting with guilt and longing. I'd missed so much... Births, weddings, milestones. Life had moved on without me, and I was just a ghost in the background.

Later that night, I found myself spiraling through old photos like a nostalgic gremlin. Roselyn, the bossy-but-lovable oldest. Kyra, the second-born with enough firepower to launch a missile and the emotional range of a very passionate raccoon. And me, chaotic baby sister who ran off to Europe like a movie cliché, minus the Christmas snow.

Diego walked in, drying his hands after washing the dishes, and paused when he saw the look on my face. Like he'd just caught me mid-existential crisis. Which… fair.

He sat beside me without a word, his presence so comforting it made my eyes sting. It was as if he knew I needed time to sort through my emotions.

I turned my phone toward him, showing him a picture of Roselyn holding her baby. "It's been three years," I said, my voice thick with regret. "Since I talked to them."

He took my hand in that maddeningly gentle way of his and said, "You should reach out."

Guilt twisted in my chest as I laughed, which came out watery. "And say what? 'Hey, sorry I disappeared into the European ether. How's the third baby I didn't know existed?'"

He shifted closer, his knee touching mine. "Start with hello."

It was so annoyingly simple, so heartbreakingly human, that it broke something open in me. I leaned into him, and he kissed the top of my head, his lips lingering just long enough to remind me I wasn't alone.

"I'm here," he murmured. "No matter how it goes."

So the next morning, after pacing the living room like I was training for an Olympic-level anxiety marathon, I did it. I sent the message to our family group chat. My hands trembled as I typed, my heart pounding with nerves.

Hey. It's been a while. I hope everyone's doing well.

Within three seconds, my phone turned into a fireworks display.

NADIA?!

Followed by a digital avalanche from both sisters. They asked about my life. Sent me baby pictures. Wedding pictures. Memes. Life updates. Kyra had gotten married (???), and Roselyn had birthed a third human, and somehow I'd missed all of it.

But even as the chat exploded, I noticed how the messages stayed... safe.

"Here's a pic of the baby!"

"Guess who got married and didn't wear the traditional outfit?"

"LOL, remember Mom's curry experiment?"

No one typed, "Why did you leave?" No one typed, "You hurt us." We were, as always, a family allergic to hard conversations.

Until Kyra dropped the bomb.

I'm going to Vienna next weekend with my husband.

423

Wanna meet us there?

I stared at the screen, my mind racing. My birthday was next weekend.

I looked at Diego. "How do you feel about Vienna?"

He raised an eyebrow from behind his book. "Austria or sausage brand?"

"Austria. Why would I ask you to join me for meat tubes on my birthday? Anyway, Kyra's going to be there with her husband. I think… I think I want to see her."

Diego smiled and closed his book. "In that case, pack your bags."

The flight felt like emotional whiplash meets reunion fever. My stomach did gymnastic routines all the way to Austria. As we landed, Diego reached over and squeezed my hand, grounding me.

When we reached the meeting point, I spotted Kyra first. Her hair was shorter, her style was more polished, but the second she spotted me, all the polish melted. She was still the same person I grew up with.

"Nadia?" she called out, like she wasn't sure if I was real.

I didn't answer. I just ran. And then we were hugging, crying, and immediately hitting each other. Literally.

A smack to my shoulder. A jab to her ribs. A kick to my shin.

To the untrained eye (Diego and Kyra's husband standing nearby in wide-eyed horror), it looked like we were auditioning for a low-budget martial arts film. But in our secret sister language?

Punch = I love you.
Kick = I missed you.
Insult = You hurt me so much, I don't know how else to say it.

Diego leaned toward Kyra's husband, whispering, "Are… are they fighting?"

Her husband shook his head, equally lost. "I think this is… affection?"

I wiped my eyes, laughing and crying all at once. "You left without saying anything, you idiot," Kyra said, giving me one more shove for emphasis.

"You never picked up my calls or texts, you jerk," I shot back, smacking her arm.

We both knew what those words really meant: *You broke my heart.*

But instead of saying that, we glared through tears until we both burst out laughing again, two disasters reunited in a train station.

When I introduced her to Diego, she looked him up and down like a bouncer at a nightclub.

"So, you're the famous Diego."

He gave her a polite smile. "Nice to meet you."

She crossed her arms, clearly sizing him up. "Do you love her?"

I groaned, covering my face. "Oh my god, Kyra."

Diego, bless his romantic heart, didn't even flinch. "Very much."

Kyra burst out laughing and yanked him into a hug. "Good. Because I was ready to beat you up."

Diego looked at me over her shoulder, amused. "I like her."

"Don't encourage her," I muttered. But secretly? I kind of loved it.

The rest of the weekend was a whirlwind as we explored Vienna together and discovered cakes, museums, and sibling chaos.

Diego won everyone over with his dry humor and impressive ability to eat schnitzel without getting crumbs in his moustache. Kyra's husband turned out to be surprisingly normal. (Suspiciously so. We kept an eye on him.)

But it wasn't all sachertorte and selfies. One evening, after dinner, Kyra asked me to walk with her along the Danube. The lights of the city danced on the water, too beautiful for the conversation I knew was coming.

She didn't waste time. "Why did you really leave?"

My chest tightened. "I told you... space, time—"

"Nadia," she cut in, her tone sharp. "Don't give me the brochure answer. You left. You vanished. Do you have any idea how angry I was? You didn't just ghost us, you ghosted your whole life. Mom cried every night for months. Roselyn buried herself in work. And me? I was so angry I couldn't even say your name without wanting to scream."

Her words landed like stones in my chest.

"I know," I whispered.

"No, you don't!" Her voice cracked, loud enough that a couple walking by gave us a curious look. "You don't get it. You didn't just run away from Singapore. You ran away from us. From me. And I hated you for it. I hated you for choosing strangers and foreign streets over your own family."

Tears blurred my vision, but I forced myself to look at her. "I didn't leave because I stopped loving you. I left because I couldn't survive if I stayed. I couldn't breathe under the weight of all the expectations, all the... everything. I thought if I told you, you'd make me stay, and I couldn't do it anymore."

For a long moment, she said nothing. Just stared at me, fury flickering into exhaustion.

Finally, she muttered, "You're such a coward."

It cut deep. But then, after a pause, she added more quietly, "But maybe I get why you had to be."

We sat down on a bench, the river glittering beside us. Her anger hadn't disappeared; it still bristled in the silence between us, but the fact that she was sitting here at all told me something.

We weren't okay. Not yet. Maybe not for a long time. But I hadn't been shut out completely. I wasn't exiled.

Kyra finally sighed, shoulders slumping. "You're different."

I braced myself. "Bad different?"

"No," she said. "Just… different. Lighter. Happier. I hate how you left us. But I'm glad you're still my sister."

It wasn't forgiveness. But it was a start.

I didn't know what else to say, so I rested my head on her shoulder. It said everything I couldn't.

Back at the hotel, Diego was waiting in the lobby with that

look. The one that says you're safe without needing to say it.

"Well?" he asked quietly.

I hesitated before answering. "She... didn't slam the door on me. That's something."

His brow furrowed, but he nodded. He didn't push, just reached for my hand like he knew I couldn't take more questions tonight.

Kyra passed us on her way out with her husband, giving me a look I couldn't quite translate. It wasn't anger anymore, but it wasn't forgiveness either. More like... *we'll see*.

The next morning, the silence in our room was thick as I folded clothes back into my suitcase. Diego, meticulous as ever, was folding his socks like he could will order back into my messy world.

"Am I at least officially family-approved?" he asked, almost cautiously.

I managed a half-smile. "You survived round one. But don't get cocky, my mom's still the final boss. And Kyra... she's not done with me yet."

He didn't grin this time. He just nodded, serious, and pulled me into a hug.

On the plane, I stared out at the clouds with a lump lodged

in my throat. The trip hadn't been a fairytale reunion. There was no bow neatly tying us back together. But for the first time in years, the thread wasn't cut clean through.

And with Diego's hand warm around mine, I let myself believe that maybe—slowly, painfully, imperfectly—I was stitching my way back to family.

CHAPTER 39 – From Free Cake to Full Tab

The warm fuzzies from Vienna didn't even have time to fade before I was hit with another emotional ambush: my birthday. Back in Barcelona. With Diego acting like the poster boy for "I'm definitely planning something but want credit for being low-key."

For the entire week, he was suspiciously secretive, texting friends when he thought I wasn't looking and making vague comments about "plans." He wasn't exactly discreet, but I played along, letting him think he was being sneaky.

"You're being sketchy," I finally told him mid-week, sprawled on the couch with a half-eaten *churro* in hand.

He didn't even look up. Just smirked. "Am I?"

"You're texting like a drug lord," I said. "Either you're planning a surprise or running an underground bull-fighting championship."

He just winked. "Just be ready for Saturday night."

"Ready for what?"

"You'll see."

When Saturday rolled around, I woke up to Diego standing at the foot of the bed with a cake box and the kind of grin that should come with a warning label.

"*Feliz cumpleaños,*" he said, leaning in to kiss my cheek as he wished me happy birthday.

I sat up, eyes wide as I beamed at the gesture. "You got me a cake?"

"Obviously," he said, smug. "What kind of monster doesn't bring cake on someone's birthday?"

I shuffled to the kitchen in my mismatched pajamas, heart full and expectations high. I couldn't wait to see the kind of decadent birthday cake I grew up with in Singapore— something layered with cream, mousse, or ganache, topped with intricate decorations.

I lifted the lid and… blinked.

Inside was a small, rustic sponge cake, much like his mother's *bizcocho*. No layers. No chocolate waterfall. No sparkly birthday message. Just a dusting of powdered sugar and a handful of almonds.

"This is it?" I asked, trying not to sound like an ungrateful sugar gremlin.

Diego chuckled at my reaction. "What were you expecting?"

I hesitated. "Something more elaborate, maybe? This looks like something you'd have with coffee."

"Traditional birthday cakes here are simple, but they're homemade and delicious."

"This looks like something you'd eat with coffee while gossiping about your neighbors," I said, squinting at it. "Where's the drama? The frosting? The danger?"

"Danger?" he repeated, laughing.

"Good cake should threaten your cholesterol."

He handed me a fork. "Just try it."

I did. And okay, fine, it was stupidly good. Soft, buttery, the kind of subtle delicious that makes you rethink your entire personality.

"Okay, you win. You're still not off the hook for the lack of ganache, but… you win."

He kissed my forehead. "In Spain, birthdays aren't about sugar highs or fancy details. They're about good company and good food."

"And cake," I added with a grin.

He kissed my forehead. "Always cake."

That night, he brought me to a bar I loved, grungy but charming, like a dive bar that read poetry. As soon as we walked in, a crowd jumped up and screamed, "SURPRISE!" even though I was 90% sure I'd figured it out.

Still, A+ for enthusiasm.

Joshua immediately bear-hugged me and thrust a beer into my hand. "Let's make some questionable decisions!"

Daniela cheered. Enrique kissed both my cheeks like the pretend boyfriend he knew he was to me. Colleagues I barely knew turned into besties within two drinks. The energy was wild.

We played beer pong with a beach ball someone mysteriously pulled out of a tote bag. Joshua tried to rap *Despacito* again and managed to offend both music and language. Enrique led a group rendition of *Viva la Vida* that was part concert, part exorcism.

But my personal highlight?

Someone, probably Joshua, because chaos is his love language, decided we should each go around and "roast Nadia lovingly." Which turned into "let's share embarrassing facts about her."

Joshua: "Remember when you asked a bartender in Spanish if his face came with the sangria?"
Me: "It was loud! I panicked!"

Enrique: "Or the time she tried to use her student ID to get into the Museo del Jamón?"
Me: "Education is priceless. So is ham."

Daniela: "Or when she wore two different shoes to work and tried to convince us it was fashion?"
Me: "Still convinced. Vogue just hasn't caught up yet."

Diego, smug and angelic: "She once tried to mop the kitchen with floor cleaner that turned out to be olive oil."

The table howled. I groaned. "That was ONE time and the floor was very... Mediterranean after."

By the end of it, my cheeks hurt from laughing, and I was two drinks past dignity.

And then the bill arrived.

"Let's split it," I offered automatically.

Enrique nearly choked on his vermouth. "No, no. It's your birthday."

"Oh, thank God," I said. "So you're paying?"

Everyone blinked. And then they all burst out laughing like I'd told the world's worst joke.

"No, you pay," Joshua said, patting my arm like I was an adorable but clueless puppy. "It's a Spanish tradition. Birthday person pays for everyone."

I stared at them like they'd just told me unicorns were real and my credit card was about to die.

"I'm sorry, WHAT?!"

Diego grinned. "Welcome to your birthday invoice."

I nearly dropped my drink. "In Singapore, I get treated. People give me red or green envelopes with money and gifts, and sometimes jewelry!"

Daniela sipped her cocktail. "Here, we give you receipts."

They all started fake-toasting me like little gremlins.

"*¡Gracias*, Nadia!"

"Thanks for this gin and tonic, queen!"

"Next round's on you, birthday girl!"

I rolled my eyes so hard they nearly relocated. "Fine. But I'm making Diego cover the tip. And the emotional damage."

He held up his hands. "Done. Though we don't tip in Spain, remember?"

At some point, someone pulled up *La Bamba* on karaoke, and the entire bar joined in. Joshua was yelling lyrics like he'd swallowed Duolingo. Enrique salsa-ed with a plant. I hit a note so high the bartender ducked.

Later, I turned to Diego and asked, "Are there any other customs I should know about before I bankrupt myself?"

He nodded solemnly. "You get your ears pulled. One tug for every year."

"THAT IS NOT A THING," I said.

Joshua was already advancing. "30 pulls, baby!"

"Don't you dare!" I shrieked, swatting him away as everyone around us burst into laughter. "Touch my ear and I swear I'll knee you into next week!"

We ended the night the way all good nights end in Spain: drunk, full of *churros*, and singing bad pop songs in the street.

Diego wrapped his arm around me as we stumbled home.

"Had fun?" he asked.

"Even with the traumatic bill, yes," I said, poking his side. "But next year, I'm bringing Singapore rules back."

He smirked. "Red and green envelopes and all?"

"Yup. You'll be handing me jewelry by breakfast."

"Challenge accepted."

When we got home, I paused and looked up at the dark sky. No stars, but I didn't need them. My chest felt full, my heart anchored.

"Happy birthday, Nad," Diego whispered, hugging me from behind.

"Thank you," I said, leaning back into him. "For the cake. For the chaos. For pretending not to see me crying during *Viva la Vida*."

It wasn't the over-the-top celebration I'd expected. It was better. Messier. Funnier. Full of love.

And maybe, just maybe, I was starting to feel like this strange, loud, ear-pulling, bill-sticking country was becoming something I never thought I'd find again: home.

But let's be real, Barcelona didn't magically fix me. I still miss my family so much that it sometimes feels like a bruise

I can't stop pressing. I still screw up, still fight with Diego, still buy glitter pens I don't need. I've grown bolder, louder, braver, but also a little lost in ways I'm still figuring out.

And that's okay. It's an ongoing process. The mess is the point.

Because maybe life isn't a five-year plan. Maybe it's sponge cake instead of ganache. Simple. Imperfect. Still sweet.

And next year's birthday? Well… let's just say if Diego keeps looking at me the way he did tonight, I might be paying for a wedding tab instead.

About the Author

Born and raised in Singapore, Nora Qin now finds herself navigating life (and Target aisles) in California. Before trading tapas for avocado toasts, she spent almost seven years living in Spain, an experience that left a lasting imprint on her worldview, her storytelling, and her expectations for dinner.

A self-proclaimed foodie, Nora loves discovering new cuisines and firmly believes most life problems can be improved with good food and better company.

She first started writing her novel in 2019, but somewhere between Spanish sunsets and real life, inspiration packed its bags. It wasn't until the birth of her daughter in 2023 and countless nursing sessions that she found the time (and motivation) to dive back in. Between naps, snacks, and baby giggles, she finished her debut novel in January 2025, fueled by chocolates, sheer determination, and a whole lot of love.